Love in The Age of

Confusion

a novel by
Byron Ayanoglu

Some Other Books by Byron Ayanoglu:

FOOD:

Byron's New Home Cooking (Penguin/Viking, Toronto, 1992)
The Young Thailand Cookbook (Random House, Canada, 1994)
The New Vegetarian Gourmet (Robert-Rose, Toronto, 1995)
Simply Mediterranean Cooking (Robert-Rose, Toronto, 1996)
Montreal's Best Restaurants (Véhicule Press, Montreal, 1999)

NON-FICTION (IN PROGRESS):

Crete On the Half Shell (for HarperCollins, Toronto)

Love In the Age of

Confusion

a novel by

Byron Ayanoglu

Love In the Age of Confusion © 2001 Byron Ayanoglu

DC BOOKS
950 rue Decarie, Box 662
Montreal, Quebec H4L 4V9

Cover painting and layout by Geof Isherwood.
Book designed and typeset by *Sasigraphix* in 10-point Garamond Book,
with titles and headings in 18- and 24-point Festiva.
Author Photo: Algis Kemezys.
Editor: Sonja A. Skarstedt.
Printed in Canada by AGMV Marquis.

Québec ▪▪

THE CANADA COUNCIL | LE CONSEIL DES ARTS
FOR THE ARTS | DU CANADA
SINCE 1957 | DEPUIS 1957

DC Books acknowledges the support of the Canada Council
for the Arts and SODEC for our publishing program.

Dépôt légal, Bibliothèque Nationale du Québec and
The National Library of Canada, third trimester, 2001.

First Printing.

National Library of Canada Cataloguing in Publication Data

Ayanoglu, Byron
    Love in the age of confusion

ISBN 0-919688-90-X (bound).--ISBN 0-919688-88-8 (pbk.)

    I. Title.

PS8551.Y35L69 2001   C813'.6   C2001-903567-5
PR9199.4.A93L69 2001

The author would like to thank Algis Kemezys, Simon Dardick, Atom Egoyan, Daniaile Jarry, Jacques Jourdain, Steve Luxton, Amnon Medad, Guy Sprung and René Lévesque for their encouragement and inspiration.

Love In the Age of
Confusion

for Nikos and Kalio, my godparents

Part One:
The Romance

Chapter 1

June, 1999. At a cafe table in Montreal.

She had been trouble from the start. There hadn't been much peace. Well, none. It was already a year. A whole year of towering highs and aching lows. Now this!

She looked at him straight on with those dark-dark eyes. Crisply, she stated: "I'm pregnant. It happened in Mykonos." Just like that. He was stunned.

It didn't end there. Even more coolly, resignedly, as if she was adding a post-script: "I'm going to have it. Yes. And it's definitely yours. But," and she stopped. A cloud or a shudder crossed that bright-white, perfectly etched face. She picked up her glass, and took a sip of the cheap chardonnay.

He had ordered a red. He hadn't touched it yet. He hadn't needed to: waiting for her was ample intoxication. Mid-June in Montreal. A lacy, just-warm breeze. Bernard Street cafe-terrace. At sunset, past nine o'clock. The late sunset of the northlands. And all around them, other young faces. Lovers, or about to be.

Ari was twenty two, medium height, weight, looks with ice-blue Scottish eyes, olive-oil skin, and jet-black Greek hair. He hated cliché. He considered himself an artist, and he knew that he must, at all cost, be Original. He could, for example, have never admitted that he was in love. He loved Arletty with all his mind and all his body. Not a single square millimeter of his entire being was ever free of this love. Yet he had not taken any of it to heart. This sort of love seemed trite, even dangerous. This sort of love was like a cancer, and like a cancer it grew and killed you. But it always happened to other, lesser people, never to oneself. Until now.

Arletty was just-older. She had told him seventeen, because she looked it, slender and child-like, a girl-woman, all-white and blondish, with a tiny waist and still forming curves. But in fact, she was twenty-three. She had lived on her own for many years. She had been happy. Except in the last year. Her lost-year, her Ari-year. She had planned a life of freedom from exactly the sort of love that Ari wouldn't admit to until this moment, and which she had recognized from the start. She had been terrified of this love, she had tried to break free, but she had failed. Because, of course, she loved him too. In the same awful way. She loved him, but it was getting in the way. And now, especially now, it had to end.

Ari thought he heard right. Arletty had just said that she would make him a father. This bit of news, coming from others, had been a source of concern, and of stress in the past. Coming from Arletty, it had felt like a panacea. As if this never-before-welcome, biological function would be the cure-all to his ills. It would bind Arletty to him, totally. Now, he would truly be her slave. Was this not unconditional surrender? Was this not love?

And then, she had said "but," and stopped. The sheer menace of that one syllable, the ominous pause that followed it, the icy sea in which it left him floundering, all of these things confirmed the love. After all Love is a sequence of "but's," most of which never get resolved. And any one of which is capable of turning ugly, destroying the love, destroying you.

The oncoming twilight had brought many more people out into the street. Families out for a stroll. Kids in tow. Grandparents, too. Taking the air. Speaking in foreign tongues. As if Bernard Street was a town square, somewhere far away. A land of palm trees, and lovers just like these, perched at tables with their bottomless glasses of wine and the longing in their eyes.

Nothing good could possibly be hiding behind that "but." She had broken their love many times. And she had made him beg to come back in. She had relented, but grudgingly, guardedly. And only for a short time, only to boot him out again. Into the cold. Again and again. And then there had been Mykonos. It had been wonderful, practically seamless, a slice of heaven. Was it any wonder she was pregnant? He should be screaming with joy. Yet her "but" was devouring him.

He looked at her with those hungry eyes she particularly feared and said: "I'm an artist. I have a right to be. I have rich parents....

"I know love. Love is my currency. Love is the cornerstone of art. As an artist I owe a great debt to love. There would be no art, if there were no love....

"I've examined love. Intimately. I have studied it. I've used it endlessly. Shamelessly. I've exploited love....

"I've been in love. Repeatedly. Serially. I have loved. Devotedly. Selflessly....

"Uselessly....

"Nothing, not one bit of it, could ever have prepared me for the way I feel about you."

Arletty had heard versions of all this before. It had amused her in the past, and it had softened her. But she was determined. She felt strong today, because she knew she was right. She loved him, yes, but there was no recourse. Not any more. No margins. She replied:

"Obviously, I'm either crazy or stupid. I can't explain it to myself, so I'm sure I couldn't explain it to you...

"What could be more natural than living with someone who adores me as much as you who has proven himself over the course of an entire year? Who has taken all the abuse I could hurl at him, all the irrational rejections, the long silences, the capricious reconciliations, all the unhappiness, the misery, and still remained as loyal and loving and ready to accept me back at any price and under all my conditions, as you?

"You who have money, when I haven't got a penny? And now with the baby on the way, how CRAZY to refuse your help and your support! How ridiculous! Bring up a baby on my own, with no money and no partner? The thought of it makes me sick. I break out....

"And yet, I can't, Ari. The alternative is worse. It's hell for me. The little family, the endless hours of your love and devotion, that same sickly-sweet thing that happens to all of them. I've watched it, believe me. I know what happens....

"I swore. Never! To me! Never. I'm sorry, Ari...

"No, I'm not sorry. It's just the way it has to be."

Ari felt tears rushing into his eyes. Tears of grief. Tears of failure. Tears of rage. Tears from all the repercussions of love.

"What? What sorry? What not sorry? What are you saying? This is the most monumental moment of my life. You're going to make me a father. What more can there be to say?"

Arletty read his rage, and she recoiled.

"I'm going to have your child, Ari, but I never want to see you, or be with you again. I called you here to tell you that. And to wish you well. To say goodbye."

Ari's eyes sunk. His jaw tightened. He could barely breath. He shakily lifted his full glass and gulped the wine, choking on it, red rivulets spilling around his mouth. He coughed painfully. He cursed. Then he stabbed at her. "You're demented. You're full of shit!"

Arletty, icily: "Yes. I am."

Ari finally let the tears come. He hugged himself and wept, loudly. As an artist, he embraced this license to react dramatically. In any case, he had much reason for despair. He had learned to both respect and dread her decisions. He knew she meant to do what she said, and that she had it in her to convince herself never to regret it. This unhappy moment could therefore be his last chance to share intimacy with her, and he wanted it to last forever. He spoke, falteringly, through his tears. "Why are you doing this to me? Why do you hate me so much?"

Suitably chastened, Arletty spoke sweetly: "The last thing I ever want is to be a family. I've told you this. I'm a unit of One. Now with the baby, I'm going to become a unit of Two. Three? No way. No. No. Not with you. Not with anyone. No. I can't. I could never."

"I want to die," sighed Ari.

Chapter 2

Exactly one year ago. Same cafe table.

Every June Bernard Street sheds its chrysalid torpor of winter sobriety. In the cold months the strip appears relentlessly wet, further dampened by the conspicuous display of encroaching decay in the boarded-up Outremont Theatre and its echo in the bourgeois-solid, all-brick, 1920s five-storey apartment blocks. In June, the whole musty package transforms itself into a ripe flower, finally being permitted to bloom.

Restaurant tables, unrestricted by any kind of fence or shrubbery are placed on the actual sidewalk, blending into the pedestrian parade. Dinner at these outdoor tables becomes eating in public in every sense of the word. And while this one human function is in progress, the foreplay for another, just as urgent and just as human an appetite, flagrantly takes place directly alongside.

Bernard Street in June becomes a leafy, joyous backdrop for the awesome spectacle of Montreal's sexiest, most fetching young adults on the make. Among them, on this particularly perfect June evening, exactly one year prior to that pivotal "I'm pregnant — I never want to see you again" scene, Ari and Arletty are about to meet each other at the same table, the corner table of *La Crevetterie*.

Situated at the crossroads of Bernard and Champagneur, which is to say, at the epicenter of the parade, directly across from the Outremont Theatre, absolutely at the mid-point of the strip, halfway between the *Café de la Nation* and the *Crémerie Barbarella*, is a table for four, set apart from all the other tables.

Uncompromisingly public, practically on the asphalt, the flagship table of the entire cruising scene has been the table of choice for our mismatched lovers, from their first meeting all the way to their last. This is the table on which Ari and Arletty's entire love-affair will have played itself out.

And this is the table, where Ari sat by himself during the magic light of the late sunset, unaware that he was mere minutes from his first-ever glimpse of Arletty. He was flushed, he glowed, he exuded an irresistible air of well-being. He was in awe of the fact that he was actually making a movie — albeit, with his mother's money. Still, making a movie, at twenty one, writer-director, which is to say *auteur*, at twenty one! What a thrill! His smile stretched from ear to ear, threatening to slice his face in half.

Arletty noticed him from the moment he sat down. By himself at the big corner table. The one usually reserved for special occasions and photo-ops, like during the Film Festival. She watched him as he practically forced the hostess to give him that table, the way he bribed her with a tip — the pig! There he was, like some kind of overlord in his preppy clothes — were those penny-loafers on his feet? She squinted for a closer look, but she was so far across the street she couldn't clearly make them out. They more than likely were penny-loafers, she guffawed to herself. A refugee from Westmount! It was written all over him. Visiting the French side. Being cool! Or, worse. Hoping to get his rocks off. Self-important, horny little creep!

What really got her boiling mad was the obscene sight of *La Crevetterie's* finest Chablis, well over $100, being served to him in an ice-bucket — complete with the whole bullshit of tasting it, swallowing it, nodding, accepting it. What a farce! As if this pork-fed, little rich-boy could tell good wine from horse-piss.

At that moment she had several choices. She could sneer off the whole pathetic scene and move on. Or, she could swing past his table, holding a gigantic, triple-scoop *Barbarella's* pistachio ice-cream — and accidentally let it fall on his head. Or, best of all, she could teach him a real lesson. It being so close to Midsummer's Eve, her only viable choice was the third.

Arletty ducked into a doorway, quickly removed all of her clothes and slipped the scarlet trench coat over her body. She wrapped her underclothes into a bundle, and stuffed them behind the hall radiator for future retrieval. She stepped back onto the street, strutting daintily, furtively looking over her shoulder, a vignette in scarlet. Cold, desperate, hunted.

She quickened her pace as she approached his table. She surprised him in mid-gulp. She sat down suddenly. She looked at him beseechingly.

"Please, please, don't throw me out. No. No! Pretend we're together! I mean it. This is not a joke. It's a matter of life and death!" Ari choked on his expensive wine. He tried to reassure her — even in the throes of choking, he noticed she was beautiful, but could only manage grunts and painful coughing, which tinted his face a deep shade of crimson.

She peeked over her shoulder apprehensively. Then she turned to him, full of fear. "I'm sorry. I didn't mean to startle you. I'm terrified. And I didn't do anything, I swear. They're after me. No. No. Don't look! They're dangerous. And here I go in English. You're probably furious that I assumed you were English. Are you? I mean, do you speak English?"

Ari, still coughing, nodded vigorously. "Oh, Eng-ish. Yes. En-lish."

Arletty, with a come-hither smile: "I'm so glad. If you were French you'd probably laugh at me. But you English understand, don't you? I'm sixteen years old, Mister. I don't know how to defend myself!"

"Sixteen!?" Ari's voice had returned.

"And they took all my clothes. Look!" Arletty opened and shut her trench coat in a flash, offering speedy, red-nippled evidence, that she was naked underneath.

"Oh, GOD! God. Were you rap... I mean, violated?" Ari's mind sped into an abyss. He had been chosen by fate to champion a teenage rape victim.

Arletty laughed melodiously. "Oh, nothing quite so glamorous. I was robbed. At gunpoint. They wanted everything, but I escaped with the trench coat. Though, I know they'll be BACK. Their leader, Carmen, has been eyeing my coat for weeks. It's just her size."

Ari's jaw was hanging open. "I think we should call the police."

"I don't think so. I have a record a mile long. They'll arrest me. No. We have no choice. You have to take care of me. They took my money. They took my keys. I have nothing. I'm scared." Thirty seconds of silent tears, followed by renewed urgency. "I'm at your mercy. Please help me! And please close your mouth, there are a lot of mosquitoes this time of year." Arletty let out a loud giggle.

Ari smiled with relief. "You've been putting me on, haven't you?"

The waiter materialized at this point, and smartly planted a wine-glass in front of Arletty. Ari took his cue. "Wine?" And he poured without waiting for her answer.

"I'm underage, but I drink a lot. I drink all the time. I'm an alcoholic." Arletty sighed as she reached for her glass. Greedily. She gulped half its contents and then she burped sveltly. Brandishing the half-drunk glass, she coyly looked at Ari. "I'm also very hungry. Can you spot me a meal?"

"Anything. I'm celebrating tonight."

She turned to the waiter. *"Des frites. Deux fois. No, fait à trois fois. Et double mayo avec chaque."*

"Oh, madame's usual," said the waiter, and receded with a fake curtsy.

"Your usual? They know you here?"

Arletty winked. "They know me. I know them."

"Right." Ari laughed. "And that's what you eat? French fries with mayo. *Deux fois.* No! Make that *trois fois.*"

"As a matter of fact, I usually eat *poutine.* But they don't make it here."

"Poutine?" He played along.

"Yes. And what do you like to eat?"

"Well, certainly NOT *poutine.* My God. I'm a gourmet!" Ari laughed out loud. "Soggy fries in nameless gravy from a powder, and tasteless, curd cheese? That's a joke, right? The *poutine?"* She stared at him hostilely. "It's NOT a joke?" She moved her head side to side no. Ari panicked. He had offended her. And now she was going to walk, he could feel it.

Arletty bristled, but she didn't walk. She was, after all, supposed to be under-aged, naked, hungry, broke and on the run. Instead she spat out her question: "SO-WHAT-DO-YOU-LIKE-TO-EAT!?"

She had trapped him. He had no choice but to tell her the truth. "At lunch I had char-grilled, fresh sardines with a parsley-red-onion sauce, followed by a warm salad with *chanterelle* mushrooms and melted goat cheese. Supper was even better. Baked lamb shanks with prunes, served on basmati rice, with braised leeks and a cherry tomato salad. For dessert, a freshly made *millefeuille Napoléon* with fresh-picked strawberries."

"What? You live in a restaurant?"

"I live at home. We have a cook and we have a berry patch. For me, my mother gets in the kitchen herself, and—"

"Your mother cooks for you?"

"And I watch. I've picked up most of her recipes."

"How retro!" exclaimed Arletty.

"Not retro. Cooking is in. It's cool to cook. I'm even writing a cookbook."

Arletty, scornfully: "Don't you know anything? The moment something is cool, it's already retro."

"That maybe so. But it doesn't mean I have to eat *poutine*. Does it?"

Arletty raised her eyebrows, but she spared him her answer, as the waiter had arrived in the meanwhile, with a huge platter of crisp, rosily fried potatoes, around which was a ring of little, plastic cups filled with oily mayonnaise. The meal in front of her, Arletty fell on it at once, grunting with greasy satisfaction, half-chewed bits sputtering out of her mouth, as if she was a slob, all by herself in some basement apartment, instead of with him at Montreal's most glamorous table.

He watched her feeding frenzy with amazement and disdain. He sipped on his wine. He coughed politely. She kept stuffing her mouth with more bundles of mayo-coated, crunchy fries. She was obviously doing this to annoy him, for his poutine put-down. Or, maybe she truly was famished. Maybe she really was a street-kid in trouble. They had only met fifteen minutes ago and already this uncertainty. Well, she was sixteen. Though she was actually twenty two.

"I just finished making a movie," he said.

She stopped chewing for a nanosecond. Without looking up, and with her mouth full: "Wan'sum?"

"No, thank you. I'm full," said Ari. "But really, it's a very good movie, not retro at all...." He paused, not sure where this was going. "It's called *They Came From The North,* and it's about life in Montreal. The troubles, you know. The English-French thing. The Separation, I mean the Sovereignty, I mean Independence, all that stuff, you know. And it's about spying. And of course it's got romance, and a little bit of Cuisine."

She let his voice dangle in the void, until she had devoured her fries down. Then she said: "You mean, it's about you."

"No. Not at all. What—" Ari was wide-eyed, as if suddenly jolted awake. He could have kissed her right there and then, if she'd let him. "YES! Unbelievable. Obviously! Obviously, it's about me. You're SO right. How could I have missed that?"

"Easy. You're a gourmet. You'll eat it if it's tasty, but you don't care where it comes from."

He didn't take her bait. Instead he refilled her glass, and then his own. He lifted his glass. She lifted hers. They clinked. She took a small sip, as did he. "If this movie is about me, then you have to be in it."

"Whatever for? I'm no part of your life."

"I think you are."

"Well, think again."

"Are you refusing a part in my movie?"

"Will you pay me?" Arletty was no longer amused.

"Of course, I'll pay you."

She lost her patience. "That is the sickest and the oldest pick-up line in the book. How trite."

"Not, if it's true," said Ari, defensively. "Anyway, I don't exactly need a line with you, do I? You already threw yourself at my mercy. You're mine for the taking. Aren't you?"

Arletty smiled sweetly. "So, what's the part?"

"It doesn't exist, yet."

"HAH! I knew it!"

"Hold on, Miss Underage-Done-it-all. This is my movie. I wrote it, I'm producing it, I'm directing it. I can do whatever I want. This movie is my own Universe. Until now, I hadn't even met you. You hadn't opened my eyes to my own movie. Of course there isn't a ready part in it for you. In fact, I thought I had finished shooting yesterday. I thought I was all done. Until this minute. Well, I was done. And then you happened to me. So, now, the movie is reopened. Because of you."

"What ARE you talking about?"

"I'm talking about creating a part for you. A postcard. We'll do a scene. Two minutes, not much more. And I'll insert it. I know exactly where to put it. There used to be a gaping hole, but no more! Now I have you."

"The HELL you do! What arrogance. I say NO. I can't do a scene that doesn't exist. I refuse to plug your holes for you. I refuse to be your cartoon. What did you say? Cameo? Oh, yeah, a postcard! I'm not a postcard. I'm REAL, mister!" Arletty picked up her glass grandly. She sipped, then she remembered she was meant to be gulping. So, she drained her glass, and set it down forcefully. She burped and giggled.

Ari was already in love, although it would take him a full year to accept the fact. He spoke persuasively: "Two minutes on-screen is an eternity. We can do a lot with that. A postcard is not a cartoon. In a movie, caricature can be ten-fifteen seconds, max. After that it becomes a role. Two minutes can be a star-turn."

Arletty peered at him suspiciously. "I'm not saying yes, but IF, then I write my own scene. I refuse to speak anyone's words. You tell me the brackets, and I'll fill in the words."

Ari bowed his head. "You're a film actress. I thought so. You understand the medium."

"I'm not a film actress. If I were, I'd be a film *actor*. But I hate films, movies, TV. They bore me."

Ari sailed right past the put-down. "I agree unreservedly with your terms. I'll set it up, and the rest'll be up to you."

"I'll need to read the script. Is there a script?"

"I'll bring it to you."

"I have no home. Bring it here. Leave it for me."

Ari's face had become bright as a moon, happy as a groom's. "To what name? The Girl In Red?"

Arletty pursed her lips. "It's vermilion." She squeezed out a thin smile. "I'm Arletty Daoust-Tremblay."

"And I'm overwhelmingly delighted to meet you. I'm Ari MacLeod. He took her hand tentatively. She held his briefly, then she let go. Ari was breathing with difficulty. "You're double-barrel French?"

"I'm double-barrel *Québecoise*. Ten generations."

"But you speak English."

"The *Québecois* are no longer *"Pepsis,"* or haven't you heard about that in Westmount?" she hissed menacingly.

"Come ON. Don't do that. You're so fluent. And... and, no accent, I mean... and, how did you...? WHAT is this about Westmount!? Please, it was an INNOCENT question."

Arletty decided to take pity on him. "I lived in the States for awhile. No big deal." She stood up. "Thanks for the meal."

Ari stood up as well. "Wait," he was at a loss, "you said you had no home. Where are you going? I mean..."

She smiled in a mature, understanding way. "I'll be alright. But, don't you forget to bring me the script, okay? Suddenly, I'm very interested in your movie."

Ari had to restrain himself from hugging her. "I'm going to bring the script down tonight."

Arletty smiled appreciatively. "I'll read it, and I'll call you. Don't forget to write down your number. Okay?" She blew him a tiny kiss — but a kiss, nonetheless — and she took off down the strip. She blended into the landscape. She disappeared.

Chapter 3

The next morning. Ari's house.

*N*umber One Redpath Crescent is high above the city of
Montreal, in Westmount. Seemingly stuck to the woodsy cliff
that leads to the top of Mount Royal, it has been home to six generations of MacLeods. Charlie MacLeod, the Edinburgh lout, who
came to Canada one step ahead of the law, built it back in 1839 as
a five bedroom safe-house: "If ye didn'a like who was approachin'
out-front, ye could always escape into the woods out back." It had
been expanded into a thirty room mansion complete with ballroom
and indoor swimming pool right after the First World War, by
Charlie's great grandson, Ross.

And now, Ross's grandson Ari — from Aristos, Greek for "the
best" — was sitting in its most beautiful room, the imported French-
glass enclosed solarium which looked out into the June-fresh rose
and forsythia garden; a scented fantasy in purple and gold.

At this moment, Ari gave nary a thought to all the hard work,
Calvinist greed and Presbyterian perseverance that had gone into
the garden, the house, the dynastic fortune, the great-big-impene-
trable package of traditions and responsibilities. To all of which he
happened to be the sole heir.

At that moment, the patio doors were open to admit the sweet
perfume of robust roses. His mother, the Greco-Byzantine Maria
— from Istanbul, the once-and-forever Constantinople — was putting the final touches on his articulated, late breakfast of grilled
brioche, Greek thyme-honey, desalinated Bulgarian feta, and fresh
peaches. However, he was luxuriating in the aftermath of the
most intense, early-morning phone call he had ever received. At
this moment, Ari had his hands quite full just thinking about his

movie, mostly about one impish Arletty.

"Something wonderful happened to me, Mama," he said, looking up at the woman who had brought him into the world, and who
would battle to the ends of the Earth, if she had to, to protect him
and to make him happy.

Maria, who treated every opportunity in life, and especially
those moments with her only child as occasions to look her absolute
best, was dressed in a breezy caftan she had sewn herself from a
design that had caught her eye in a Milan shop-window. She was
wearing some light morning make-up and freshly-styled hair, its
original blue-black restored by a master coiffeur, who had cleverly
masked the premature gray.

At 39, Maria was by all counts a beauty. Tall with lush hair and
fiery, brown eyes, she was endowed with the full figure of a Sophia
Loren, the proud posture of an Irene Pappas, and a uniquely
expressive face. Her physical attributes, in conjunction with her
position as First Lady of the MacLeod household, gave her immense
clout, as well as an aura of privileged unattainability; qualities that
played well on the social-philanthropic circuit, wreaked havoc on
her by-now loveless marriage to Duncan MacLeod, and painted her
a hero, a rock, a CHAMPION, to her son Ari, who, after all was said
and done, was the only lasting joy, the only element that made her
life worth living.

She set down the breakfast foods in an attractive arrangement
before him. Ari barely looked down, sipping absently on his coffee,
letting some pre-tears glisten on his eyes.

"Whatever this wonderful thing is, it's making you sad, and it
made you lose your appetite. Aren't these signs?"

"Of what?"

"Of being in love!"

Ari smiled painfully. "No, it's not love. I'm not so crass as to fall
in love, mama. But," he winced, "I need money."

"Already?" Maria's eyebrows arched and then relaxed with a dis-
approval that could never quite lead to a scolding.

"It's not what you think. It's for the movie."

"You said the movie was done. I can't really give you more.
Your father will notice."

"Oh, my father..."

Maria sighed. She sat down next to Ari, and caressed his cheek,
turning his face towards her. "Listen to me, Aristaki!"

"Do I ever not?" he asked demurely.

"Stop conning me. I've had enough of your embezzling ways," she said laughing merrily. "Your father would cut us both off without a penny, if he knew I was giving you his money to make a film that promotes Quebec separatism."

"What do you mean his money?"

"That is how I think. Where I come from, the husband controls the money. I spend as much as I like, but I have to be prepared to be accountable."

"And he has never asked for an accounting before. Isn't that what you said?"

"I did, and that's not the point. The point is that the money is finished. $350 thousand was it. My private chequing account. The household budget. Even the salaries of the staff. God knows how I'll pay them this month. It's all gone. You've taken everything. We are bankrupt, my darling."

"Oh, Mama," moaned Ari.

"What is it? The end of the world? The final destruction of life as we know it? The deluge?"

"Stop laughing at me. This is much worse than any of that. It's the end of Inspiration. The death of Art. My film career? Wiped out. I mean it, this is desperate!"

"Okay. Now, tell me. What's this really about?"

"It's about a scene. A two-minute scene, that will refocus the story. The spark. The decisive moment of any artistic creation. That, which propels the action to its next level of sophistication, to its intoxication, and that which validates its logical conclusion. Like the mad scene of Lucia, or the death scene of Gluck's *Orpheus and Euridice*. I have the scene. I have the actress. All I need is about five thousand dollars for a day's shooting and some recutting."

Maria withdrew her hand and raised her eyebrows again. This time they remained arched. "This actress. She wouldn't by any chance be the person you're so desperately NOT in love with, would she?"

Ari lowered his gaze. "She would."

"Oh, Aristo. When did you meet her? Only yesterday, I suppose." Her disappointment was palpable. "And now you want money we don't have, to put her in the movie, to impress her, and then what? To buy her affection? This is not worthy of you. Dirty old men do things like that. If you need to play games to make someone love you, then they're not worth loving."

Ari raised his eyes, and spoke with an urgency his mother had never heard before: "She called me this morning. She had only one hour to read the script. But she understands it totally. She understands everything. And she knows what to do, and has the courage to do it. This is what I was missing all along. I didn't know it yesterday, but now it's clear. Very clear. I'm sorry. I should've known before, I didn't, and it wouldn't have mattered, because without her, it couldn't have been done. With her, it'll be perfect. It'll be perfect because of her. My movie, my life, the entire Universe. Everything depends on this. Everything."

"Well, if that's the case," Maria laughed weakly, "I suppose..."

"PLEASE, Mama!"

"Zizanio. Monster. You're IMPOSSIBLE!"

Ari pouted, aiming low, and scoring. "I'll pay you back, mama, every penny. You'll see. We'll go to Cannes with this movie, and... and, well, with this scene in it, WE CAN'T LOSE!"

Maria pinched his cheek. "I suppose I could borrow against some jewelry..."

"Oh, MAMA. You saved my LIFE!" Ari bounded out of his chair, and hugged his mother, leading her in a mute waltz, kissing the air all around her.

Maria struggled out of his hold. "Stop. You'll ruin my hair! And if your father ever finds out—"

"He won't. How can he, unless you tell him." Ari continued his dance round and round, giggling and yelping like a puppy.

"Now, I have to turn into a liar because of you."

"No, mama. Not a liar. A weaver of dreams. An enabler of fantasies. An artist. And a champion! You do what you do, so that I can become what I must become."

Maria looked at him puzzled. She stood up to pour herself a coffee. "I don't know what you just said, but I'll let it go. And I'll only help you if you sit down and eat. You've lost weight with this movie, God knows what you've been eating. Not much, I know that. Day and night. Movie, movie, movie."

Ari sat down and dug into his meal with gusto. Maria sipped on her coffee, content to see that this desperate love had not actually diminished her son's appetite, yet. "And this actress... What's her name?"

Arletty. Arletty. "Ar-let-ty-y-y-y-y," sang Ari, through a mouthful of juicy peach.

Chapter 4

That same day. Lunchtime in the Plateau.

Down the hill from Westmount, and a couple of miles to the east, is the Main, otherwise known as St. Lawrence Boulevard. Historically and geographically, the Main represents the dividing line between the English and the French, money and poverty, West and East.

East of the Main, stretching to *Parc Lafontaine* and beyond, is a densely populated area of narrow streets with mixed-and-matched low-income architecture. This area that once housed working-class families has been reinvented as the *Plateau*, short for *"Plateau Mont-Royal."* Now in the process of being renovated and gentrified, this is the district where Arletty grew up, and where her parents, Louis-Marc Daoust and Josette Tremblay still live.

Arletty walked quickly, oblivious to the charm of the tree-shaded streets, the exterior, metal staircases winding up to doll-like, two and three storey, skinny houses, all the new little restaurants, florists, and hair-dressers, the brave new daintiness of a neighbourhood for which prospective new tenants and home-buyers were lining up, and from which she hadn't been able to move out fast enough.

Arletty's memories of the *Plateau* were tainted with youthful contempt for everything her father stood for, and therefore everything she had hated for as long as she could remember. Here in the Plateau was the motherlode of the little life. Dysfunctional marriages, unruly children, endless financial worries: a repetitious, trite and petty cycle in which unhappiness was a foregone conclusion and forced cheer, the only recourse. The same relentless pattern, day in, day out. Christmas was always a momentous occasion, as if one day a year could possibly salvage a lifetime of suffering.

She had moved out at fourteen. Made a beeline for New York City, where she had, teflon-like, escaped unscathed for two years, despite living on the edge, in clubs and video arcades and tiny, communal apartments. She had returned to Montreal at the age of sixteen, seasoned and matured, even more of a cynic than when she had left.

A cynic in the Classical sense. As in, a higher being, who believes in virtue, self-control and independence. Her father had taught her about the Cynics when she was six. He had made a fatal error. He had provided her with the ammunition to despise him with. Ever since, she had seen him as a person of little virtue, no discipline whatsoever, and utter dependence on everything and everyone but himself.

For the sport of it, she had set out to become his exact opposite, and to flaunt it in his face as often as possible. In fact, she was on her way to see him now, and she was braving her distaste for the *Plateau,* because he refused to travel outside it. She urgently wanted to taunt him with her news, and by happy coincidence, the meeting was being held at his insistence.

She entered *Le Resto Dali* on Gilford Street, far east of St. Lawrence, almost at Papineau, at a corner that used to, in the old days, house a snack bar, the purveyor of ordinary hot dogs, but the very best *poutine* in the East. Now it was redecorated with ripped-off replicas of the crazy Figueran's warped surrealism; its all-female waiters sporting glued-on, stiletto mustaches, and the place reeked of too much garlic, which went into all of its medium-priced, extremely popular, so-called *Costa-Brava*-style *tapas.*

Dali was her father's favourite restaurant, and he swore by the authenticity of its Catalan cuisine even though he had only been anywhere in Spain only twice. Both of these occasions had been spent at the Madrid airport, waiting endlessly for his cheap, Montreal-Casablanca charter connections when he was a hippy in the late sixties.

From what she could see, the only item he enjoyed in his favourite place were the heavily-garlicked shrimps, surely a vestige of his childhood, when crustaceans bathed in garlic butter were *Québecois* families preferred treat during dinners-out. Sure enough, Louis-Marc was already tucking into the first of three or four orders of his *gambas al ajillo,* when she unceremoniously slipped into the chair opposite his window table — from one could "breathe and taste the *Plateau,*" as he reminded her every time they met there. "Ah, finally!" boomed her father. "You're late, but no matter. Sit and enjoy. The June weather. The *Plateau* air, its taste, its spirit. Let it carry you away, Arletty. And let it bring you back home. To us."

"Ah, what a surprise! You've ordered garlic shrimps," she said with a barely disguised sneer. She was disdainful not only of the clichéd shrimps, but also of his never-changing appearance, his uniform: skinny pony-tail set on his increasingly balding head, John Lennon granny glasses, ironed lumberjack shirt, intentionally weathered jeans, and — horrors — the Birkenstocks. A parody of himself, but worse, some kind of terrible joke on her.

Louis-Marc had learned to live with his daughter's sarcasm. "Sample one. They're delicious. Go on. Share with me. Go on."

Arletty spotted several bread crumbs in the garlic butter. "No, thank you."

Louis-Marc caught her gaze. "You're supposed to sop up the sauce with your bread. That's how they do it in Spain. You eat from your half of the plate. It's untouched."

"*Bof!*" exclaimed Arletty. "I told you I hate the shrimps here. They use garlic salt instead of real garlic."

"They do NOT!"

The waiter arrived to take her order. She hoped he hadn't heard her slur, and take revenge by spitting on her food. "I'd like an omelette," she said to him, politely. "Please, no tricks. Just eggs. And fries. Lots of them. A salad, with no garlic. Just oil and vinegar. And a Coke. And quickly, please. I'm starved."

"We might as well have gone to a snack bar," scoffed Louis-Marc.

"Next time we should," shrugged Arletty. "So, what's the emergency? Why did you make me rush down to see you? Are the English planning to invade the *Plateau?*" She stifled her giggle: making the joke was risky enough.

Louis-Marc wound himself into an attack posture. He engaged Arletty's attention, and stared at her dangerously for a long second. Then, gravely: "There is a very important meeting on the referendum tonight. It's imperative that you be there."

"You're mad."

"You're refusing to come?" Feigning surprise.

"Why should I come? I never did before," Arletty said defiantly. Louis-Marc was reaching his Arletty-exasperation limit sooner than he had intended. To calm himself, he ate a shrimp, and took a gulp of wine. He wiped his mouth with exquisite self-control. The waiter brought Arletty's lunch. He started setting down the dishes with Iberian disdain. Louis-Marc acknowledged this affront to Spanish cuisine with a humble shrug. He waited until the omelette, the fries, the salad, and the glass of Anglophone Imperialism — the Coke — were firmly placed in front of his daughter. She started to eat immediately.

"This is our nation's greatest historical moment," began Louis-Marc, as if delivering a manifesto. "We are a mere dagger's thrust away from success. IF this next referendum is held, we will finally be able to evict the colonizer-oppressor English, and at last regain our independent, fully empowered *Québec*. Our HOMELAND, Arletty. Why do you resist? What's wrong with you? How can you allow this opportunity to slip through your fingers? Don't you have any decency?"

Arletty paused her chewing, to seethe: "Do you mind? I'm eating."

"I mind GREATLY." seethed Louis-Marc right back at her. "I didn't— I didn't invite you here so you can EAT!"

"Really? Well, I only came for the meal. I haven't eaten well in days."

"Fine way you have of taking care of yourself! You can't even afford eggs to make yourself an omelette? You're going to die, you!"

"Times are tough, but not quite deadly, yet. I can afford eggs; I can't afford to go to restaurants! You know I don't cook."

"Yes, just like your mother."

"And what's wrong with my mother?"

"Nothing at all. I love your mother, almost as much as I love you," smiled Louis-Marc, trying to regain the upper hand. "The problem with you young, is that you are relativist. For you, the communal aims and values of society mean nothing, because you are hedonist, and have no concern for your duties as citizens. You'd rather have your fun than lay down the foundations for your future."

Arletty stopped chewing, and looked at him incredulously. "What? Again with the famous condemnations of Charles Taylor, that senile, Anglophone ass-kisser of yours? How many times are you going to ram him down my throat?"

"As many as necessary. Charles Taylor speaks of you. You're exactly the kind of person who'll flourish in the New *Québec*. You have so much to gain. Oh, Arletty, whatever I've done to you, forgive me, and change your mind. I implore you." Louis-Marc was beginning to crack.

Arletty finished off her drink, and wiped her mouth on her sleeve. "I'm NOT coming to the yes strategy meeting. Nor to the yes demonstration. Nor am I wearing your stupid yes button. Nor am I voting yes. I don't care. Yes free *Québec,* No free Quebec, it's all the same to me. I'm not interested in your outdated politics. It'll do nothing at all for me when you've won your tired old war, and no one is allowed to speak English in Montreal any longer. It no longer makes any DIFFERENCE! The whole situation BORES me."

"Enough. Stop slapping me!" Louis-Marc fought back the desire to scream at her.

Arletty, suddenly humbled, gave her father a conciliatory smile. "Sorry, pops. Really. By all means. Go on with your war. And who knows, maybe one day, I'll see the light, and join the struggle. Except, tonight, it's impossible."

"Why?"

"I'm busy tonight. I'm being paid to act. I came here all excited to share my happiness with you. Really, it wasn't just for the omelette."

Louis-Marc allowed himself a slight sneer. "Ah, yes. Your acting career. Are you going to remain clothed this time?"

Arletty sneered back. "I took off my clothes last time for the Cause. The rock-video I was in became an *Independentiste* anthem. I thought you'd be proud of me."

"Proud to see my daughter nude on TV?"

"Well, I won't be nude this time. It's a REAL film. A feature. And it's pro *Québec*. Really." Arletty settled back in her chair, which, having been inspired by that master of cruelty Salvador Dali, provided scant comfort. "I'm getting more than scale. Twelve hundred dollars for five hours' work. Not bad, eh?"

"Who's behind this? Who hired you?"

Arletty had been waiting for that question. She savoured this pregnant pause for a few seconds. Then, deliberately: "A new friend. The director. His name is Ari. And he's an Anglo." Arletty lit a cigarette, further provoking her violently anti-smoking father.

"An Anglo?"

"From... Westmount." *Touché.*

Louis-Marc let out a derisive snort. He was back on familiar ground. This was the old Arletty, fencing with him, and she was enjoying her little victory. He looked at her with exaggerated pity: "Well, yes. That makes sense. That's exactly what I expect from you. But watch out, my lovely one, my only one. Westmount is full of inbred Anglos, self-centered and mean, hungry and greedy; so hungry that they suck up everything in sight, and when there is nothing left, they eat each other. They are cannibals. I'd be very careful, if I were you."

Chapter 5

Afternoon that same day. Duncan MacLeod's study.

Duncan MacLeod, Ari's father, had never cared for the rose and forsythia garden. For his office, he had chosen a second floor suite of rooms facing the front of the house, as far away as he could from any smelly, conspicuously cheerful foliage. Instead of flowers, he looked down the hill at the city, which rolled out beneath him, an apparent miniature of itself, with the bridges and installations on the St. Lawrence River, a mechanized municipal boundary.

He felt quite pleased with himself. He had just pulled off a nifty coup. Working on an insider's hint, he had sold off $350 million worth of stock in an Ontario mega-company that had been secretly planning to sell off its assets and declare bankruptcy. This lightning bankruptcy wasn't a particularly legal maneuver, and someone down the line would eventually go to designer jail for it, but it certainly had poleaxed the stockholders' capital when the news exploded half-way through the afternoon's trading. Everyone's capital, that is, but Duncan's.

In the course of one brief exchange at 2:22 p.m., Duncan had beat the announcement by thirty minutes, sold his stock for a decent price, and reinvested the entire amount in a U.S. company — bless those Yanks! — which had itself been contemplating a questionable gesture — a surprise merger — within that same half hour. By 2:56 p.m. both events had taken place, vapourizing the value of the Ontario company, while doubling that of the American.

At three o'clock sharp, Duncan sold his stock in the U.S. company, ending up with $700 million instead of the zero he would have struck, had he not made the transactions. It had taken thirty-eight minutes, which meant a profit of $18,421,052.00 per minute. Bill Gates, screw YOU!

Duncan decided to take a ten-minute rest before resuming his trading. He got up and and pulled his vest tight. He fondled his tie-knot, making sure it was in place. He decided against putting on the jacket of his three-piece pin-stripe and left it on the clothes horse, where it had hung since the morning. He walked over to his picture windows to indulge in his favourite pastime: looking down on Montreal. It had been such a fine town... once. So charming, so accommodating, so fully-functional, so lucrative, so... HIS.

He ground his teeth, tight-lipped, as he always did when the spectre of Quebec separatism crossed his mind. Such fools. Cutting off their collective pecker to spite their crotch. Peppers. Frogs. Dumbos. *QuebécOIS!* Yeah, right! *QuébecOIS*, who want their *OUI*. But, YES to separate from WHAT? Idiots. Nevertheless, what a pretty town.

Duncan smirked at the view of the city. The funny thing was that, if he wanted to, he could buy all of Montreal. He had actually sat down and figured it out. His own $750 billion, bolstered by another couple of trillion from the banks, would be sufficient to buy every property worth buying, with the exception of the parks and the churches, which would effectively be his anyway if he owned everything else.

A city-state with Montreal's strategic location, under his control and with his business acumen, would flourish like none other in history. It would outdo Ancient Athens, even rival Rome. But, to buy Montreal, and serve the French masters up there in Quebec City? He'd rather buy one of the new republics in the former Yugoslavia!

To enter into either of these equally dodgy ventures would have made his noble ancestors collectively churn in their graves. All of them, that is, going back to his great-great-grandfather Charlie MacLeod. Because before him the family had been riddled with Edinburgh-slum style peccadilloes: illegitimacies and public hangings. Not exactly the kind of folk with traceable family trees and ancestors who tend to churn in their graves.

Charlie, an accomplished pickpocket by the age of six, and leader of the most notorious sheep-rustling operation in the Lowlands at sixteen, had basically founded the MacLeod family — it was not his real name — when he escaped to Canada in 1826, at the age of eighteen. He had lucked out because this was a time when business opportunities abounded in Montreal, especially if one happened to hail from Scotland.

Given a legal license to make easy money, Charlie had embarked on a business involving imported cast-iron machinery, in which he succeeded because he had savvy, even though he knew nothing about either importing or metal. He did so well that by his 30th birthday, he was able to start a family by marrying the spinsterish but highly respectable Augusta McGill, daughter of Duncan McGill, the publishing giant, as well as to build a supposedly impenetrable home up on Redpath Crescent.

During the next twenty years, Charlie became certifiably rich by scrapping imports in favour of opening his own foundry, to cast iron from his own mine — which he acquired for free from a government eager to promote development — and manufacture the machines in his own factory, which he had won in a poker game, by cheating another Scots ex-hustler, this one from Glasgow.

In 1859, at the age of 50, Charlie met his maker in the form of an aggrieved ex-partner, who extracted revenge for a thirty-five year-old grudge, by sailing all the way from Scotland, eliminating the bodyguards and the gardener, and gunning Charlie down in cold blood, before he could reach the safety of the woods out back.

Charlie and Augusta's only child, James — never Jaimie or Jimmy — grew up in a hurry that evening, at the tender age of eighteen. He had had to outshoot his father's assailant and therefore kill a man in order to save his mother's as well as his own life. Thus, he got to inherit and take over Charlie's sprawling, secretive, and highly profitable business, while still a teenager.

James, who was born in that original five-bedroom house, died in it at the age of seventy one, fifty-three years after that fateful, bullet-ridden night, without ever finding the time to renovate it. The MacLeods shat in outhouses well into the Twentieth Century, even though indoor plumbing had existed in Montreal for decades.

Instead of concerning himself with the creature comforts of home and hearth, James devoted his fifty three years in business to working around the clock, seven days a week. His only recreation was the Sunday morning church service, and grudgingly, the entire day of Christmas. In the process he had transformed Charlie's burgeoning business into an empire, and by the time of his death in 1912, every home and every enterprise in every Province of Canada and in several States south of the border owned something manufactured from scratch by the MacLeod Company.

The original mine had become fifty mines, the original factory grew two hundred times bigger, and James owned a major chunk of the cross-continental railroad, which was built expressly for the purpose of transporting the interminable freight of products like his. In 1897, at the height of the Victorian era, the year of the Queen-Empress's Diamond Jubilee, the MacLeod Company employed 20,000 people. Somehow, in the midst of all that, James found the time to personally review and appraise the productivity and efficiency of each and every worker.

During a moment of sheer frivolity, in the summer of 1873, the thirty-three year-old tycoon took off valuable Sunday afternoon accounting time to marry Edwina McAllister, the frail, sickly daughter of Ross McAllister, the fur baron. The accounting suffered another delay that evening, as James bedded his new bride, to consummate the marriage. It must have been a fruitful session, because Edwina, who took ill directly after her wedding night, and slept separately from James for two months, discovered she was pregnant at the end of those sixty days.

Edwina spent the next seven months in agony, her skinny frame barely able to contain her developing offspring. She died giving birth to a healthy, beautiful boy, whom the officially-grieving James named Duncan — after his mother's father — and not Charlie, fearful of eponymously ascribing his father's awful fate to his son.

Little Duncan, overcoming the doting of his forever grieving — for Charlie — grandmother Augusta and his twice-bereaved, widower — grandfather Ross, grew into a champion of a man, his father's great hope for the future of mankind. He was that sort of heir to a fortune who usually exists in pulp fiction. Perfect in every way; a model son, a delightfully devoted young husband at eighteen to beautiful Elsie MacDougal, daughter of beer and tobacco king Finlay MacDougal; handsome, compassionate, smart, an athlete, natural-born businessman, and excellent father to his first-born daughter Jaimie, named after his father, and younger son Ross, named for his maternal grandfather. This guy had it all.

Nevertheless, and despite the precautions his father had taken to name him anything other than Charlie, Duncan MacLeod was not able to escape an early death. Only thirty-eight years old, but at the height of his prowess, besieged by pleas to enter politics and seek high office while James was still in charge and could spare him. Duncan and his forever glamorous, beloved wife Elsie both perished in the hostile waters of the North Atlantic during the early morning hours of that infamous date, April 15, 1912. They had been sailing luxuriously on the Titanic, back from England where they had gone to accept James MacLeod's knighthood from King George V. The newly — and by proxy — knighted Sir James, who had at 71 enjoyed fine health, received the news of his son's death very badly. He went into a rapid Dickensian decline and died not more than four months later, during a rainy-muggy August morning — of grief, they had all agreed. The MacLeod Company, with assets of almost a billion pre-First-World-War dollars — enough to buy Montreal, at the time — was thus suddenly in the hands of eighteen-year-old Jaimie MacLeod and her twelve-year-old brother Ross.

It took the various trustees, vice-presidents and major business affiliates of the Company exactly two hours to comprehend that Jaimie was cut from the same wool as all the other MacLeods. With neither her youth — she was the same age, after all, as her grandfather James, when he had taken over — nor her sex serving as impediments.

Jaimie boldly led the Company through The First War, a gold mine of opportunity for the cast-iron industry; cautiously through the devil-may-care Twenties; ruthlessly through the Great Depression — MacLeod was the only company in Canada to be consistently in the black throughout the Thirties; and brazenly, masterfully, through the bonanza of The Second War, during which she had supplied arms to both sides: England and her allies directly from Canada, and Hitler and his allies from her subsidiaries in the States. This she did openly until 1942, and not so openly after that, when America was sucked into the war against the Axis.

She continued her assault on the marketplace by diversifying into plastics and aluminum in the Fifties, nuclear fuel in the paranoid Sixties and Seventies, and heavily into silicon, which she manufactured into computer chips just in time for the dawn of the Cybernetic Era in the early Eighties. She did the company proud, right up to her death in 1990, at the age of ninety six. And she'd have lived longer if her brother Ross, the only love of her unmarried-childless life, hadn't died and broken her heart earlier that same year.

Ross MacLeod, born on New Year's Eve 1900, was truly a child of his century. He spent his ninety years on this Earth conspicuously care-free, unashamedly pleased that his sister Jaimie, whom he loved with a passion equal to her own for him, took care of business, so that he could dream and remain young, almost childish, right up to the end.

At the magic MacLeod age of eighteen, Ross undertook the rebuilding of the family home, and upon completion of his *oeuvre,* a vast improvement on the original house, he spent almost a year to plan and execute the most lavish party *tout-Montréal* had ever tried to crash, in order to celebrate it.

At twenty-five, during the height of his Gatsby period, Ross founded a symphony orchestra and an opera company, both of which disintegrated with the onslaught of the Great Depression. At forty-one, during the worst of the fighting over in Europe, he built an ostentatious museum, which he filled with artwork that had been stolen by the Germans and clandestinely sold to Company agents in Europe. The museum quietly shut down at war's end, when the rightful owners, several brand-name art museums in France and Holland, reclaimed the art, and he had no choice but to return it all for free.

In 1946, only a year after the war, Ross spent considerable money to convert some unused factory space into a movie studio for talented film-makers who had been persecuted by Hitler, and who were now about to be persecuted by Stalin. All of them gratefully accepted his patronage, happy to be paid to come to Canada and escape the ravages of eastern Europe. But once on this side of the Atlantic, the best of them promptly departed for Hollywood. The studio faded away, and by 1948 no one on Redpath Crescent mentioned it again.

Jaimie forgave Ross all his follies, and worked overtime to recoup whatever she could from each succeeding debacle, because she loved him, and because he reciprocated by taking care of her. Ross was a gentle and good-humoured, but exacting and thorough housekeeper. He was in charge of the staff, he was in charge of the kitchen — he had taught himself to cook light but full-flavoured dishes, decades before such things became fashionable — he was in charge of all diversions, parties, vacations. In every way, he provided the home life and the sense of family — as well as the nice, healthy diet — Jaimie needed to be able to succeed in business.

Ross provided Jaimie with an empowering nest, and Jaimie gave Ross the latitude to indulge his fantasies. The two of them quite happily lived, played and earned their place in history, always together — tongues wagged, despite their innocence — a tight society of two, a closed circle. However, there was a problem: no heir.

When he was almost fifty years old, Ross suddenly married the awkward, young and strong, eminently-divorceable Cornelia MacDermid, daughter of Alexander MacDermid, a modest grocer of particularly sturdy genes — members of his family generally lived to a ripe old age. Exactly nine months later, Cornelia gave birth to baby Duncan, who was named after his Titanic-drowned grandfather, with no heed whatsoever to any possible historical repeats of bad luck. Within six months, Cornelia moved out of Redpath Crescent at the legal request of a battalion of lawyers Jaimie had hired to oust her — or, more accurately, to buy her out. The MacLeods took custody of the child, and handed her a court order to stay away forever.

Duncan the Second grew up to be the focus of his father's unadulterated attention — no more arts projects — and the careful grooming of his aunt Jaimie. His business training, which began at the age of ten, was as rigorous and calculated as the preparation of an heir to a throne. This quickly aroused his appetite for power and acquisition, and it surprised no one that he quit university and joined the company on his eighteenth birthday. He was confident that he could learn all he needed to know from his aunt Jaimie at the office.

In 1990, when Duncan was forty, married to Maria and sire of the pre-teen Ari, his father and aunt both died within months of each other, and left him in charge of the MacLeod legacy. He didn't waste any time. Fueled by his disgust for Quebec's abstract nationalism, and facilitated by the plutocratically-inspired Free Trade deal with the U.S., he immediately and systematically started selling off the vast MacLeod holdings in Quebec to opportunistic American companies, and reinvested his capital internationally.

Clever, almost clairvoyant, he executed a series of enviable trades, profiting even from recessions and market implosions, a chess master of the financial game, a Michelangelo of the pin-point deal, every detail thought-out and seamlessly timed, every decision correct. He had tripled his treasury in less than a decade, to its present three-quarters of a trillion — enough to buy the island of Montreal, or any of the new republics of the former Yugoslavia.

And for what? So that he could die and hand it over to an altogether-useless, mama's boy. An empty-headed fool who had the nerve to proclaim that he had no interest in business, only in Art —

brazenly using his grandfather Ross's deplorable art-ventures for leverage. What the hell was art anyway, if not a reflection and a celebration of the World? And where the hell would that World be without MONEY? What kind of an idiot would one have to be to show even a hint of disinterest in three-quarters of a trillion dollars? Only one who resolutely refused any and all preparatory business training, thus breaking the most sacred MacLeod trust. And succeeding in this act of execrable omission by hiding behind his mother's skirts. AND one who spent his eighteenth year, the fateful MacLeod year, bumming around Europe, sleeping in cheap hotels, whiling away his days in movie houses and pretentious, cafe-society hangouts, more than likely smoking dope or, worse. His only son, and unless he did something to prevent this, his heir. Ari. Aristos. The best. What a joke. What cosmic irony.

Obviously he would eventually have to induce the boy to marry, as Aunt Jaimie had done with his father Ross, buy himself a grandchild along with some fresh hope. But not this minute. Any plans for this happy event would have to wait. Duncan was now through with his rest period. He returned to his desk, determined to hit on the market again, stir up another little windfall. $300 million would be just right. Added to the $700 million already in his pocket, it would put him at a cool billion for the day. A personal best, and surely a world record.

Chapter 6

Early evening that same day. In the Daoust-Tremblay house.

L ouis-Marc, looking comical in his late mother's frilly apron, yet deadly serious about the task at hand, fussed over his table set-for-two. Candlelight, wine breathing in a decanter, napkins folded into a peacock shape, crystal gleaming, antique china, still unchipped, as fragile and elegant as the day his grandmother had first received it fresh from *Sèvres*. Bread warmly nestled in Egyptian cotton in its basket, unsalted butter softening in a silver dish, and the tablecloth underneath all that, starched and ironed.

This was going to be a great dinner, yet another great feast for his forever-fascinating Josette. The star of his Universe, the singularly most worthwhile event in a life otherwise dedicated to reading and research, teaching Political Science part-time at UQAM *(L' Université du Québec À Montréal)*. And endlessly composing his definitive manifesto/business-plan for a free, prosperous, fully Francophone *Québec*, where Anglos would only be welcome once they were assimilated — or at least, learned the academic French required for filling out government forms, as well as *Québec*'s dialect Joual — to facilitate communication with their neighbours.

His work was performed mostly at home on his computer and according to his own schedule. Josette, on the other hand, worked in a high-powered travel agency, 9:45 a.m. to 5:55 p.m., six days a week. He considered it his duty and the high point of his day, to have dinner ready for her, exactly at 6:16 p.m. This was the earliest she could arrive, after a hurtling, European-style drive in her convertible, vintage BMW — red, of course — from her Bernard Street office.

It was no stretch for Louis-Marc to cook and cater to his wife every day but Sunday, when they ate out, over the entire twenty three years of their marriage. Food was in his blood. He had traced five centuries of the Daoust family tree, three hundred years of it in *Québec,* and he had unearthed a steady line of his male ancestors, all named Louis something-or-other, all of them illustriously employed in the food business.

The earliest Daoust he had uncovered, Louis-Anthelme, was a chef in the court of Louis XI, the king, who had reconstructed the homeland in the 15th century, following a hundred years of mind-less, Anglo devastation. Fast-forwarding to Louis-Archange-Gabriel, who had brought the family to the New World on a royal charter from Louis XIV in 1699, to open a fancy guest-house in Montréal, in case any courtiers ever happened to visit La Nouvelle France. And right up to his own grandfather, Louis-Télésphore, who as a young man at the turn of the century invested the family money in open-ing Montreal's legendary *Daoust Met Fins,* purveyors of prepared fine foods and imported delicacies. Located smack on the corner of Ste. Catherine and Peel, the once-but-no-longer centre of Canada, it thrived for seven decades until his death in 1970.

Old Louis-Télésphore lived and breathed Food, right up to his last minute: fittingly, he died in his shop, behind the fish counter, while sampling a fresh batch of dry-smoked Gaspé salmon. Always with his ear to the frying pan, he readily tempted his well-heeled customers with the latest, astronomically-priced, cutting edge cui-sine, and the rarest, trendiest ingredients imported from all four corners. Boxes and shopping bags emblazoned with his *fleur-de-lis* insignia — courtesy of Louis XIV — were status symbols. No Westmount hostess of social consequence was entirely free from the obligation to regale her guests with something wonderful from Daoust.

Unfortunately, Louis-Télésphore took such a long time to die that none of his eleven children, including Louis-Polycarpe, Louis-Marc's father, managed to survive him and continue the store. All forty-five grandchildren, among them Louis-Marc, were already grown-up, and had chosen other, mostly-academic careers.

The store's assets were sold, and its proceeds added to the siz-able estate. The money, as per the will, was placed in a trust, which provided each grandchild with cash to buy a home, and an annuity of $20,000. As a result, Louis-Marc owned his comfortable, second-storey flat, with its front and back balconies, its ornamental wood-

work, its Habitant-style eat-in kitchen with its special alcove table
set-for-two, in the heart of the Plateau, his private paradise. The
annual five-figure cheque was the cherry on top of the sundae, his
toe-hold on financial independence: it was all the license he needed to afford himself the luxury to earn very little, and immerse himself in political philosophy and the struggle against the Anglo-
Conqueror.

Cooking for Josette was Louis-Marc's nurturing gesture of love
to her. At the same time it afforded him the opportunity to get in
the kitchen and pay homage to five-hundred years of Daousts, who
had laboured there, so that he could be who he was, and save his
country.

He had been extra-diligent today, outdoing himself, hoping to
definitively floor Josette with the evanescent lightness of his pike
quenelle appetizer; the profound flavour of his labour-intensive,
home-made veal demi-glaze for the Madeira sauce of his *veau à la
dauphine;* and the silky richness of his ice-like burnt-sugar-coated
crême brulée — her favourite dessert. All because he wanted no, or,
very little trouble from her, when she learned he'd be going out for
the rest of the evening, directly after dinner.

She arrived a few minutes late, demonstrably tired, rattled by
the never-changing slow traffic. In this town, every June it was
always the same, stupid work crews pretending to mend pot-holes,
combined with every holiday-driver and his dog, out there showing
off fancy cars they never dared take on the streets in winter. Closed-
off lanes and bottlenecks, just to make the working stiffs' lives even
harder.

She sniffed the air, its subtle scent of treats-in-store. She sighed.
She kissed him. Then, as was her custom, she quickly washed her
face and changed into a loosely flowing caftan which she had
bought on sale at *La Baie,* so that she could sit down at table, and
wordlessly start her second day. This moment of peace, the promise
of Louis-Marc's cooking, which she never took for granted. The
inexplicable happiness she derived from being at home with this
introverted, methodical man, the diametrical opposite of her own
exuberant self. A man who had anchored her life as she believed no
one would be able to, ever.

Louis-Marc, respecting Josette's need for silence, held off on the
news of his evening plans. He waited past the *quenelles,* which
floated like sheer palate-magic on their exquisite *beurre blanc;*

through the tender-as-butter veal and its amazing sauce; until after she had had a chance to drink her usual two glasses of white wine, and even utter a few sighs of bliss. Sitting back in the crisp June light of late afternoon, looking down at the small, haphazardly-landscaped backyards, she was becoming human again, after an overly long day on the phone, booking and unbooking plane and hotel reservations for customers who could never really make up their minds until the last possible moment.

He served her the *crème brulée*, unable to hold the peace any longer. "There is a *Oui* meeting in about half an hour," he blurted.

"Oh, yes?"

"Want to come?"

"Will there be any dancing?" she chuckled through a mouthful of double-cream custard with its melting shards of glazed sugar.

"Not this time," he chuckled back, weakly.

"You go, baby. But be back by 9:30," she said, and winked.

"Nine-thirty? What's at 9:30?" he asked feebly.

"You forgot? Louis-Marc! How could you FORGET?"

"What did I forget? They called this meeting at the last minute, and I said yes. Did I do wrong? What did I forget? Please, Josette, stop enjoying my discomfort. Tell me."

She shook her head, like at a truant child. "*Omerta* on TV? Remember now? Gangsters, vendettas, guns. You know how horny all that Mafia stuff gets you. The way the Italians bled *Québec*, and did it mostly in English. And then, after the show, you know... we were supposed to...?" Her disappointment had become palpable. "You promised me. An early evening, *Omerta*, then *Jean Philippe Rameau*, a shot of Calvados, a little AFFECTION for your wife. I've been looking forward to this all day. It's the only thing that kept me going, I swear to you! Anyway, go, but be back by 9:30. *Omerta* starts at 9:30. That's all I'm saying." She finally took another bite of the *crème*. It sent shivers down her spine. She had yet to stop being grateful to her fate, which had granted her a husband who could make better *crème brûlée* than *Caprices de Nicolas*, even better than the best *L'Eau à la Bouche* had to offer.

Louis-Marc was at an impasse. He decided to deploy his ultimate weapon: the *Brillat-Savarin* inspired, quadruple-chocolate cognac-truffles, based on a secret recipe of his grandfather's, and the old store's all-time best seller. He set a heaping portion of them before her, and though she normally ate these instinctively, she didn't even look at them. Instead she stared straight at him, her eyebrows raised as far up as they could go.

"It's the poker, isn't it?" she asked menacingly.

"You know we always play after the meetings." He could avoid the issue no longer.

"Didn't you play just the other night?"

"The other night? Josette, that was five weeks ago, after the last meeting."

"Really? It feels as if it was just the other night." She took a truffle and stared it down, practically to its melting point, before dropping it in her mouth.

"It's traditional, Josette. We've been doing this forever. You know about this! You're just teasing me, aren't you?"

"No, I'm not. This time I'm serious. This one time, you could change your routine, and make me happy."

"Josette, please. You're being impossible. There is no way I can get out of the post-meeting poker game. It's as important as the meeting itself. Everyone on the organizing committee has done this. Even René Lévesque!"

"At least he used to win."

"It helps us focus after the meeting. We play, yes, but we continue a serious dialogue on the issues."

"Don't make me laugh. You play so that so you can bash each other's brains out, and take each other's money. I've seen you gloat for days when you've won, replaying the major hands, feeling like a million dollars. And rather energized in other ways too, I must admit. NEVERTHELESS, it's a disgusting habit, gambling, and I wish you'd stop, because it's robbing me of my romantic evening. That's all I have to say on the subject."

Louis-Marc, almost desperate, flew off into the kitchen to make Josette's coffee. Strong, dark and thick, the perfect accompaniment to her post-prandial cigarette.

"You don't understand poker, and that's why you're so against it," he started, as he set down the coffee. "It's not just gambling. It's a game of pure strategy and steely nerves. It's a true contest of will and skill, much like our greatest, most challenging life-concerns. Very much like our battle with the Anglo-Oppressor. It teaches all of us to stay on our toes. Alert. On the edge. Poker is a magnificent game, and it was invented in France. I love it."

"It's just about all you love anymore," she said matter-of-factly,

sipping her coffee and lighting a *Gauloise*. This was her one irrev-
ocable indulgence of the evening, and the only cigarette Louis-Marc
permitted her to smoke inside the house.

"I don't love poker any more than you love your cigarettes," he
said all-sufferingly. "I love *Québec* much more than that, and even
beyond *Québec,* a thousand times more, I love you."

"Really?" laughed Josette. "Then prove it."

"What? Now?" Louis-Marc feared that he had stepped into a
puddle.

Josette stood up and extended her hand to him. "Come on. Take
me to bed, my beautiful husband, and SHOW me how well you can
love me. Come on."

Louis-Marc stayed seated, miserable. Josette sat back down, and
lit a second *Gauloise*. It was getting late, but he knew he couldn't
quite go, yet. "I saw Arletty today," he said.

"How wonderful," smiled Josette. "I haven't seen her for a week
myself. Except through my window. I see her scooting down
Bernard Street, glorious in that red trench coat. Oh, I adore her."

"I'm worried about her," said Louis-Marc, to divert his wife's
attention. Arletty was an over-riding concern at all times. "She was
very hungry. She told me she hadn't eaten in days."

"She was pulling your leg," said Josette comfortably.

Louis-Marc laughed out loud. "You're right! She was sparring
with me right through lunch. Yes! That's what it was. Part of her
strategy to derail me. Ah, Josette. It was like old times. Challenging
me, angering me, and then pulling me back from the brink at the
last possible moment. What a fast brain. What confidence. What
poise. We did well, Josette."

"She did it mostly on her own. She is a true Tremblay.
Independent to a fault. Nimble as a brain surgeon. And impetuous?
My God. Like a volcano."

"She is a Daoust too, you know. Hard-working, grounded..."

"Sorry, baby. She's a sorry excuse for a Daoust. She hates cooking, she hates gourmet food. Hey. You know how long it took ME
to get used to your recipes. Well, she's worse. And she hates poker,
almost as much as I do."

"Both of you are missing out on one of civilization's greatest
and most diverting entertainments."

"We both have better ways to spend our money. Plus, we have
you to uphold the civilized standards of diversion. So, GO. Your

buddies are itching to take your money. Go! I'll wash the dishes, don't worry."

Like a teenager who just got permission to borrow the family car for the night, Louis-Marc yelped for joy and jumped out of his chair. He hugged Josette, giving her a sloppy, full mouthed kiss, the kind she liked. He flung off his apron and he fled out the door, before she had time to change her mind.

"Tomorrow night. Television and affection. I promise!" he yelled as he raced down the stairs.

Chapter 7

The same evening. A loft in Old Montreal.

*L*ow-budget — independent — film-making has historically been accomplished in weird and wondrous ways. By magic, as it were. By the scruff of one's neck. By relentless will-power.

Ari had spent three years pursuing *They Came From The North,* working on it ceaselessly ever since the idea came to him in an Amsterdam coffee house specializing in hashish — at least thirty daily offerings, available by the joint, all of which Ari tried but never inhaled. It was a simple idea: a movie about a runaway Toronto teenager who escapes to Montreal, hides out with some *Québec* revolutionaries, gets involved in the struggle, and dies for the cause.

He had envisioned it as a monochromatic picture, a drug-induced paranoid daze, composed chiefly of his heroine's shadowy face in *film noir* close-ups reacting to plot elements, most of which take place off-screen. By the time the script was deemed ready for filming, he had rewritten it seventy-two times, ending up with more of a cavalcade on *Québec* life, and therefore a satire on his own life, than the taut portrait he had originally intended.

The rewrites were occasioned by the inevitable screenplay-by-committee that victimizes all first-time movie scripts, where more of the key personnel assembles around the cinematic project of a *wanna-be auteur*-director. The fact that the movie was being produced solely by Ari, with whatever money he could scrape off his mother, didn't make a difference.

The various players he needed, the actors, the line producer, the locations manager, the continuity person, the camera crew, even the production assistants, all of whom he had had to persuade to work for less — all seemed to know exactly what the script was lacking.

So they bullied and badgered him on a daily basis, to incorporate their endless suggestions into his one fragile idea.

When the cameras started rolling on the first day of principal photography, Ari's original concept was barely recognizable, lost in the inane gags, fast-paced stunts, and gratuitous sex he had been forced to personalize and then write into the story in order to garner the cooperation of his underpaid staff. They needed to feel that it was a group creation, in order to give it their best effort.

His most profound regret with the final shooting script was that it no longer contained the pivotal scene upon which he hoped to peg the turning point of his plot. The scene was a two minute phone call from the heroine's best friend, another down-and-out teenaged girl from Toronto, who speaks desperately, defeatedly, beseechingly, and then kills herself, while the heroine listens and reacts.

This terminal act of intimate violence propels the heroine into a free-fall, reckless and self-destructive cycle that leads to her own violent death. And to a powerhouse ending invoking Hope through Death and Rebirth, or something along those lines.

He had been talked out of the scene, because they persuaded him that the money would buy more production value if they did a fast-edited, music-video style clip in a dance club. They did grant him that the story twist was valid, but that it could be served by one quick, inexpensive shot of the heroine listening to her friend over the phone, followed by the gunshot and the big shock. They said the shock was the point of the scene, not what the other girl was saying.

Ari had relented, mostly because he had never found a young actress talented enough to summon the raw emotion that could, in the span of two minutes, credibly lead to her violent suicide. Arletty was that actress — sorry, *actor* — he was certain of it, and she had surfaced just in the nick of time, while it was still possible to re-edit the movie.

He already had the footage of the heroine listening on the phone, and freaking out from the gunshot at the end. Now, with Arletty, he would be able to show the other side of the phone call, the fully-loaded side. He would thus be able to reclaim some of the power of his original scenario, and also finally get to work one on one, with the camera and the actor, serving as the only link between the two. With no peripheral interference; just like a real director.

To accomplish this, Ari called the crew back, paying them handsomely for once — under further pressure, Maria had found $7,500 for him, instead of $5,000 — and thus securing their cooperation. For a set, he rented a famous, vacant loft in Old Montreal, the dismal top floor of a once-proud Art Deco building, with loose plaster and a grimy floor.

It was a favourite shooting location of young, local cinéastes, because it was comparatively cheap, it had room for camera movements, and it was quasi-condemned, which appealed to the nihilist tendencies of these budding geniuses.

Ari was using the entire floor as his set. The idea, which he had worked out with Arletty during their morning phone call, was that her character had been squatting in a derelict factory, with a filthy, bare mattress, a handgun and cell-phone, her only possessions. She had already been referred to by the heroine in earlier scenes. All that was needed from this night's shooting was a quick establishing shot of the surroundings, and the fatal phone call.

Arletty refused to tell Ari what she would say, or how she would play the scene. All he needed to know was that she would do the entire two minute scene on the mattress which he should light harshly and with shadows. And, that she would do it "only once, take it or leave it," because she was "no Thespian, too bad." As she couldn't possibly memorize lines anyway, she planned to ad-lib most of it.

Throwing caution to the Fates, Ari agreed with all her terms. He ordered a second camera, eating into a big chunk of the extra $2,500 so that he could cover himself from two angles during his one permissible "take."

He set the first camera on remote control, camouflaged against a pillar. He focused this camera on the mattress for a continuous close-up of the playing area. For the second camera he laid down tracks, which ran from the farthest corner of the huge room right up to the mattress. His notion was to do a continuous, slow-moving dolly shot, that would start with the image of a lonely girl in the distance, in a tiny part of the frame. The camera would then travel through the hostile cavern, inexorably enlarging the sad image of the girl, timing its approach to the heart-beat of her own deterioration, as her agony and her despair overpowered her. This slow-ride-into-hell would finally come to a stand-still on an extreme close-up of the gun-barrel-in-the mouth ending.

Ari and the crew worked without a break from early afternoon on. They were ready to shoot at 9:29. Arletty arrived one minute later, dressed in her vermilion trench coat, looking gaunt but still radiant under tons of pale makeup and extra-black mascara. She was exactly the girl Ari had envisioned in this role, ever since Amsterdam.

She walked in menacingly, with a gait that was simultaneously small/vulnerable and big/dangerous. She examined the set, and approved the slow-dolly idea, agreeing that it was a brilliant use of the second camera. Ari beamed.

The crew perused her with suspicion. A skinny unknown, in a loud coat, who would speak lines SHE had written, and who would do it all in only one take? Meanwhile they had no idea that not even Ari was privy to what she intended to say.

Arletty took off her trench coat and electrified the room. All she had on was a pair of dirty, slightly torn underwear. She had very realistic bruises, one on her breast, and one on her thigh, while the rest of her skin appeared to be streaked with the kind of body waste that results from a prolonged stay in an abandoned factory with no running water.

She checked herself out in the mirror of the dressing table, and pasted down her hair with Vaseline. She walked to the mattress and addressed it. She chose a spot on the side which was particularly soiled, with a large circle of brown, crusted spots.

She sat down and swiveled into the brown circle, trying to grow into it, become a part of it. Ari brought her the cell-phone and the gun. "Whenever you're ready," he whispered.

"I need my trench coat. I left it on the chair," she said, as if from a great distance.

She seized the coat and crumpled it, leaving one flap free. A bright flash of colour. The only colour. She herself, the mattress, the room were a relentless black-grey-white. She stuffed the gun deep inside the crumpled part of the coat. She took the phone in her hand, and squeezed it hard. Her face was in pain, solemn and angry, very angry, but also fey, like that of someone who knows she must soon die.

"Ready," she muttered, through clenched teeth.

Lights, microphones and cameras came alive. Film was rolling. She was on. She intensified her suffering manifold. She stood absolutely still for a long quarter minute.

Suddenly she hit herself on the head with the phone. Hard.

Several times. Thud. Thud. Thud. THUD. Ari, watching it, gasped inwardly, feeling the pain of each stroke.

Arletty threw the phone on the mattress, cursed, then retrieved it. She punched in a number. She waited the appropriate time, and then she closed her eyes.

"Christine? It's Sal," she whispered. Then she lowered the phone and let a tear drop. She brought the phone back up to her face.

"I CAN'T DO IT ANYMORE!" she screamed into it. "They're everywhere. I can feel them. I can smell them. I wanted you to know. I owe you, Christine. I wanted you to know that. That's why I called. You're the only one — the ONLY — You're my — it's hard to say this — it's been a while — I've had your number for awhile — we never had to say things like this, did we? Remember, Christine? We used to have a GOOD time. You and me. A good TIME."

Big, numberless tears were now flowing, carrying along traces of mascara, down her hollow cheeks. She curled herself around her trench coat, and pulled its loose flap across her belly.

"It's cold in Toronto. But then again, it's always cold in Toronto. I hear Montreal is okay. I hear you're okay. I want you to be okay. I want one of us to be okay." She paused, as if unable to go on. Then she winced, and she continued. "I just wanted to hear your voice. Like, one more time, you know?" Her tears had turned to gasp-like giggles.

"Let's hear it for Christine and Sal. Let's hear it one more time. Yah. Louder! Let's hear it for the girls. LOUDER! For the GIRLS! LOUDER!!! The girls, who never done you wrong. Yah. It's getting dark in here, Christine. LOUDER, sister. Like you screamed, when the cop punched you. Louder, like I screamed, when he punched ME! Louder, Christine. I can't hear you. And I'm scared. MUCH LOUDER. Let's hear it for Sal, one LAST time. ONE LOUSY, FUCK-ING, PUKING LAST TIME; do me, Christine, DO ME. One last TIME!"

She fished under her coat with her free hand and found the gun. "Louder, Christine. It's goodbye, CHRISTINE! Louder, please. CHRISTINE!" She dropped the phone. She shoved the gun into her mouth. Terror filled her eyes and she pulled the trigger.

No one stirred. She held the pose. It was done. The jump edit would be to Christine's face, screaming into the phone, when the gunshot sounds — which was already filmed. The scene was done. Exactingly, exquisitely, heart-wrenchingly, in one clean, continuous take. Just as she had promised.

She looked up from her gun and beamed at the crew. No one moved. She removed the gun from her mouth, and blew some air at its tip. In a sweet, tiny voice, she said, "Cut!"

Then, the crew erupted in a roar. Shouting and applause. The grips and camera crew, who had meanwhile recognized her body from the pro-*Québec* rock video, and being fervently pro-*Québec* themselves, approached her and bowed, as if to a princess.

Arletty acknowledged the acclaim, and stood up. She lifted her trench coat and smoothed out some of its creases. She put it on and buttoned it up to the neck. She gazed at Ari, who was a pace to her left, awestruck, ready to swoon. She extended her hand to him.

"Take me out for a drink," she winked. "I think you need one."

Ari grabbed her hand greedily. "Print it!" he yelled, at no one in particular, and pulled Arletty away, to the door, and down the stairs.

The cobble-stoned streets of Old Montreal were alive with drunk, American teenagers, on the prowl for tourist-style action. Arletty huddled close to Ari. "Take me to my place. I want to be alone with you," she said.

Ari's knees turned to jelly. He almost fell down. But he recovered. And he found his car, a convertible, mint-condition, 1954 Chrysler roadster, and he drove to a back street of Outremont not far from Bernard, and he entered her small, basement studio: books, a desk, a chair, a bed, a kitchenette whose only useful appliances were the fridge and an espresso machine; a minuscule bathroom, and a horizontal slit of a window that let in light during winter when the trees were bare. He tossed back a quick shot of Bourbon as he waited for her to take a shower, from which she emerged all clean, no more bruises or streaked-on body dirt, no make-up, no subterfuge, only the lithe body of a lean woman, round pertinent breasts, a pre-pubescent mound, velvet smooth and virgin fresh, and she helped him undress, running her hands up and down his olive skin, voluptuous with its Levantine promise of secret desires, smooth with its Scots fragility, and hairless except for the tuft around his sex, and she led him to her bed, where they stayed the night, and into dawn, with its fingers of early light filtering in through the leaves, birds singing refrains for two lovers who had become one repeatedly and again, until neither of them could move anymore, let alone make love, until neither could even sleep anymore. So they lay there, spent, on Arletty's bachelor bed, with eyes

half-open and arms around each other, uncovered, shivering somewhat, as the morning breeze lifted perfumed dew off the flowers,
and settled it on them.

They drifted off at last and slept without stirring, until noon.
Arletty woke first, gently pulled away, made coffee, and brought it
to him in bed. Thick and strong, topped with a touch of milky foam.
She showered while he drank it, and returned clean and purpose-
ful. He tried to lure her back into bed, but she declined. She pointed him to the shower.

When he came back, she was dressed. Slacks and a boy's shirt.
She looked even younger than sixteen, even though she was twenty two. Ari dressed and let himself be led out of the apartment vol-
untarily, because he thought they were going out for a bite, or some
fresh air.

She took him to their corner table at *La Crevetterie* and started
to talk the moment they were seated. She told him how great it all
had been, meeting him, filming the scene, making love. She thanked
him and assured him that she would never forget him. She
explained that she was afraid she would fall in love with him. Which
would ruin her completely. Completely! Which would change everything for her. Everything! Which was therefore something she could-
n't possibly live with. She never let him say a word. She talked until
the waiter came, and then using him as foil, she got up, she slipped
away, she ran off with Ari's heart and several other of his vital
organs. She left him crushed, shattered, paralyzed. She left him permanently, never to see him again, never to love him again. Or, so
she thought.

Chapter 8

A month later, in mid-July. On Bernard Street.

Ari had been watching them for more than half an hour. Hidden in a steamy doorway next to the Outremont Theatre, itchy-hot and sweaty, he had a perfect view of that famous corner table at *La Crevetterie,* where Arletty and a flashy middle-aged woman were sitting, the two of them sheathed in breezy lightweight dresses and wide-brimmed sun-hats. Drinking, eating, laughing, having a good time.

Ari was overdressed in his signature Brooks Brothers cleanwear, and overwhelmed by his distress. It had been a miserable month since that perfect night of filming and sex — the kind of sex one can only dream about. Thirty days of longing: of driving by *La Crevetterie* and then down her street, many, many times a day, parking down the street, his eyes peeled to the entrance of her apartment house, his heart pounding every time the door opened, only to stop beating altogether, when all the other someones exited instead of her, his mind always on her, wherever he was, hoping to spot her, to bump into her accidentally. Hoping for a moment with her, hoping to regain her favour. But she had vanished.

Now, she had just as suddenly *un*vanished. There she was, not twenty yards away, having a good time and eating French fries with mayonnaise. All he had to do was to walk across the street and sit down at her table. As if nothing much was at stake. A couple of old friends, colleagues chancing upon each other. Happens all over Montreal, all summer long, as the citizens live outdoors, and eventually all of them re-meet everyone they have ever known.

Now that his prize was within range, he hesitated. Was he savouring those last few moments before the kill? Would the extra delay render their encounter all the sweeter? Or, was he simply embarrassed? There was no denying it: he had been stalking her, albeit unsuccessfully. No different than any other ordinary pervert. On the other hand, there was nothing ordinary about Ari. Nothing at all. He decided he needed to relax for a minute, and then, when he was good and ready, he would stride over to her confidently, as if he had every right.

Meanwhile, across the street, unaware that she was on the verge of witnessing a defining moment in her daughter's life, Josette kept up her candid, free-association chatter, punctuated by melodious outbursts of laughter, a combination for which she was famous all over the sidewalks of the city.

She spent all her summers sitting outside, in the sun, as often as possible, and in as many of the countless *al fresco* tables of Montreal as possible. She had brought Arletty up on outdoor tables every summer since she was an infant, with *La Crevetterie*'s corner table, their special place. Eating, drinking and gossiping within two feet of passing traffic, in the midst of a hedonistic city's most dedicated hedonists, thus became Arletty's summer-camp, as well as her proving ground.

While other kids swam in the Laurentians and, covered in mosquito bites, did arts & crafts in converted barns, Arletty sailed through her summers trading quips and matching double-edged pleasantries with the best of them, growing up very fast, learning the ropes of urban survival and defensive socializing. She was empirical proof that cafe-society behaviour can be taught if tutored hands-on by an expert of the sport, especially if that expert happens to be one's mother.

Josette, on a roll, hit her stride, directing her rhetoric to everyone else on the terrace as much as to Arletty. She puffed on her *Gauloise,* sipped on her wine, and continued as if she hadn't paused at all:

"You can stay out of the sun all you like, Arletty. My generation has no knowledge of skin cancer. We grew up with only one axiom in mind: get as tanned as you can, and you'll be happy. Why do you think I put up with all the headaches of the stupid travel agency? For my health?" She chortled and sipped some more wine. "Well, in a way, yes! I need my seven trips to the sun a year. I'd get sick and die without them. And speaking of trips, you should save up your pennies. We're doing San Andres in December. It's cheap and it's

Colombia, if you know what I mean! Otherwise I'd have to sit at home and listen to your father. He's obsessed. As if anyone can make a master plan for the way people want to live! As far as I'm concerned, we're already Independent. And not because of any plan. It happened organically, like we knew it would, when we were young and René was our god and we would go barefoot on Ste. Catherine Street, screaming his name, and fighting for Separatism. "He had no master plan. He just knew what to do. He smoked his cigarettes, he had sex with his gorgeous wife, and when he wanted something for us, he just called Ottawa and got it, without ever having to beg. We don't need a master plan, we need another René Lévesque, okay? We certainly don't need your father's theories. I swear, even though I vowed to stay married to him and only him, I could divorce him in a minute over this. Except that, he's still excellent in bed!" She punctuated this with a major laugh, and was rewarded with a small but enthusiastic ripple of applause from the neighbouring tables.

Arletty, blushing, *"Maman!"*

"What?" shrugged Josette. "It's a compliment. You should be proud of your old man."

A deep shadow, like a scar, crossed Arletty's face. As if she were in imminent danger. Josette felt it, too. "What's the matter?"

"I'm being stalked. Is there someone crossing the street towards us?"

Josette looked up. "Yes. A very handsome young man. Blushing like a rose. What pink cheeks!"

"Oh, no. It's him," whined Arletty. "Damn! Damn!!"

"Wha... What's wrong? Who?"

Josette's questions were left dangling in the air, as Ari was already upon them, with a fake shock of surprise and a shit-faced grin. "Arletty! Hi! What a coincidence!"

"Yes. I'll bet."

Ari pulled out a chair, and speaking rapid-fire, managed to rattle off: "I'm so glad I ran into you. You don't mind if I sit? I've been watching the rushes. Well, every day. You are MAGNIFICENT. Sorry to be disturbing you. Only two seconds. I'm Aristo MacLeod," while sitting down and proffering his hand to Josette.

"I'm Josette Tremblay. Arletty's mother," she smiled, as she took Ari's hand and shook it caressingly, fighting off the temptation to pinch his peach-like cheeks.

"Your two seconds are up," said Arletty sternly.

"Oh, let him stay a minute, beautiful," chuckled Josette, keeping her eyes on Ari, "it's summer. We have to be lenient and— a little generous, no?"

"Stop flirting with him, maman. He's an intruder."

"I'm only teasing, for Christ's sake. Mind your manners, Arletty. I'm your elder. And I flirt with whoever I please. In fact, I'm flirting with the whole world, all summer-long. This is my new policy. In the winter, it'll change."

"I'm sorry. You are right. I am intruding," mumbled Ari uncomfortably, while slowly rising, as if to leave.

Josette's hand tightened vice-like on Ari's shoulder, and slammed him back down on the chair. "Don't talk to Arletty. She obviously doesn't care to talk to you. Tell ME, please, Mister Aristede, or whatever your name is, why are you stalking my daughter?"

"STALKING? Who? Me?"

"Yes, *you*," said Arletty impatiently. "Up and down my street, then up and down Bernard. How many times a day? You tell me! And then you park. And you think I can't see you. But that car! Who can miss it?" She turned away from Ari, in disgust. She continued to her mother. "He's a criminal, maman. I'm scared. I've had to go in and out of my own house through the back alley. I told him I never wanted to see him again, but..."

Josette shook her head disapprovingly. "We'll have to let the police deal with this. He's obviously abnormal to want you this madly." She fished out a cellular phone from her bag. "So, what kind of car do you have?"

"Maman!"

"A 1954, convertible Chrysler roadster."

"Nice," said Josette, while dialing 911. "I have a 1965 BMW, 106i series. Convertible, also." Her phone came to life. "The police, please," she purred into it, sweetly.

"Cut it out," snarled Arletty, grabbing the phone from Josette. "False alarm," she said into it, and switched it off.

"Thank you," said Ari.

"Don't mention it. Just beat it, okay? And quit hounding me! I mean it!"

Josette drained her glass, licking her lips. "Not Aristede. Aristo! Now, I remember that name. Isn't that the name of your director chum? The one who put you in his movie?"

"It's me! I'm that Aristo," said Ari, beaming.

"No kidding!" said Josette. "Well, you must have made some impression on my Arletty. She's been talking about you non-stop for a month."

"That's NOT true!" growled Arletty, furiously.

"It makes me SO happy to hear that," moaned Ari.

Josette was suddenly animated. She had spotted a woman across the street. "*Syl-VIE!*" she shouted in her rich soprano. "SYLVIE. WAIT. I'M COMING!" She turned back to Ari and Arletty, while locating her wallet, placing a couple of twenties under a glass, packing her cigarettes and vintage *Zippo*. "Sorry, kids. Wish I could help you, BUT Sylvie is the last person I need for my group, and then I get my free trip to Mykonos. In late September, just as it starts to cool off over here, and there it's a steady 80 sunny degrees every day."

Josette got up smartly, and handed Ari her business card. "Call me if you decide to travel. We can fly you anywhere you could possibly want to go." Meanwhile, she had hugged Arletty — "Bye-bye, my darling!" — and she was already on the pavement, dodging traffic, defying anyone to obstruct her from capturing Sylvie's participation in the Mykonos adventure. "It'll be like *Shirley Valentine,* or your money back," she had promised all of them, relying heavily on the prowess and mostly the stamina of the Mykonian studs, after a whole summer of relentless *Shirley Valentines,* female and male.

Arletty, now alone with Ari, settled into her chair smugly, pulling down her *chapeau* until her eyes were completely in the shade. She was in control. "You have some nerve, though, eh?"

"I'm sorry. I couldn't help it. It was like... it was beyond my powers. I could've set out to go to any part of town at all, but somehow, my car—"

"So, your car was to blame?"

"I don't know. Somehow, I always found myself on a detour. Through Cote Ste. Catherine, then down McEachran, and onto Bernard, and—"

"So, what's the story? You're in love. Is that it?" asked Arletty with the glow of someone who has decided she'll soon be having excellent sex.

"In love? I don't think so. Nothing cliché for me. And I've been in love. Believe me. I know love. This is no mere love. I swear to you."

"So, you just want to fuck. Is that it?" asked Arletty, as if the idea didn't exactly repel her.

Ari blushed. "I have enormous regard for you. Trite as that might sound. I'm talking as an artist, and a thinker. I'd like to hope that one day you and I could create a great work of art. Together. I don't want to lose sight of you. I can no longer envision life without you, even if we never fuck again." Ari blushed even deeper.

"Yeah, sure," smiled Arletty.

Ari had rehearsed a million beautiful things to say to her. Philosophical... Artistic... Funny... All of it was on the tip of his tongue. But now that he was actually face to face with her, all he could think of was her mouth glued to his mouth, her hands clutching his hands, her body pulsating thirstily against his, her mind and her seemingly-untamable self entirely at his service.

Arletty, though dead-sure that it would be best to simply get up and walk out on this needy little sap, instead took his hungry libido by the hand, authoritatively, and walked him back to her place. There, she made love with him into the late afternoon, without ever exchanging a word. Words weren't necessary. It was more of a dance, a choreography of sweat-slicked hands and breasts and lips and genitalia, performed in the cocoon-like July heat. And then, when both of them were satiated, having simultaneously exploded and imploded several times — with enough voltage to light up Times Square and all of Broadway — just as wordlessly, she indicated to Ari, that he must now leave, and never try to contact her again, never comb the streets looking for her again, never imagine that he could have sex with her again. To just forget all about her.

Chapter 9

Three weeks later, in August. On Redpath Crescent.

All Montrealers will boast about the enormous and powerful winters, the relentless ice, snow, and howling winds, that comprise the legacy and folklore of *Québec*. From Cardinal Richelieu's disparaging *"quelques arpents de neige,"* to Gilles Vignault's *Ski Doo* anthem, *"L'hiver c'est mon pays,"* winter is a subject for both dread and exaltation in this part of the world. It is used by the inhabitants as proof of their sturdiness and their forbearance, not to mention their ability to have fun even in adversity.

Wherever the *Québecois* travel, they can be counted upon to volunteer awesome details of the homeland's cold months, without ever mentioning how treacherously hot it can get in the summer. How a mercury-hike toward a hundred degrees, combined with a hundred percent humidity day and night, can turn people into lizards and melt them into the pavement.

The famous heat-wave of 1998, already in effect for three debilitating weeks, still had another eight days to peter out. When coupled with the more famous Ice Storm of the Century that had occurred earlier that January, the heatwave made this one of those years the weather-pundits would eulogize for decades.

The unforgiving heat roared like an oven over Maria MacLeod's annual garden party plans. This was the social event of the year for Montreal's meritocrats, whose invitation list was strictly limited to a mere two hundred. It bestowed acceptance and recognition upon a clever mix of over-achievers, artists, business people and socialites of all ages. It was meant to be a lighthearted, entertaining evening, and its first-Saturday-in-August placement usually assured it ideal skies, heat-waves and mosquitoes left behind, autumn rains yet to come.

Tonight, the oppressive heat — in tandem with an ancient out-door air-conditioning system installed by Ross MacLeod in the '60s, which she had neglected to have repaired, and which now randomly switched from the fine mist it was designed to emit, to a light drizzle — boded disaster.

This stroke of bad luck, exacerbated by her anxiety for Ari, convinced Maria that she was under someone's evil eye. Ari seemed in control of himself, but she was a mother: she knew something was horribly wrong. It had to be that actress Arletty. She had caused him to lose his *kefi*, his sense of enjoyment. Her final proof, if any was needed, was that he had begged off the party. For Ari to miss a party he had attended since he was an infant, and now, especially now that he most needed the exposure, was not right. The situation called for serious counter-measures.

She had spent the afternoon sticking cloves into oranges, and then burning the cloves, while invoking names of possible enemies, plus some other, more controversial evil-eye self-remedies her mother had taught her. Nothing had helped: the heat intensified into the evening, Ari left the house looking like a wet mouse instead of her valiant son, and now Duncan had barged into her dressing-room as she was fixing herself up for the party.

He was in a foul mood, the kind he reserved for his displeasure with Ari. Maria guessed immediately. He must have discovered the missing $357,500! She had dreaded the fact that she gone overboard. It was far too great a sum. She rearranged her kimono to cover her breasts, and she spoke first, in an effort to pre-empt him.

"This is a very bad time to discuss it, Duncan," she said, while starting to carefully apply the new, purple eyeshadow.

"The future of our family is at stake, Maria. There is no such thing as a bad time to discuss it. This is a matter of life and death!"

"Don't you think you're exaggerating just a little?" She turned from the mirror to face him squarely. She looked odd, with half of her face in make-up and the other half untouched.

"No, I'm not. When my wife conspires with my son to embezzle more than three hundred and fifty thousand dollars—"

"Now, hold on, please. That is too strong by half—"

"So that he can spend it on ambitions usually reserved for half-wits!"

"Embezzle? Conspire against you? What are you talking about, Duncan? You are going to make me cry."

"Kindly do not cry. It upsets me, and it'll be only half as effective as it would be if the make-up could run down both sides of your face." Duncan smiled wryly.

"Yes, that would be funny. And God forbid anything should ever make us laugh. Not in THIS house!" Maria turned back to her mirror.

"Wife! We're talking about the corruption of my only son. It is wrong to make him believe that he can buy a career in the arts with family money. And not little money! WE'RE TALKING three hundred and fifty KAY, my dear!" Duncan was controlling his renowned temper beyond the call of duty. In reality he was angry enough to hurl the vase of red-pink-cyclamen peonies right through the bay window down onto the elaborate buffet table in the garden below.

"He made a feature film with that money. The whole industry is proud of him. It is a tiny budget by all standards."

"Oh, yes. His brilliant movie about a teenaged degenerate from Toronto. That'll have them lining up at the multiplex to be sure," said Duncan sarcastically.

"They won't have to. Ari can make the money back, and even turn a profit with a limited release and then video and sales to TV," Maria echoed Ari's sales pitch, while adding silver sparkle to her eyelids, so that her every blink would twinkle with starlight.

"Jesus H. Christ! You're so naive," hissed Duncan as he flopped down on a chair, loosened his tie and let out a frustrated howl.

Maria, now fully made-up, absolutely splendid and leonine, turned and slowly rose to her full height. She let the kimono slip and settle back on the tips of her shoulders. A wide slit up front revealed tightly fitting, shiny-black lingerie. She stood facing him, towering over him, even though he was sitting far away, across the room.

She remained perfectly still. Like a warrior queen, thought Duncan. So sexy. So strong. "It sounds as if it'd please you to hit me, my husband," she stated unflinchingly.

"No. Never. But, I wouldn't mind giving that son of yours a royal wallop," said Duncan without blinking.

"You'd be better off to kill me, sir. Because if you don't, I'll become an evil woman, like Clytemnestra," said Maria, as she moved towards her clothing, which lay in waiting, pin-pointedly ironed, smooth, caressable.

Duncan glowered at her for an instant; then he burst-out laughing. "There you go again. Turning our life into one of your operas."

"Into one of my ancient Greek tragedies, actually. Iphigenia in *Tauris*. Euripides, you know," said Maria, as she let the kimono slip off her shoulders onto the Persian. "And the funny thing is, Duncan, I've made it my life's work, from the beginning, for more than twenty years, to save you money. This dress, for example." She liberated the dress in question from its hanger. It was a confection in *crêpe de chine* and silk, with strikingly scarlet highlights against a base of pale rose, discreetly detailed with 1930s patterns.

"This dress would've cost you $8,000 if I had bought it in Paris. Instead it cost less than $300 to copy and sew it myself. After seeing it only once at *Givenchy*. 'Not too shabby, eh?' Isn't that what you'd say?"

"Not too shabby, my dear. Yes, that's what I'd certainly say," said Duncan, admiring her fine craftsmanship, as she stepped into the dress, and wiggled it over her contours.

"Be a gentleman and zip me up, will you, Duncan?" she implored him with feigned helplessness.

Duncan rushed over to her, as he always did for the "zipping-up."

"And please don't worry about your money," she continued. "I'll pay you back every penny. I have decided to accept a position. It's what I always do, you know, fund-raising and such, but as a job. For a salary, plus bonuses. I have two offers to choose from."

"I forbid it," said Duncan, carefully doing the catch on top of the zipper, and gently smoothing out the rounded collars.

Maria allowed three seconds of pleasure from his touch. She then turned around, and he dropped his hands. "Thank you," she said, moving back to her dressing table. "And why do you forbid it?" She flipped open her jewelry box.

"Professional fund-raising is one notch from prostitution," stated Duncan, resignedly sitting back down in his chair.

"You're probably right," agreed Maria. She picked out the sapphires her mother had given her. A giant's blue tear-drop for her neck, and a round blue boulder for her finger. A zillion blue-tinted fires to clash with the red-pinks of her dress. She would be easy to spot at the party.

"There goes my pay-back," laughed Duncan.

"Not at all, my darling. I'll go onto plan "B". The same people from the fund-raising are also itching to invest in and open a sewing school for me. We even have a name. *Maria's*. Do you like it?"

"Great. I love it. Just make sure you charge tuition. And speaking of money, I've invited a little group for baccarat in the library. I trust you'll keep your guests away from us."

"If you lot stay away from us," rang Maria in a peal of *mezzo* mirth.

"They were told to come late and duck straight into the library. They'll be clutching their money, which they will soon thereafter lose to me. You won't be seeing them, trust me. But, I'll be with you at the start of the party. You do want me there, don't you?"

"If you don't show up, I'll divorce you," sang Maria, standing up and walking to him in a waltzy rhythm. She extended her hand to help him rise. "Which means, you'd better go and change."

Duncan stood up, holding onto her hand, caressing it lightly. "For you I'll dress up. But, I'll come to the party only because I'm hungry, and you've ordered enough food to feed an army."

"I agree to your terms," smiled Maria, extending her cheek for his peck. He brought his face closer, and kissed her on the lips instead. She pulled away, as if stung by a bee. "Careful! You'll ruin my hair," she complained.

Chapter 10

The next day. At La Crevetterie.

Ari sat waiting at the corner table, sedated, practically numb, over-whelmed by the power Arletty wielded over him. She had called him that morning, and sweetly asked him to meet her for lunch. He had dropped everything and driven to Bernard Street in a blind rush.

That he would do so was perplexing to Ari. He had imagined himself to be a little stronger, somewhat more dignified than this puppy-like persona. By all rights he should have been angry at her, or at least standoffish. She had insulted him and terminally blanked him out since their last encounter in her steamy basement apart-ment, twenty two days ago. Twenty two days of sheer agony for Ari.

He had restrained himself from combing the streets for her, and absolutely from parking outside her house. It had taken great will power, but he had managed. Instead he had sent her a dozen pink roses a day, for seven days running, with a new poem included in each bouquet. A poem for each day of the week, seven poems about longing and desire.

On the eighth day, a cardboard box had arrived for Ari at Redpath Crescent. In it he had found his roses, all of them in their original wrapping; seven bundles, some dead, others dying, poems crumpled, the whole lot crushed to fit into the box. By foot, judg-ing by the imprint of a Doc Maarten sole. And a special something on top, a small note, with a neatly written, two-word message: "Fuck OFF."

All this had made Ari laugh, at first. He had to admire her ges-ture as a formidable answer to his own. Finally it had made him hard. He had even considered cutting Arletty's scene out of the movie — a sorry revenge, at best, since it turned out to be the one remarkable moment of the entire opus. Then he had relented; and again he had hardened. And so it had evolved for two weeks, fourteen unspeakable days, which had taken their toll on Ari. He was frequently nauseous, and unable to sleep, he felt twisted and confused. Finally, yesterday, he had cracked, and called Josette, to ask an inane travel question, a barely disguised appeal to her, to intervene with Arletty on his behalf.

This morning Arletty had called and he had responded with unmitigated alacrity. Forcing him to forego his most sacred duty to his mother: to console her for her debacle of a garden party the previous night.

Sitting in the air-conditioned solarium, looking out at heat-wilted roses and flowerless forsythias, Maria had just finished telling him how the faulty, outdoor air-conditioning had gone totally berserk, drenching the guests in ice-cold rain, ruining everyone's silk shirts and having to be turned off; and how two rival, government-subsidized film-makers had gotten too drunk too quickly and had come to actual blows over some idea that one had allegedly stolen from the other, kicking and screaming when they were pulled apart; how the cutting-edge band she had hired proved a bit too progressive even for this party, when, during their second set, they had all unzipped their pants and exposed themselves and started to masturbate in unison before having to be physically ejected from the house. How the *sous-chef* had tripped while carrying a large bucket of beef gravy, sending it all over all the desserts on the sweets table. AND how, to top off the nightmarish, stiflingly-hot-in-every-way evening, Duncan had lost at baccarat, and made a HUGE scene, accusing herself and Ari for his lack of concentration at the table, and for his losing attitude; vowing blue murder were his own family to ever undermine him again, and punctuating his sentences with stiletto-sharp exclamation points, not shouting, but hissing. STORMING out of the bedroom, making her fear that the gap between them had widened irreparably. "Oh, Ari, I'm so miserable."

Ari, under the double onus of having been the cause of their argument, as well as having been absent from the party, was just about to open his mouth and offer his encouragements. He was searching for the opening words that would express his concern, while making her see the amusing side of the mishaps, the words that would let her know that at least his love was unswerving. Just to comfort her. At that moment his phone had rung and Arletty's invitation had galvanized him, mesmerized him.

So, he had left without a single word to his mother, without even a goodbye kiss. He had driven like a madman and here he was at the appointed table, too-warm in the summery version of his preppy outfits — white tennis jersey, beige chinos and yes, penny-loafers — fragile, anxious, bewildered.

Arletty appeared from out of nowhere. Very elegant in a wide-brimmed straw hat, sun-glasses, and the sheerest, bluest — practically sapphire — halter-top sheath, that lightly caressed and suggestively hugged every precious part of her body. She sat down opposite him, and eyed him angrily.

"You're a bastard, Ari," she said. "You're a prick."

Her words were like slaps. They woke him up.

She raised her voice somewhat: "How dare you call my mother?"

Ari's pedestal shattered. She hadn't called him because she broke down and wanted him. She had called to give him more hell. "I called her to reserve some tickets," he said defensively.

"For Cannes? For next May? Nine months in advance?"

"It gets very busy at Festival time. Especially the Paris-Nice segment."

"And how would you know?"

"We have an apartment in Cannes," protested Ari, pleased with his small victory. "I've been there often. I've been to the Festival, too. And once, when I booked at the last minute, I was nearly shut out. Anyway, this time, it's imperative to book way ahead. I need two tickets. One for me, and one for you." Ari looked away, demurely.

Arletty widened her eyes, until they threatened to engulf her forehead. "What presumption! How dare you believe I would go anywhere with YOU, let alone Cannes!"

"We'll take the movie. We'll have a good time."

"NEVER MIND my good time. You are not involved in my GOOD TIME. Okay? And you are never, NEVER to call my mother again. You hear? My mother is nosy enough as is. You are NOT to give her any further ammunition to meddle in my life. She likes you, because she smells money, and she thinks she won't have to worry about me if I marry you. MARRY YOU! What a joke! WORRY ABOUT ME? I forbid it. I've been on my own since I was fourteen! Eight years!"

Ari was no math-whiz, but he caught the discrepancy. "Two years?"

"Fine. Two years. That's long enough. I've learned freedom. I refuse to regress. She thinks you're the most handsome man in Montreal. The Catch of the Century. As far as she's concerned, I should want to spend the rest of my life in bed with you. *Bof!* Even my father. She discussed you with him, and he, who hates all the Anglos and all the ethnics, HE wants me to marry you. He thinks he can convert you. He thinks you'd be an asset to the Cause. Balls!"

"I promise never to call her again. I'm sorry," muttered Ari.

"Tell me," said Arletty, narrowing her eyes to slits, "is your father Duncan MacLeod?"

"Ye-es," ventured Ari, dreading this detour in her attack.

"Great!" exclaimed Arletty. "Just great! Exactly what I needed at this time of my life, an attachment to the son of the arch-villain of *Québec.* Your father, buster, is single-handedly trying to destroy our economy, because he doesn't like the sound of our voice. He's a fascist pig, and the mere mention of his name would give any civilized person the creeps."

Arletty spat on the ground. Ari had no idea how to defend his father, having never before had a reason to try. A shiver went through him, and it reacted violently with the heat in the air. He broke into a torrent of sweat and his face flushed crimson.

The waiter, having waited a break in Arletty's verbiage, approached to take their order.

"Let me buy you a drink," pleaded Ari, grateful for the interruption.

"No. I'll buy the drinks. Do you like *Pernod?*"

"I love Pernod. It's like *ouzo.* I'm half Greek, you know," smiled Ari.

"*Deux Pernods,*" she said to the waiter, without turning her head. "Yes, I heard about Mister MacLeod's Greek wife. From Constantinople. Isn't that Istanbul? And doesn't that make her and YOU Turkish?"

"I wouldn't say Turkish to my mother," laughed Ari, with fake terror.

"I wouldn't say anything at all to your mother or to your father. Believe me! And also not to you. This is my final, FINAL warning to you. Get out of my face. Get outta my sight. I don't need you. People like you and your family scare me."

The drinks arrived. Arletty sipped hers. Ari downed his in one gulp. It radiated in all directions from his throat, in a series of minor implosions. Arletty continued:

"There is a very fine line that separates us from chaos. From most angles it is very difficult to perceive that line. One can therefore ignore it, and pretend it doesn't exist, and plug-on as if everything is all right. But, there is one special angle, a perverted perspective, which I'm unlucky enough to possess, from where the fragility, the utter idiocy of human life, and the ludicrous course of its evolution are painfully obvious. This line, Aristo MacLeod, is threadbare. People like your father, and therefore people like you, have been mercilessly tugging and stretching this line, hoping it'll break — thinking you'll be able to enjoy the spectacle of human suffering, because you yourselves will escape the deluge, cocooned in your money. Well, maybe you will. As for me, I intend to go on cleaning houses and making my little money, and waiting, waiting for the end with dignity."

Ari had to restrain himself from applauding. She had made a moot point sound extraordinary. She took such great pleasure in putting him and all the other MacLeods down. Might there be some kind of hope for this relationship after all? But, then it clicked in his mind. She had said she cleaned houses for a living.

"Did you say you cleaned houses for a living?"

"If it's okay with you, yes, I did. Another drink?"

"Only if I pay."

"I pay, or no drink."

"No drink will do. The mere thought of you on your hands and knees scrubbing someone's toilet to earn the money for these drinks—"

Arletty stood up before he could finish his sentence. "In that case, this meeting is over."

"No. It's not!" Ari spoke with such authority, that she sat down, in spite of herself.

Ari pinched his face into a condescending smile. The sweat had blended into his sun-darkened face and arms. It gave him a stained and rugged look. Like a gardener or a farm-hand. Arletty's carefully-kept-from-the-sun whiteness shimmered in the heat. They were like a pair of porcelain figurines. The unattainable princess, and her lusty, swarthy, infinitely inferior admirer. An admirer who has suddenly accepted the obvious: that he had so little to lose, he could therefore throw caution to the wind.

"You're such a child, it's pitiful. For you, everything is black and white. A series of somber occurrences, seemingly random, but in actual fact tacitly coordinated, a chiaroscuro conspiracy, with you at the epicenter: the nihilist super-hero who refuses to save a world, because she can't be bothered. A situation beyond redemption. Simple, clear-cut problems, right? No discernible cures, no possible solutions. An entire Universe of unexpressed fear and loathing. A life of imminent pain. The whole enterprise, an exercise in futility. This is beyond simplistic, Arletty. It's a formula for inevitable and terminal failure."

He had said too much. And it had exhausted him. He closed his eyes and turned his face to the scorching sun. Searing light flooded in, through his eyelids, incinerating all the images. He hoped she would leave during this blinding whiteness. But she was in no mood for mercy. When he turned back towards her and opened his eyes, she was very much still there, ignoring him and settling the bill for the Pernods.

She peered at him over her shoulder. "No, it's not," she adjudged. And she quickly but not hurriedly, got up and dashed away. She became one with the heat, just another speck of inconsequential matter on the steaming pavement.

Chapter II

Seven weeks later, in early Fall. On Mykonos.

It was only six p.m., but the sunset was already in progress. The clutch of Mykonian widow-tycoons, uniformly drab in black — head-scarf, socks, and everything in-between — all black, in perpetual mourning for husbands and even sons they had out-lived, all clucked in unison at the sight of the scores of colours filling the sunset sky, from mauve to gold. Yes, summer, glorious, license-to-print-money summer was quite over.

The widows were gathered by a door-stoop around the corner from *Braggadocio,* the new sunset-watching bar on the backside, so called Venice, of Mykonos' port-town, with its unrestricted view into the western Aegean: tiny islets on shimmering waveless waters, the Homeric wine-dark sea that stretches from this Cycladic island into mythology.

Braggadocio was housed in a minuscule sea-front shack, with a few square yards of sidewalk for outdoor tables. They had paid old Thodoros one million American dollars for this property, which he had been using to store his fishing gear, and which he couldn't have sold for more than fifty of those dollars before the tourists came.

The widows clucked and chuckled over Thodoros' luck: he had died *in flagrante,* in a Parisian brothel. The "forgiven" one having gone quite mad, trying to spend all that money after a lifetime of abject poverty. They inwardly clucked at their own amazing luck for good measure, to ward off the evil eye and the wrath of God.

The same sort of business wizards who had paid Thodoros his million — *Braggadocio* was rumoured to have recouped its investment after just one season of sunset-watching drinkers. He had also dished out ludicrous amounts for previously-neglected chunks of family properties on which they had slapped up cash-cow "package-tourism" hotels and nightclubs. The Mykonos boom, which had started in the late 60's and escalated dizzyingly to its present state of relentless, sexually-charged mega-tourism, had turned the traditionally impoverished Mykonians into overnight plutocrats.

These women, and many others like them, remembered the beginning very well. They remembered how, a mere thirty years ago, while in their prime, and not in the least widowed, they used to have to collar the few tourists, freshly arrived at the port, and offer to house them in their own homes for something less than a dollar a night. Now secure with their U.S. dollar accounts in foreign banks and their ongoing businesses — charging fortunes per night for wee rooms — they, like capitalists the world over, resented the interruption to their cash-flow the approaching winter and its early sunsets represented.

They resented the newly-emptied streets, the necessary seasonal closings of many restaurants and shops, the dwindling numbers of tourists disembarking from the reduced-schedule ferry-boats. But there was always Kiria Maria, the rich Constantinopolitissa from Canada who unfailingly showed up at the end of each September, to reopen her villa and to add one last touch of *kefi* and spice to the spent season.

This year, Maria had left Montreal for her annual Opera-&-Mykonos pilgrimage with mixed feelings. Ari had gone from bad to worse, now given to spending much time locked up in his room, editing his film. When out and about, he was always melancholy, a cross between Hamlet and Romeo, a composite Shakespearean victim of smoldering, irrepressible passions. Duncan, seemingly still angry at her — and the world — for losing at baccarat (only fifty thousand, but it was the principle that mattered), had avoided her since that awful night, exchanging only strained pleasantries during their obligatory early breakfasts together.

The larger-than-life house seemed more cavernous than ever, unbearable in view of all the unhappiness it sheltered. Even so, Maria had seriously considered canceling her trip, right up to the last moment. Yet the prospect of missing out on the one time of the year — her precious three weeks that she reserved entirely for herself, a tradition that she had maintained despite all odds, ever since Ari was six years old — depressed her, threatened to reverse her optimism and to diminish her enthusiasm: the two qualities that had sustained her and kept her sane.

The final factor in her decision to go ahead with her plans was the complete indifference, with which both Ari and Duncan had reacted to the announcement of her imminent departure. Ari had looked away vacuously, wishing her the habitual *kali antamosi* (until our reunion), while Duncan, too preoccupied to wish her anything, had at least promised to replenish her bank account, which he did with exactly $357,500, just to underline her calumny.

Leaving behind such sordidly emotional surroundings actually proved very easy, even therapeutic for Maria. Her elation started when she settled into her business-class airplane seat — upgraded from economy through Duncan's favour-banking: a true MacLeod never paid full price for anything — and reached festive proportions once she reached the *Teatro dell'Opera* in Rome.

Maria was an opera fanatic. She attended throughout the year: in Montreal, where she was chairperson of the board of the M.O.C., and also during quickie trips to Toronto and New York. However, her major outing was this annual late-September jamboree. She chose a different European opera-city every year, wherever the most interesting and most concentrated program was being offered; her ideal being a different work a night for ten nights, before going onto Mykonos for the subsequent ten days and nights.

This year the choice had been obvious. Rome's major opera house, which had started its life in 1880 as the *Teatro Costanzi,* and renamed *Teatro Reale dell'Opera* after its renovations in 1928, was by now just another financially challenged, cultural antique. It was staging a fund-raising festival, a re-mounting of ten of the most famous operas that had been premiered inside it during its heyday. The whole affair was serendipitously scheduled to coincide exactly with Maria's preferred dates.

She was swept away by evening after evening of exquisite stage and music craft, with the finest interpreters of Italian opera singing their hearts out for the benefit of the venerable auditorium. She was grateful for the two *Respighis, La Fiamma* and *La Bella Addormentata nel Bosco,* which she had never before seen fully staged. They were not exactly the kind of stuff that the parochially facile programming of North American houses was likely to yield. Yet she was overjoyed with *Tosca,* which premiered in Rome since it takes place in Rome: a melodrama she knew note for note, but one she never tired of hearing, since she identified with the firebrand Floria, admiring her bravado and secretly envying her dramatic-heroic death.

Her eyes and ears satiated — at least for a while — she fretted yet again about her menfolk back home. Bags packed, clutching her tickets for Athens and Mykonos, she phoned Redpath Crescent, as she always did at the mid-point of her trip, just to set her mind at ease before going on to the second part of her vacation.

She spoke to Betty, her housekeeper, an ancient model of high efficiency and dedication, who had been trained by Ross MacLeod. Impossible to replace Betty had made it her life's work to serve the family, informed her that Mister MacLeod (Duncan) was very jittery and out of sorts, while Master MacLeod (Ari) appeared on the verge of some kind of collapse.

She then suggested that Maria should cut her trip short and repair home. It was obvious, Betty opined, that Maria's men needed her. Desperately.

Maria, though concerned, responded in a way she would have never thought herself capable of. She gave a transatlantic shrug and almost mirthfully said, "Oh, they're big boys. They'll manage. Please give them my love." Upon which, she hung up, sparing herself Betty's self-righteous gasp, and headed for the airport.

It took Maria the usual two days to get re-accustomed to the incandescent eccentricities of Mykonos: its all-white, light-reflective clay structures, minimal and functional, arranged in a circular formation, a maze of outstretched-arms — wide, whitewashed alleys and byways, all of which eventually let out to the weathered port. Potted basil and red carnations on darkly tinted wooden balconies and staircases; plump adobe churches — the island of Mykonos has 365 churches and chapels, the majority of them inside its port-town; jagged vistas of twisting rooftops interspersed with cuneate peeks at the eternal Aegean: thin, reversed triangles of sapphire-emerald-aquamarine waters, where legends begin, and lithe, luxuriously swaying yachts repose. Little spears and shooting stars, piercing and bouncing off the ripples.

On the third day, she shed both her shyness and awe. In the morning she went to Elia beach on the other side of the island, where you can clearly recognize the colour of the rocks twenty feet below the surface of the sea, and take the sun on the white sands of a primordial cove. She ate lunch at *Acroyali,* on the promontory overlooking the beach and the expanse of sea to the south, from where Aegeus's son Theseus, it is hoped to this day, will have returned from Crete and the Minotaur, bearing a white sail, not a black one, and save his father from that deadly plunge off the top of Cape Sounion.

In the late afternoon, somewhat sunburnt, feeling disconnected, as if her entire life had been just a prelude to this glorious moment, as if nothing else but this island and its intoxicating possibilities mattered, she got all dressed up, make-up, jewels, the works, and stepped out to watch the sunset from *Braggadocio,* to meet some new people, to remeet old friends. To start the process of believing that she lived here year-round, and that her house was always full of laughter, that her nights were always caressed by silken breezes under the pale glow of a full moon.

She started to feel dizzy in front of the *Presto* snack-bar, just before reaching the Cathedral. She considered returning home, or at least sitting down for a moment. But the dizziness passed — it must have been the smell of French-fries cooking in old oil. Besides, the sunset was beckoning. The sky had added a third layer of colours. She pressed on, walking faster. Somehow, she thought, if she could just reach the bar and sit down in front of the crimson sea, she'd be fine.

She swayed past the widow-tycoons, smiling wanly in response to their enthusiastic greetings. She rounded the corner, and there it was. An explosion of a sunset. Like fireworks. Like an uncontrollable vortex of colours, spinning wildly, blending into sheer white. She felt faint. Her legs were giving out. She grabbed for the back of a chair. She so very much needed to surrender, and let herself melt into the ground. But she resisted, gripping the chair even tighter. She heard some distant noise, or many noises, as she fell into a pair of strong arms. Unforgettable arms. Aromatic, bronzed, jeweled, soft, supportive, a comfort, a joy to let herself go and to become one with those arms.

The one to whom those arms belonged — a certain, charmingly capable Josette Tremblay — fussed over Maria, whom she had rescued from falling, and had eased into a chair. She stroked Maria's forehead, cautioning the concerned and curious to stay back, give her air. Maria opened her eyes and slowly focused on Josette's face. "Would you like some water, sweetheart?" asked Josette. "I'm not sure," said Maria groggily. "Did I faint? I'm sorry." "Sorry for fainting? Come on, girl, this is Mykonos. You can faint all you want. Here, have a sip," encouraged Josette, holding the glass near Maria's mouth. Maria raised her hand, and caressingly took it from Josette. She drank from it and set it down on the table. She smiled.

"Oh, you'll be just fine," laughed Josette with relief. The onlookers applauded Maria's recovery. On this island life and death are celebrated with equal zeal. Josette returned to her seat on the other side of the table.

"I should move to another table, I'm intruding," said Maria lazily, happy that her strength was returning, and happier still to have met this expansive person, despite the circumstances.

"You stay put and stop worrying about everything," advised Josette. "So, what happened, eh? A bit too much *ouzi* at the port, watching the yachts going in and out?"

"*Ouzo?* No," sang Maria. "I never touch the stuff. Well, only sometimes. No. It must have been the sun. I guess I was on the beach too long."

"Too long in the sun? I didn't think that was possible."

"Neither did I. That's why I did it," laughed Maria. She extended her hand. "I'm Maria, from Montreal."

"From Montreal? Fucking hell! Now, that is rich. Boy, there's no getting away from us, is there? One day, we'll conquer the world. I swear it. Well, at least all the resorts in the world. Josette, also from *Montréal.*"

"I'm really happy you're here, Josette! I couldn't have chosen a better person to save my life."

"Which group are you here with?" asked Josette, fishing for some insight into the competition.

"I'm here by myself. I own a house. I come every year," recited Maria.

"Lucky you. I'm here only my third time, and I have in tow a group of thirteen crazy, forty-something *Québecoise* divorcées, all looking for the same stud so they can bring home a memory."

Maria raised her eyebrows. "Maybe I should do that. It must be good for the soul."

Josette laughed. "It's excellent for every part of the body. Except the soul. At least I'm stupid enough to believe that."

"Me too," agreed Maria. "Frankly, I couldn't do it in a million years. Even though I suspect that my husband doesn't let anything get in his way."

"Your husband cheats on you?"

"I said I suspect he does. Anyway, if he does, he thinks it's to save our marriage."

Josette was all ears. "How come you tell me this? We've barely met."

"Yes. But we have barely met on Mykonos. This island has no shame and no secrets." Maria smiled resignedly.

"So, tell me more?"

"I am from Constantinople. Well, Istanbul."

"You're Turkish?"

"God, no!" said Maria, horrified. "Greek. My ancestors are the Byzantines and the Romans and the Ancient Greeks. I come from a very conservative family. We trace our descent from Xenophon, from the fifth century B.C. He left his calling cards during the retreat of the Anabasis. The Turks didn't take Constantinople until 1453."

"Hold your horses," laughed Josette. "I'm a little shaky with the Greek. I'm still trying to master *paidakia me patates.*"

"Ah, lamb chops with fries. I love them, too."

"So, okay. You're from Istanbul, and you're more Greek than feta cheese..." encouraged Josette.

"Right. So, I was eighteen. Just graduated from the American college. A virgin, naturally. And suitors a mile long. My mother wanted her prize daughter to marry the best. Unfortunately, all the best were at least fifty years old. And then I met him. My young Canadian. Twenty six, looking nineteen, pink skin, blond hair, blue eyes, tall, athletic. I wanted him at first glance. It was a reception at the college. I don't know how he got in. Funny. I never asked him. That's how it started. And he fell for me in a big way, too. He liked the exotic types. I had long, black hair, and I was very trim. Don't look at me now."

"You're gorgeous, darling."

"I take that as a compliment, especially coming from a beauty like you." Maria extended her water-glass and Josette clinked it with the remains of her *Campari* and soda, a drink she believed to be highly Mediterranean. "*Yassou!*"

"*Yassou,* to you too. And your parents agreed to let you marry this pink Canadian?"

Maria sighed. "They threatened to kill me, if I ever even thought about him again. Fortunately, he turned out to be a very rich Canadian. And not pink at all. True blue."

"Blue?"

"Old money. Blue-chip. Establishment. So, he went home and flew back three days later with his father, the two of them dressed in pinstripes and silk, red ties, in the middle of summer, and he officially proposed. We had two weddings. One in Istanbul, in a Byzantine church, with Gregorian chanting. And then he brought my whole family over, and we had another one at the Ritz, with champagne and ducks swimming in the pond, among three thousand gardenias, my favourite flower."

Josette let out a loud whistle. "Hah! That's exactly how I got married."

"At the Ritz, or at the church, or both?" marveled Maria gullibly.

Josette answered with her ringing soprano laughter. The others at the bar turned away from the sunset, toward the sound, but they soon turned back. The sun was about to perform its final treat of the day: sinking into the sea, and setting it on fire. Josette waited for the miracle to occur before continuing:

"Neither. I'm pulling your leg. I met my Louis-Marc at a rally for René Lévesque. We had both been at the demonstration all day. It was summer, very hot. Walking up and down Sherbrooke Street. We passed the Ritz twice, actually. Screaming insults at the Anglos. Maybe you and your gardenias were inside on one of those occasions. Anyway, we were sweaty, and I had lost my shoes, so my feet were almost black, and his face had a smear of ketchup dried up across it. I'll never forget it. They had catered the rally with millions of French-fries and a ton of ketchup. So, we fell madly in lust. You know how it used to happen those days. Come to think of it, you probably don't. Anyway, believe me, it used to, in spades! We had sex in *Parc Lafontaine.* All night. On the grass. And there were pebbles or something. I had bruises all down my back, as I discovered afterwards. But that night I didn't care. When morning happened, he grabbed me by the hand to take me to City Hall and marry me on the spot. I said: 'Whoa, Louis-Marc. Stop right there! I'm no virgin bride, baby. I like to fool around. And I love traveling. ALONE! And I hate husbands, and I hate children. I want to live! Okay?' And he looked at me, with that smear of ketchup somehow still on his face, and he said 'Okay!' And we went to Notre Dame Street and did it. We were the first in line. For some reason there were lots of people getting married in City Hall that day. But, you know, I'm glad. We don't cheat on each other sexually, but otherwise I'm my own person, and I do whatever I want. And I have my Arletty."

Maria felt queasy. She thought she might faint again. "Arletty?"

"My daughter," said Josette proudly. "I chose the name. From that actress in *Les Enfants du Paradis*. I love that woman."

"Your daughter's name is Arletty?" Maria's queasiness was giving way to wonder.

"Yes. Why?"

Maria, with a wide-eyed smile: "My son is madly in love with a girl called Arletty."

It finally dawned on Josette, too. "Fucking hell! You are Ari's mother."

The two women nodded knowingly to each other, as if romantic miracles were commonplace on Mykonos.

"Let's order drinks," said Maria.

"Oh, yes. Many. We need to talk."

They both burst out into their respective and celebrated laughter, one several octaves higher than the other, until together they producing a chord of pure harmonic verticality. The kind that Rameau himself might have used as the basis for his musical theories.

Chapter 12

The next three days. On Mykonos

Maria's villa was a modern structure, two levels of white walk-through's, with windows everywhere and a small swimming pool on the side, the whole affair carved into the rock-face of the cliff just outside the port overlooking *Megali Ammos*.

It was a piece of real estate the famously-frivolous Ross MacLeod had bought and developed for a song back in the early '60's, hoping it might lure his sister Jaimie for vacations-away-from-everything. Jaimie had finally agreed to indulge her brother's concerns for her well-being in 1967, at the height of Mykonos' hippy invasion — which kick-started the island's reputation as a haven of permissiveness. This was at a time when the place boasted a total of three, clunky, overseas telephones and cellular phones had yet to be invented.

Jaimie had lasted all of three days, driven out both by the shoe-less, disorderly, drug-addicted youths, and by being almost totally out-of-touch with her office. She had politely advised Ross to sell the house and rushed back to Montreal. Ross, who was much shrewder than he had proven, recognized the potential of this island, which had been a song-and-sex vacationland during Antiquity, a place where nearby, somber Delos's sybarites could celebrate. Now, 2,500 years later, it was showing signs of a belated, but exuberant comeback. He held onto the villa, and eventually found the perfect use for it.

It became the all-around ideal wedding present for a bride years later, when Duncan decided to fall in love with and marry a Greek girl. Not only was the family able to offer something they didn't mind parting with, it was also a heaven-sent acquisition for Maria.

It became immensely valuable in time, and even more than that, it represented the sum-total of Maria's private wealth. She had received nothing from her own family, and Duncan never considered registering her name as owner, or even co-owner, on any of his numberless parcels of real estate.

Duncan himself accompanied her to Mykonos once on their honeymoon, and enjoyed it to the hilt for three days. After which, exactly like his workaholic mentor, Aunt Jaimie, he had forced a retreat back to Canada. The chalet in Georgeville, Eastern Townships was the setting for a continuing honeymoon of sorts, endlessly peppered with phone calls and far too many suit-and-briefcase visitors who stayed for a few minutes, *please excuse us ma'am,* arriving at all hours of the day and deep into the evening.

It took Maria almost seven years to organize herself to return to her villa, and she found an immaculately maintained house where no one had slept or eaten since the honeymoon. Its sterile and antiseptic smell was an oxymoron in a town whose every square inch was devoted to pleasure.

On this second and pivotal visit, Maria fell under the spell of Mykonos, and formulated her plan to return every year, albeit for only those precious ten days. And she solved the problem of the other idle 355 days by assigning an agent to rent the place to those who could afford it. From the proceeds she deducted basic costs, including a new master mattress for her October arrivals, and donated the generous remainder to local charities.

Thus she endeared herself to the Mykonians, who love money in all its forms. The whole deal finalized without requiring any measure of Duncan's approval. The Mykonos experience was the liberating nucleus of Maria's life, wherein she felt free, the total master of her destiny. It was the best, and arguably only forum, in which her relationship with Josette — a safe harbour in which she would so often need to take refuge during her upcoming trials — could have germinated and taken root.

It did not require much arm-twisting for Maria to persuade Josette to let her group — exhaustively serviced and very satisfied: repeat customers, for sure — return to Montreal on their own, and extend her own stay as a most welcome guest in the villa. The clincher was the revelation that the two women shared a birthday on October 4th, a respective milestone for each this year, a double-whammy of decade-enders, Maria's fortieth, and Josette's fiftieth.

During the two days leading up to their birthdays, the absolutely inseparable women did the rounds. The beach; the seaside meals; *Braggadocio* for sunset; sitting back on snow-white adobe stoops, listening to brooding geniuses sing lovelorn Greek songs, self accompanied on weepy guitars. They briefly attended a couple of parties in Maria's honour, but most of their time was spent poolside at the villa, taking the obligingly warm Autumn sun, and talking, talking.

The birthday plans were all-encompassing. Maria's birthday, already a virtual national holiday on the island, joined to the birthday of her engagingly warm new friend, was enough to throw the party-addicted Mykonians into a frenzy. Facing a party-deprived winter with small reprieves at Xmas, New Year's and *Mardi Gras,* then nothing until Easter, this was a double-birthday to cherish. All the bars and restaurants that were still open, along with a number of private homes had issued their intentions to fête them in the grand style. There was everything short of a parade, including a twenty-one gun salute by a navy ship conveniently parked in the harbour that evening.

Thus the parties and celebrations unrolled and they were enormously successful; everyone had a great time, and no one got hurt — not even during the twenty-one gun salute — but the guests of honour never showed.

The women spent that entire festive day and night in the villa. It started with Maria breaking into serious sobbing while making the morning coffee. Josette was taken by surprise. Tears for yet another spent year, she could understand. But actual, uncontrollable, inconsolable sobs?

"I'm sorry... I'm sorry," babbled Maria.

"Oh, you're sorry about everything, you. It's that Anglo you married. Fake British humility. Please. Excuse-me. Thank-you. I'm-sorry. Before and after each statement, you can commit the worst crimes and it's okay! *Bof!"* snarled Josette, not in the mood for any niceties before her first coffee and cigarette of the day.

Maria suddenly stopped sobbing. "I meant, I'm sorry to disturb you, not sorry for crying."

"Tears do not disturb me," snapped Josette, though with a diminishing edge: the coffee was ready, she could smell it, she could almost taste it. Maria poured a cup for her. "I love emotion. I live for it. I welcome it. I thrive on it." She took her first sip. "Aaah, you make good coffee, Maria." She lit her *Gauloise.* "So, girl. Happy Birthday. You're an adult now. Welcome to the club. Now you can do as you like, and no one is allowed to contradict you."

Maria blew her nose into a napkin and took a sip of her own coffee. It was good. She had brought the beans with her from Montreal. "Am I really supposed to believe that you don't care why I'm crying?"

"Why do women cry, Maria? Does anyone really care anymore? They handed us some fake independence, and now we're on our own. Of course I want to know why you're crying. I'm praying it's not because of any bad news from home. But I'm fairly sure it's not. Those tears had a different label. Something old, from the past. Something beyond repair."

"I'm crying for my mother, *Eirine.* Like Irene. She died five years ago, but for me it's just like today."

"I know how you feel. Mine died ten years ago, but it still wrings my heart."

"How did yours die?"

"In her sleep. After a night of drinking, and probably sex. My father took that information with him to his own grave. They both died happy, I suppose."

"Well, mine did not," retorted Maria with spite. "My father wasted away from organs that kept giving out one by one, until all he had left was pain. With my mother it was even worse. She was broken both in spirit and body. When my father died, he left everything to her, with provisions for my brothers to inherit after she died. Nothing for me, but that is another story, and it's cultural. Meanwhile the estate included a business and lots of rental properties. It required management. Conducting business in Turkey is not easy, especially for a woman, and even more so for the few Greeks who still live there. On top of that my brothers, are very greedy. So, they got her to sign everything over to them, and told her not to worry, she would continue to be the Queen. Needless to say, she had lots to worry about. Both of the sisters-in-law had hated her all along — oh, we're a very normal family, to be sure — and before she knew it, she was on a plane, penniless, thrown out, to come and live with me in Montreal. A queen, alright. Queen Lear."

"Lear? Isn't that Racine?"

"No. Shakespeare," said Maria, surprised by the interruption.

"Yes, I know," sighed Josette.

"She came in the middle of the winter. She was like a blizzard, piled on top of all the other blizzards. She was so... angry. She ranted on endlessly about the calumny of her sons and their wives. Pacing through the house — you'll see the house, Josette, it's immense. But, she would make the whole tour again and again, cursing, cursing, refusing to eat, refusing to sleep. And then, one day I saw all this blood in her toilet, and we rushed to the hospital. It was colon cancer, her worst nightmare. We are Greeks, but we have lived with the Moslems for so long, we share their horror of anything abnormal... down there. Not being able to go to the toilet properly, unable to wash oneself, to have doctors prodding and looking and asking you questions. This is abomination. For her, to develop such a cancer in that place, was some kind of awful proof of unforgivable sin. So terrible you'd rather die than admit it. Can you understand, Josette? It turned out, she'd had it for ten years. Ten years before, when it hadn't turned malignant yet, the doctors told her they should cut it out, and she would be completely cured, except that she'd have to wear that... bag."

"Colostomy bag? Oh, my God."

"That's what she said. She told them she'd rather commit suicide."

"I wouldn't go that far, but, you know..."

"I know. She said that elegant women do not wear those bags. She was a true Duchess, my mother. She never left the house unless she put on all her make-up and the right clothes."

"Aah, a diva," sighed Josette.

"Yes, exactly. The mere thought of carrying her... excrement in a plastic bag hanging from her waist... well, you can imagine. She went into total denial. She refused to see a doctor for ten years, even though that thing was getting bigger, and more painful. By the time we went to Montreal General, she was beyond help. Nevertheless, they gave her chemo and radiation, making her even weaker, ever sorrier. And she wept for months, and got thinner and thinner, but she went for her treatments always neatly dressed and fully made-up. You have to admire her for that. And then, she got a little better. She could sit up. She started eating. And she even stopped crying and cursing. Instead, she got on the sewing machine. She altered a couple of her dresses, to go out in, or so I hoped, but she knew better. She did it so that there would be a choice of outfits for her funeral. I didn't know, I feel so guilty, I refused to admit it. Instead

I hoped, I really hoped, that she had turned the corner. So guilty..."
Maria refilled the coffee cups. "And, in September, as usual, I got up
and left. To the opera, then to Mykonos. I called every day, and
every day Betty told me Mama was fine. Duncan had told her to,
thinking he was doing me a favour. By the time I was back, she was
already on the death-floor, the tenth floor of the Montreal General.
If they ever tell you they're checking you into the tenth floor of the
Montreal General, refuse to go, hold them off at gunpoint. Do you
promise me, Josette? I could never face that floor ever again."

"And who said I was going to the tenth floor before you?"
snapped Josette.

"Oh, yes, I forgot. You're only ten years older than me, and you
smoke like a chimney, so-o chances are I will indeed end up on the
tenth floor before you! Oh, my God, listen to me. I can't believe it!
Making stupid jokes about death. Me! I cross myself three times, at
the mere sight of a funeral home. God, Josette, you're good for me.
Do you promise never to leave me?"

"Why should I? You have a better villa than I've ever seen in my
wildest dreams," said Josette, offhandedly. Maria, already fragile,
shuddered. Josette shook her head and came closer. She hugged
Maria, rocking her. "It's not your fault the cancer spread while you
were gone. That's how it happens. I watched my friend Jeanine go
through it. She fell just like that. She went in less than two weeks.
We also all had thought she was getting better. We were wrong."

"My mother was only seventy."

"Jeanine was forty two. She had an eight year old, plus two
teenagers."

Maria started sobbing again.

"Crying for your mother, or for yourself?"

"For Jeanine," said Maria. "I can't help it. I do feel guilty. Truth
is, I never loved my mother as much as she loved me. I couldn't wait
to leave home. I was in heaven when Duncan came along and took
me to the other side of the world."

"You were young. That's the duty of the young. To grow wings
and fly as far away as possible from us. At least you did it with
someone who could take care of you. Arletty got up and headed
into the unknown. Into the abyss of New York City, for Christ's sake!
All alone. At fourteen. She called me only three times in two years.
I went through hell. It's been eight years, but I still get the shakes."

"Eight years? Are you sure?"

"What do you mean, am I sure?"

"She told Ari she's sixteen!"

"That imp. She lied to him. She's short and skinny enough to be sixteen, but she's twenty two. I should know."

"Why would she lie to Ari?"

"And how dare he pursue her, if he thought she was sixteen. Your son is a scoundrel, Maria!"

"I agree. But, he assured me he wanted to marry her."

"Good luck!"

"Really? Is it that hopeless?"

"Listen to me, Maria. My daughter is a very strange creature. She wants. She doesn't want. She wants and doesn't want at the same time. She tests people. She mistrusts people. She drives them to the edge. She does this to her own father. I've quit trying to figure her out. I just enjoy her for being my daughter. My flesh. But, there's one thing I do know about. And that is Love. Yes, she's in love. Deeply in love. I would say, for the first time in her life."

"Ari too. Indisputably. I would bet the villa on that."

"We're in trouble. I'm telling you."

"But, we are two mothers. Now that we're a team, they don't have a chance. Isn't that so?"

"Indisputably. They have no chance."

"He's such a baby, my Ari. So protected."

"Well, he did make a movie about terminal despair. Maybe..."

"Yes. You're right. And Arletty, so... so independent."

Josette lit another *Gauloise*. "It's all an act. At heart, a lamb."

"Are you sure?"

"No, of course not. Are you sure that Ari is such a baby?"

"No. Obviously not. Maybe he grew up while I wasn't looking."

Josette took a deep breath. "I believe all this uncertainty will eat away... what did you call it, our *kefi?*"

"Yes, *kefi*. Our birthday mood. Gone."

"No way! Come on, girl, don't be stingy, open up that bottle of *ouzi*. I'm ready for some *kefi.*"

And so it went, throughout the day, all evening, and deep into the night. A little *ouzo,* some tears, and lots of motherly plotting. Plotting to set their kids' lives straight, to see them happily married to each other and out of their hair, so that the two of them could take trips to Mykonos as often as they liked, carefree and duty-bound only to themselves. To have as good a time as possible, now that they had found each other so that, when that tenth floor eventually beckoned, they could take the final elevator ride with a few less regrets.

Late, late at night, far more tipsy than either of them would have admitted, Maria and Josette stepped out of the villa just in time to greet the drunks who were rolling home after drinking all night in their honour. Most of them were so blotto, they had already forgotten what they were drinking to this night, as opposed to every other night.

The two women, daintily propping each other up, walked into the white-washed maze, and let themselves get lost. Finally, they sat down on an adobe stoop, to regain their breath. A brooding genius, guitar jauntily across his back, appeared from behind a tiny church. He was young, much younger than his songs would suggest. Both of the women recognized their own child in him. Somehow, to them, he looked like both Arletty and Ari simultaneously, even though Arletty and Ari didn't resemble each other at all.

They gave him a bundle of 5,000 drachma notes, a total of some seventy or eighty dollars. He sat down under a tree of frangipani flowers, and sang for them a song of unrequited love whose melody, wrapped in the perfumes of the night, floated up to the cloudless, starlit sky to amuse Eros and his own over-protective mother, Aphrodite.

Chapter 13

Mid-October. On Redpath Crescent.

Arletty's phone came while Ari was in the middle of a very tricky edit. Installed in his room with his own digital, movie-editing equipment — no first-time film-maker hardships for him — with his best friend Benjamin Cohen next to him. Ben was playing on the electronic keyboard, composing what would eventually comprise the soundtrack: a lone saxophone, wailing, echoing the melodramatic plot twists.

Ben, more emaciated and scruffier with each passing year, was exactly the kind of person whom the prissier MacLeods — Ari's great-aunt Jaimie and his father Duncan, for instance — would rather kill than acknowledge as a visitor in their house. Born a Jew, raised as an agnostic by leftist-hippy parents, a high-school drop-out, permanently hashish-dazed, arguably a closet-homosexual (no known girlfriends), unkempt and rarely washed with no visible means of support, yet solvent — obviously a dope-dealer — and a musician to boot.

But, what a musician. Never formally trained — his parents deemed music lessons too bourgeois — he could play any instrument he touched, and was able to express his emotions in any musical style he chose, from baroque to hip-hop. He was far too good to play music for mere money, and his many compositions — cantatas, concerti, rhapsodies, tone-poems and lyric-less songs — existed solely in his head, since he did not know how to write musical notation, and he was too busy forever creating new material to ever find the time, or the money, to record anything he had finished.

Benjamin's only real audience consisted of Ari. The two outcasts, Ben the drop-out and Ari the ludicrously rich kid, whom no normal person would dare befriend, had met when they were four-teen, at a park in winter. Ari, decked out in a million dollars worth of goose feathers and fur collars, was walking back from seducing — and yes, deflowering — yet another of his girlfriends — never to be talked to again, after giving in to his teenage lust. Ben was on an icy bench, flimsily dressed, oblivious to the elements, playing a complicated tune on a wooden flute.

Ari sat down in the snow and listened to the music. He was too ignorant to recognize it for the masterpiece it was, but he recognized a soul mate when he saw one. If it weren't for his mother, Ari would have gladly taken up a life of playing music, under-dressed on a wintry park bench. That is, if he had had any musical talent to begin with.

Two if's removed from being Ben, he adopted Ben as his alter ego and sounding-board for his free-flowing libido. Intimate details of frequent one-night stands with girls of all descriptions were willingly shared by Ari and eagerly attended by Ben, who was too spaced-out to have any kind of sex-life of his own. Ari, in return, listened to and applauded everything Ben composed and played on the electronic keyboard, the only present of Ari's he had accepted, and which he carried with him everywhere he went.

Ben had been the main inspiration for *They Came From The North*. His leaf-in-the-wind existence had been the model on which Ari had drawn his main character, a girl — some sort of Freudian field-day, that — but more concretely, it was the music. Ari had barely finished relating the bare bones of the original story to him when Ben got on the keyboard and extemporized musical themes, to give the as-yet-unmade movie its sound, its feel, its life.

On this chilly October morning, Ben had sneaked through the woods out back, up the trellis to the window and into Ari's room. Just as he had been doing for years, ever since the day Duncan had first found him in the house and physically hurled him out the front door, injuring him slightly on the unforgiving stone steps.

The two collaborators spent ten minutes discussing Ari's ongoing pain for Arletty, watching yet again the completely edited, scored and sound-synced scene of her warehouse monologue, bracing themselves for the enormous challenge of crafting the rest of the movie to sound and look anywhere near as compelling as those precious two minutes.

Today's chore: to doctor a segment that had been particularly badly-acted by the lead actress — the heroine, Christine — and try to drown out its faults with music. They had almost gotten it, Ben's plaintive notes easily replacing the botched dialogue and even adding heart-felt emotion where none had existed, when the phone rang. Ari, who normally let the answering machine take his calls, lunged for it during the first ring, somehow convinced that it was Arletty reaching to him out of the blue, after two and a half months of absolute silence.

Arletty started with a simple "Hi, Ari, how are you?" as if contacting him was routine. Without waiting for his response, she plunged into an uninterruptible monologue, in the manner of all her important lectures to him, including her speech in the movie. Chidingly, but not exactly angrily, she informed him that she had been right all along, that her mother, and now his mother had been conspiring behind her back, and that they had arranged back-to-back matchmaking lunches in their honour: herself in Westmount with the MacLeods, and himself in the Plateau with the Daoust-Tremblays, starting with Westmount tomorrow. She'd be there, but only because she could use the food, and could he please make sure there were some French fries on the menu? Then she abruptly hung up, without a goodbye, and without having to hear anything he had to say, except for his initial "hello."

Ari clicked off the phone, and fell back on his chair, stunned. After some silence, which Ben restrained himself from breaking with appropriate music, Ari, still in shock said: "She's coming to this house tomorrow." He didn't have to say who she was. There was currently only one "she" in the entire world, who had the power to thrill him like this.

Ben smiled mischievously and reached into the pocket of his ratty vest. He whipped out a ready-rolled joint of hashish. "Well, this calls for a celebration," he winked, "doesn't it?" Like Arletty, he didn't wait for Ari's response. He lit the joint and passed it to him.

The next day, Arletty arrived fashionably, forty-five minutes late. Ari opened the door for her, and smiled shyly. She was dressed in summery clothes to reflect the unseasonably warm day, sunny and dry, possibly the last of its kind until next spring. She kissed him lightly on alternating cheeks, three times, as per *Québécois* custom. He didn't expect the summery look, and he couldn't have hoped for the kisses, but he welcomed the whole package. The vision of Arletty in thin, curve-hugging fabric, in tandem with the sound of her lips kissing, aroused in him a sexual awareness he hadn't felt for two and a half months.

She walked into the ornate foyer un-self-consciously, as if she too lived in a palace. Carved wood, plaster relief, a three-storey atrium with stained-glass windows that scaled the high ceilings, and rising out of the middle, a rich-man's dream: one staircase for going up, one for coming down, and a third one between them, just for show, for making grand entrances to celebrations held in the ballroom to the right.

The one sobering feature of this exuberant foyer was a rigidly hung battalion of oversize portraits, six of them, set three to a side, glowering at each other from opposite sides of the gleaming, Carrara marble floor. The visages, painted in different periods over more than one hundred years, had all been executed in the style of English, upper middle-class portraiture. Dark colours and corpse-like faces lacking warmth, but resounding with self-proclaimed grandeur. This was the kind of art one buys in countryside antique stores for the quality of the gilded, filigreed frame, intending to chuck the picture and replace it with, if nothing else, a good mirror.

Arletty whizzed past the five portraits of the men and stopped in front of the sixth one, which depicted a woman. "Ah, so at least one guy in your family had a wife," she scoffed.

"That's no one's wife," laughed Ari, "that's Great Aunt Jaimie. They say she was ruthless and mean, but she was very nice to me. Let me introduce you to the rest of them. This is Charlie MacLeod, a gangster from Scotland, though we don't talk about it. That's James, his son. Sir James, I should say. And here's Duncan the First, James's son, and a spectacular fellow, by all accounts. A kind of cross between Prince Hal and a philosopher-king— "

"Oh, I'm sure!" interjected Arletty.

"Well, whatever. He died young, and he had two children. Jaimie, his daughter, you already met, and this fellow next to her, is Ross, Duncan's son, and my grandfather. He was great. He's the only ancestor I have whom I'd be proud to introduce you to. He loved art, and he didn't care who knew it." Ari arrived at the last portrait.

He feigned embarrassment. "And this super-serious dude over here, he is my father, Duncan..."

"Ah, yes. Perfect," said Arletty peering into the oils, as if trying to burn holes into the canvas. "Let's not forget Duncan."

"Well, lucky you, you're about to meet him in the flesh. Then you'll never forget him. But then again, you'll also meet my mother."

Ari offered his arm, and Arletty tentatively took it. Some invisible servant threw open big, reddish-brown, mahogany doors, inviting Arletty and Ari to step through them, arm-in-arm, like two extras posing as a couple engaged to be married in a turn-of-the-century Paris costume-drama. They promenaded like that through the western wing of the house, past the library, the drawing room, the gentlemen's smoking room, the ladies' smoking room, the billiard room, the movie-screening room and into the solarium, whose French-glass doors had been opened onto the sunlit garden. There, many full-bloom gardenia plants had just been delivered from Madame DelaSuffrance's shop on Laurier Street, filling the air with the sweetest, most feminine perfume of all.

Duncan, who had eagerly welcomed the opportunity to meet the woman who might make an honest man out of his son, sprung to his feet when he heard them enter. Then, he unwittingly shuddered. This little waif would never become a child-bearing woman! He wished he had made an excuse and stayed at his computer. His obvious distaste at first sight froze Arletty. Ari gulped, and as usual when facing his father, he regressed to a preteen, bracing himself for a scolding.

Maria sashayed in from the garden, to the rescue of all concerned. She was bearing gardenias for the table. "Hello, hello, hello, *yassou!* I'm so glad to finally meet you!" she sang. She briefly embraced Ari on the fly, and surprised the hell out of Arletty with a big, juicy hug and several wet kisses on each cheek.

"Take it easy, Maria. You'll drown the kid," said Duncan wearily.

"I'm not a kid. I'm Arletty," said she, extending a hand coldly.

Duncan shook her hand formally, with a small bow. "I'm Duncan. Nowhere near as beautiful a name as yours. What was she? A poet? No. A sculptress?"

"She was the whore in *La Traviata,*" retorted Arletty.

Maria laughed. "No, darling. That was *Violetta.* I must take you to the opera. Are you a fan?"

"Don't know. Never been," smiled Arletty, who was enjoying the uptight situation just as she thought she would.

"Come on, Duncan. Pour some wine. Everyone, let's sit down. We're starving!"

Duncan obliged, carelessly pouring a very expensive white wine, spilling it. "I wouldn't bother with opera if I were you. Just endless screaming by people who can't have what they want."

"It's not necessary to scream to get what you want," observed Arletty, as she sat down. "Sometimes it's better to say nothing."

Duncan pursed his lips, and nodded in agreement. Saying nothing, he sat down across from her and looked at her closely. It wasn't a definitive ogle; it was more of a re-evaluation. Maybe he had underestimated Ari. She did have a rude sort of sexuality that counterpointed her underfed delicacy in a very exciting way. He smiled. She did not smile back.

Maria arranged a couple of gardenias beside each place setting. "They speak to me of summer," she announced to all of them, daring anyone to contradict her.

Sophia, Maria's kitchen ally, wheeled in a rolling cart, groaning with enough food for sixteen. A childless widow from the old country, overweight, a little smelly, she was the only person permitted to cook in Maria's kitchen. Sophia was a little-bit-of-Constantinople, Maria's last line of defense against the MacLeods, which was to say, her husband Duncan and Betty, the housekeeper.

"Arletty's lunch first," instructed Maria. Sophia chose a silver-domed serving dish and placed it on the table in front of the guest of honour. She proudly uncovered it, and sank a spoon in it, for Arletty to serve herself.

Arletty opened her eyes wide, and let out a small scream. *"Poutine!"*

"Our version of it," beamed Maria. "The potatoes are fried in olive oil. The gravy is made with pure veal stock, and thickened with a *roux* we got out of an old *Québecois* cookbook. Josette lent it to me. And for cheese, we used raw-milk curds from the *Auvergne*. Made of sheep's milk. For the flavour. I'm desperate to know what you think."

Arletty picked a fry out of its hot sauce by her fingertips. She put it in her mouth and then she twisted her face. "I don't think it's *poutine.*"

"But, it's okay? I mean, you won't mind eating it?" Maria floundered, hoping for a compliment. Meanwhile, Sophia prepared the other three plates. Grilled swordfish with lemon-oil-caper sauce, *arugula* salad — an old Constantinopolitan favourite with full-fleshed fish — and some of the same fries, minus the gravy and cheese. She deposited additional portions of everything, covered on a hot-plate on the sideboard, and was about to exit, when she noticed Arletty continuing to dig into her *poutine* by finger, sloppi-ly, dripping gravy on the tablecloth, eating noisily. Sophia giggled and shuffled out.

Ari took a bite of the swordfish, and rolled his eyes. "Fantastic," he exclaimed with his mouth full.

Maria smiled gratefully, and nibbled on her portion. "Yes, it's fine," she pronounced.

Duncan didn't even glance at his own plate. He stared at Arletty, instead. She stepped up the tempo. Now that the gravy was cooling down, she was plunging her entire hand into the *poutine,* and stuff-ing her mouth with more than it could hold. Bits of potato and drib-bles of gravy came sputtering out as she tried to chew and breathe simultaneously.

Duncan, aware that he was being baited, followed suit. He poked around at his food by hand, and gingerly picked up a chunk of the fish between thumb and index finger. He put it in his mouth and smacked his lips.

"It really does taste better by hand, Maria. You should try it, too. And get used to it. They'll be passing a law soon, which will be enforced by the language police. Once they've eliminated the English language, they'll start banishing cutlery."

Arletty stopped chewing and winked at him quizzically. "You're getting the idea, sir. But I'm afraid you're too late. They already know all about you."

Aha! Now she had walked into his trap. "Dear, dear. Do they, now? I suggest they leave me alone, and take a good, hard look at History. At the mother of all French Revolutions, for instance. All that blood and all that rhetoric, and by the end of it, first a war-mon-ger with pants too tight for his own good, and then back to the Bourbons. Louis the XVIIIth, an ineffectual sap. Give me Marie Antoinette, anytime. Quebec? The same thing." Duncan had her attention. He refueled with a few, hand-picked leaves of arugula, and a sip of wine. "The history of Quebec is just about to begin," he continued. "Our place in the sun is about to be granted. And what happens? Some idiots are busily drawing the blinds to block out the light. Canada is a well-oiled machine that has been sitting dormant for three centuries. Waiting its turn. Well, our number is being called, but we've gone fishing. Haven't we? Fishing for laughable, Nineteenth Century dreams of nationhood and insularity and the preservation of one language at the expense of all other languages, life-styles, ideas. At the expense of worldliness and sagacity. At the expense of evolution and achievement, and of course, at the expense of success."

Ari and Maria continued eating with gusto, as if there was no war raging at the table. Arletty had finished her potatoes. She lifted the silver dish and drank down the last of the gravy. Then she wiped her mouth and hands on the creamy, damask napkin. "It was actually excellent *poutine,*" she said to Maria, "once I got used to it. Maybe the best I've ever had. Thank you."

"There's more," said Maria, pointing to the sideboard.

Arletty ignored the offer, and turned to Duncan. "Was that supposed to be funny. Was it, like, a joke?"

"I'm dead serious," smiled Duncan dangerously.

"Really? Ari did warn me that you were a very serious person."

"Ari is a silly, pampered boy, and he would do well to mind his own business. It would also be a good idea to let go of this pretentious cinema career of his, and think of his future."

"And you think I should be the one to help him find his true path in life? Is that what you expect after preaching at me for under two minutes?"

Duncan gave a dismissive shrug. "Frankly, my dear, I expect about as much from you, as I expect from him."

Arletty snorted derisively. "In a world according to you, you would be stupid to expect anything from anyone. Except, maybe to get your head chopped off, like your friend Marie-Antoinette. And, no. You don't have to call the body-guards. I don't give a damn what happens to you. I'm not even going to be at the square to watch. I'll be too busy cleaning someone's house, Yes, I clean houses so that I can afford to survive the rules and the greed of people like you."

She raised her glass to Maria. "Maman told me you're one hell of great lady, Mrs. MacLeod. I hope I get the chance to find out. Now, you must please excuse me. I have to leave, I have an appointment."

She stood up. Both Ari and Duncan jumped to their feet. Arletty nodded to Duncan. *"Enchantée."*

"Oh, me too," mumbled Duncan. "Charmed."

Arletty turned to leave with a mere glance at Ari. He puttered after her like a puppy. They walked back to the foyer wordlessly. She opened the front door. She blew a kiss to Ari. "And tomorrow, you'll meet my father." She winked and stepped out into a light rain, which had just started to sprinkle.

"Wait. Let me drive you," he helplessly shouted after her, but she was already out of earshot.

Chapter 14

Next day at lunchtime. On the Plateau.

The return engagement of the bipartite Maria-Josette-organized, match-making lunches took place in the respective solarium of the Daoust-Tremblay home. The solarium in question was no more than the alcove next to the kitchen, but it was splendid this lunchtime, dressed to kill in all manner of heirloom china, cutlery and linen. It was marginally floral outside the bay window, albeit of spent, small, Plateau gardens, looking rather defeated under the dark October rain. The weather had spared Maria's gardenias yesterday, but seemed to be taking pleasure in pissing on Josette's lunch today.

Josette, who measured her happiness by the amount of sunshine on any given day, winced at the depressing sight. The steady rain would surely prove a deterrent for the bubbly, care-free ambience that had to be generated to offset the near-fiasco of yesterday's Arletty-Duncan debate. But the insistent rain, an irrefutable harbinger of winter, presented yet another danger. It never failed to spur Louis-Marc to extreme nationalism and doctrinaire speechifying. He had sworn not to do this today, but it could well just gush from his mouth on its own.

Despite her fears, the lunch had started out wonderfully. Both Arletty and Ari had arrived cheerful and on time, only minutes apart. Louis-Marc had hastily greeted them, sizing Ari up and down, seemingly pleased with what he saw, and had hurried back to his kitchen to put the finishing touches to his surprise dish for the special guest.

This had left Josette the floor, to entertain them with her little stories of Mykonos, and of Maria's very particular role on the island,

her benevolent-queen status, her ability to knock back *ouzis* with
the fishermen on the wharf, as well as to rule the most elegant parties, with important people lining-up just for the privilege of having
spoken with her. This was all of special interest to Ari, who had
never been invited to join his mother on her annual jaunts, and
couldn't imagine her sitting on a dock, swigging *ouzo* from a communal bottle while waves crashed on the jetty, spraying her hair
with salt water.

Louis-Marc returned from the kitchen, announced that the meal
would be ready in ten, and led the party to the table to start the
wine. Josette tried to maneuver her husband into the seat facing the
room, but in the final shuffle he had insisted on his usual seat, in
full view of the rain.

Arletty was the first to read the warning signs: a certain glint in
the eye; repeated brushings-back of his thinning hair towards the
pony-tail; impatient clearings of the throat. She gestured to her
mother to intervene. Josette had already noticed it. The self-satisfied
grin; the tiny twitch of the cheek; it was happening. Meek, house-
husband, part-time lecturer L-M Daoust, was transforming into
Louis-Marc, Defender of Enslaved Francophones. Josette desperately grasped for escape-subjects, but she drew a blank. She slumped
back in her chair miserably, ready for the worst.

Louis-Marc engaged the unprepared Ari's attention with a piercing "Ahem!" and asked him what it was about *Québec* that he liked.

Ari, unaware that he needed reasons to like a place where he
had lived since birth, did his well-bred best to say what Louis-Marc
wanted to hear. He dredged up all the usual reasons: the *joie de
vivre,* the friendliness and compassion of the populace, the beauty
of the land, the world-wide importance of *Montréal, Québec City,*
and even *Trois-Rivières,* where he had never been, enhancing his
list with passable enthusiasm, a sincere effort to please Arletty by
pleasing her father.

Louis-Marc heard him out, then smiled broadly. "When sovereignty has been achieved, people like you will be alright. I can't
vouch for your father, not even for your mother. Sorry. But you? No
problem." He sipped his wine for punctuation and added his zinger:
"Et maintenant, tout l'affaire, encore une fois, mais en Francais."

Josette and Arletty sighed in unison. Ari gulped. "You know, I
speak French, I mean, I understand it perfectly, but it's difficult."

Louis-Marc cut him off with a roll of his eyes, and a flick of his

wrist. "Don't you think, in that case, that you should make more of
an effort? How can you contemplate a life in *Québec,* and not be fluent in our language?"

Ari was stymied. He made a small noise, appealing to Josette for
help. She laughed expansively, and stroked his cheek. She smiled
warningly at Louis-Marc. "Leave the man alone, Louis-Marc. When
we separate, he can be our ambassador to London, or something.
Maybe Washington. Hey, how about Ottawa?" She turned to Ari.
"You see, sweetheart, my husband hasn't declared his intentions yet,
but he's a shoe-in for the first President of the Republic. The top
banana. He can give you any job you like."

Louis-Marc hissed at her in French, through clenched teeth:
"You are not to make fun of me in front of him. I cannot permit
that!"

"Then quit sounding like an asshole." she replied calmly, in
French.

Louis-Marc's entire face twitched, then he recovered, and turned
back to Ari, smiling benignly. "The future of this land is indisputably
French. Anyone who can't see that, will perish. And the rest of us
will succeed. It's that simple. And yes, we do have a plan. A workable plan, which is based on empirical evidence, on tangible facts.
Look around you the next time you're out in the streets of *Montréal.*
The pace, the mood, the creativity. God, it's hard to remember
where we are. Is it Paris, or is it Grenoble? Well, it's definitely not
Toronto, and it's absolutely not the *Mont-ree-yall* I grew up in. There
are no longer many signs of petty Presbyterian uprightness. Very
few shackles left, my friend! And those that are left, are bloody well
deep in the closet. Hiding! Because, we no longer tolerate them, and
no longer have to tolerate them!

"René Lévesque told us. We possess all the human and economic resources to create and organize our own affairs... BUT, we
are drowning in the mud by a federal system that is dictated by
interests other than ours!" Louis-Marc took another sip, to punctu-
ate the thought, let it sink in. "Do you understand the significance
of that deduction? We must, we have to, take our life in our own
hands. It will be US this time, who sells *Québec* to the Americans.
The Anglos have sold it to them repeatedly, but always the money
has gone to Westmount, and to Ottawa. This time it will stay *chez
nous,* and because it is our very home we are selling, we'll make a
bloody-good deal. A *maudit-tabernacle* of a deal. We'll get big

bucks for it, and we'll sell our services, not our land. And how do we do this? We break down that antiquated, Victorian business arrangement they call Confederation, and declare Independence. Finally, we revise our criminal code to serve *our* needs, not the needs of Nineteenth Century Scots. We hold onto the best parts. We like innocent until proven guilty, versus Napoleon's guilty unless you can prove your innocence. Fine, BUT, we dismember all the laws, which were part of the British-Catholic Church conspiracy. I'm talking about laws that regulate our morals and belittle our free will. When we have achieved that, then we decriminalize gambling, make way for fun and prostitution!"

A loud gasp by the two women crashed Louis-Marc right off his podium, making him wince. He had gotten in trouble with them over this issue in the past. This time, with Ari in the room, they were furious.

"Shut *up*, Louis-Marc," said Josette in English.

"Oh, no! Not THAT again!" echoed Arletty, in French.

Ari, who had been on the verge of boredom with Louis-Marc's long argument, and had only half-listened to its non-conclusive conclusion, was jolted back to full attention by the violent reactions of the women. Had Josette really said *shut up?* He shuddered to think what calamity would have to befall them, before either of his parents would express such ire to the other in front of him, let alone a guest.

Louis-Marc continued to address Ari, though visibly less confidently: "Just like they do in France. We decriminalize, but then we monitor, to make sure it's healthy and crime-free, instead of now, when it happens in the closets, full of disease and Anglo underhandedness."

Josette had heard enough. She stood up menacingly. "A legal bordello! You and your friends want to make all of *Québec* a gigantic whorehouse!

Louis-Marc cowered as she towered over him. "No, we are not," he tried to reason with her. "All I'm doing here, is trying to prove a point!"

Now Arletty stood up and said in French: "Your point can only be proven if we all agree to become whores and attract American sex-tourists, to build up the *Québec* economy. I, for one, refuse!"

Louis-Marc, now enraged, lashed out: "You have joined the other side. Your opinions do not count! And I never suggested you should become a whore!"

Josette crossed herself. "I should hope NOT! My God!"

Arletty defiantly: "In your opinion, I'm already a whore."

"I don't have an opinion on that. Are you?"

Everyone froze after that. Louis-Marc for having said it, Josette and Arletty for having heard it. Even Ari, though he had barely understood anything, since it had all been in French.

Josette, switching to English for Ari's benefit, said: "Oh, for fuck's sake! You've gone *mental*, Louis-Marc!" She left the room in a huff,

Arletty followed suit, with an equally corrosive: "You're alone, now, pops. You've gone too far. I think you've actually flipped." And out she stormed, leaving the two men on their own.

The surprise dish had reached its point of readiness, infusing the air with a comforting aroma. Louis-Marc was too shattered to get up and remove it from the oven. Ari was bedazzled. He had just witnessed an all-too-real family scene, which couldn't have happened in his own home in a million years. It made him want to become a part of this family evermore.

Louis-Marc let out an exasperated guffaw, attempting to regain control of the situation. "It is so hard to deal with women," he sighed. "Do you find that, too? I was just trying to make a point. A small point of my theorem, and next thing I know, I'm mental and I'm driving my own daughter to prostitution! You know, if there's one true obstacle to a successful Sovereignty, it is that women will have to be part of the decision-making!"

Ari motioned with his index finger in front of his lips. "Sh-sh. They might hear you."

Louis-Marc laughed. "Oh, you are a diplomat, my friend. Maybe we should make you an ambassador. But, let them hear me. Let them hate me. They love to gang up on me. It's part of our lifestyle."

"They don't hate you. They love you. It's obvious."

Louis-Marc stood up chuckling. "It is true. I am very lovable. And fuck them! Let's you and me eat. Now, remember. This is not Westmount. This is the *Plateau!* You're getting *Ragotte des pattes,* the way my mother used to make them."

Ari feigned a swoon. *"Ragoutte des pattes!* I LOVE *ragoutte des pattes!* With mashed potatoes?"

"Of course." Louis-Marc coquettishly sauntered over to the kitchen and took a steaming serving dish out of the oven. He brought it to the table and set it down on a trivet. Meaty pork hocks, meltingly reposed in thick, brown gravy. He rushed off and returned with an earthenware bowl, which was overflowing with creamily mashed spuds, and set it down next to the stew. Arletty and Josette came back into the room, smiling and hungry, as if nothing had happened. Louis-Marc portioned out gargantuan helpings, which they all wolfed down with great appetite, much wine, and pleasant chit-chat. Even Arletty gorged on the potatoes and the gravy, nimbly avoiding the meat.

The meal over, Ari, much kissed by Josette and warmly hand-shaken by Louis-Marc, was fully prepared to walk out the door with at most, the habitual triple-kiss from Arletty. She surprised him by asking if he would give her a lift home in his car. The two of them, raincoats in place — hers the scarlet showpiece, his, a London-bought, regulation beige *Burberry's* — walked out arm in arm into the rain.

They sauntered past his car and continued into a narrow street of tiny two-storey dwellings, all attached to each other. Ari waited for her to say something, his heart pounding, his face drenched by fat rain-drops.

"So, you see what it's like," she finally whispered, "married life! God forbid what's going on in your house. And though I'm sure you found it amusing, God twice forbid what's going on in mine. Is that what you want for us? Is that what you're hoping for? Or, are you really stupid enough to believe we could be different?"

There was a narrow break between the houses. A thin alley, just wide enough to walk through single-file, it was a mid-block conduit to the backs of the little buildings. Ari peered into the depths of it. Dark and wet, absolutely private.

"Come on," he said, "I'll show you my tree-house."

"No. No way," she objected, but she must have meant yes, because she followed him into the hideaway, even though he had dropped her arm, and walked in without looking back.

At its rear end, the alley was blocked by a wooden door that had not been opened since it was installed. The door had grown into the sagging walls on either side, a solid shoulder to lean on. Ari stopped in front of it. Here was the impasse, the end of the road. Cornered. He hugged the rotting wood, pasting his face against its clammy surface. He let out a sigh, which sounded very much like one of his mother's at her most Hellenic.

Arletty hugged him from behind. And, though he was twice her size, she engulfed him. He turned into a little boy, then an infant, then an embryo. He was inside her now, surrounded on all sides. The door in front, she behind, and leaning against his flanks, the hopelessness of it all.

"I am not stupid. Not at all. And it's not love and marriage. Who needs it? I don't want to be in love. I know what it does to people. I've seen it, just like you have. Love is nothing more than a dramatic device to me. It makes for excellent plot lines. That's all. I don't want to shackle myself anymore than you do. I want both of us to be free. I mean it. So that we can create. Together. I told you all this before. I want to be friends. That's all I want..." Ari's voice trailed off. The rain had gotten stronger, and a cold wind had picked up. Now it was washing down his face in icy sheets. The few tears that escaped his vigilance were quickly melted away.

She turned him around and looked into his eyes. She kissed him. His lips were trembling as he kissed her back, hungrily, painfully. Moaning. "But, it's not all is it? I don't believe that," she said. "I don't believe that of either of us. That's the problem."

She unbuttoned her trench coat. He unbuttoned his. She circled his chest with her arms and drew him to her. They kissed again, longer, fleshier, more tenderly. The rain seeped between them, penetrating them. Their clothes clung flimsily. It was as if they were naked.

They held each other close, rocking to a gentle, self-regenerating beat. He climaxed first, and sensing it, she did right after he did. They stayed like that, swaying imperceptibly, continuing their climaxes, coming, coming, glued to each other as the rain, now in buckets, cleansed them and slowly dissolved their desire.

Soaked and shivering, they ran back to his car, and he drove her to Outremont. She quickly kissed him his three times, opened the car-door, and stepped out. She ran up the steps to her building and fumbled with the key. She ducked inside.

He sat at the wheel, the engine running, the wet street darkening after the early sundown, his clothes drying off and smelling of stale sex. He stared straight ahead, seeing only bleakness, months and months without her, an eternity of want.

Chapter 15

Early December. At La Crevetterie.

"I've been dreaming of her. Every night. It's making me terribly, terribly sad."

"Why? What happens in the dreams?"

"The dream. There is only one. The same every time. There is a waltz. Blue Danube. Her favourite. She's dressed in a cream-coloured ball gown. Third-Empire style. She always prided herself on her ability to wear *empire*. The right figure, the right size bust. She looks like the Empress Eugénie. Even like Romy Schneider in Sisi. I'm young. Maybe eleven years old. I'm dressed formally. White-tie. Very proper. I'm tall for my age. Almost her height. Suitable for a dancing partner. But she's leading. Like she used to, when I was really eleven, and she was teaching me to dance. We make a nice looking couple. We turn gracefully. One, two, three. *One, two, three.* First to the right. Then, when the music pauses, we change direction. To the left. She does the steps quickly and effortlessly. She was a great dancer. It's hard for me to keep up. I concentrate, but I trip once in a while. I'm a little stilted. Then, suddenly, the music swells, and the entire orchestra — yes, there is an orchestra, and we're in a ballroom, with a huge chandelier, like the one at Redpath Crescent. And we're the only dancers. It would seem there are others, off to the side, watching us. But I cannot see them — anyway, at that point, I begin to get it right. My feet take flight. I switch arms. I'm leading her, now. We're dancing fluidly, almost liquid movements. Round and round. And she laughs. And I laugh with her. Round and round..."

"And what happens then?"

"Nothing after that. The dream dissolves. I fall back asleep. But,

I wake up sad in the morning."

"You shouldn't. It sounds like a fabulous dream. I'd love to have this dream. When I dream of my mother, it's always in the kitchen, and she's teaching me how to cook. I'm terrified that I'll burn myself. She forces me to put my hands in the hot oven, and stir the browning flour. For the *roux*, you know, for the *sauce brun* of the *ragout*. Then I do burn my fingers. I wake up in pain. And I rush to the fridge and munch on Louis-Marc's leftovers. And thank my lucky stars that I resisted the cooking so he has to take care of it," said Josette with a twinkle in her eye. Then she burst out laughing, her trademark upper-register trill.

Maria relaxed. She reached for the *ouzo*, but it was done. She lit a cigarette instead. It made her cough but she liked it. Josette was teaching her how to smoke, to relieve *la stresse*. Josette was also helping her expiate the guilt she had accumulated in the five long years since her mother's death. Josette, as well, was bolstering her through that nightmarish romance of her son's.

And what was she doing for Josette? Next to nothing. Josette wouldn't have it. "Even-Stephen, or we can't be friends," she had said when they had returned to Montreal. "Your house, on your Mykonos, okay, I accept. But, *Montréal* is my town. Here, I require NO hospitality. Here, I GIVE hospitality!"

She had visited Redpath Crescent once. She had squealed with delight at the discovery of yet another gorgeous bedroom, of yet another priceless sitting room, the numberless alcoves, the fine library, the wood-paneled smoking rooms. The ballroom had floored her. "What a place, Maria. My God!" And the solarium, which Maria had kept for last, had absolutely demolished her.

She had sat down to feel the space. A long silence. Five, maybe ten minutes. It was as if she were sipping the room, the delicate furniture, the gleaming cut-crystal, the forever-flowering, sun-drenched garden — this was in early October, when they had first come back from Greece — as if it were a rare Cognac. As if she were tasting little spoonfuls of the finest of Louis-Marc's *crème brulées*.

After the obligatory tea and crumpets Josette had suggested that future meetings — and there were to be many — should take place on neutral ground. She told Maria, as kindly as she could put it in English that she would never feel comfortable in this grand house. And that, having experienced this house, she couldn't possibly invite Maria to the *Plateau*. But she was acquainted with every worthwhile bar and cafe in town, while Maria probably didn't know a single one outside of Westmount or Downtown. "Am I right? So, let's see each other out there, sister, and get you out of your shell a bit, eh?"

Josette had then given Maria the grand tour of Montreal's cafe society. St. Denis. St. Lawrence. Mount Royal. Various little corners of the *Plateau. Carré St-Louis.* Old Montreal. Duluth. And of course, Bernard Street.

Of all of them, it was *La Crevetterie* that drew Maria — she did have taste. It was at *La Crevetterie*, where the two mothers had engineered their reciprocal, match-making lunches. La Crevetterie where they had consoled themselves when the lunches had backfired and the kids were now further apart than ever. Arletty had moved out of her apartment to a secret location with an unlisted phone. Josette's sole means of contact being an e-mail address. There were weekly lunches together, following which Arletty became more distant and aloof, more palpably unhappy. Meanwhile, Ari had become equally invisible, stashed away in his fully equipped room at Redpath Crescent.

And here they were again at *La Crevetterie,* though regrettably inside. The terrace a thing of the past, and of the future. Now in December, with its snowy sleet and dark skies, it was the table at the window, and a couple of spent *Pernods* — the next best thing to *ouzos*. Maria and Josette looked into each other's eyes, and now, in the stark winter setting of their home town, knew absolutely for sure that this Arletty-Ari thing had at least one very refreshingly positive aspect: the two mothers' pleasure in each other's company.

"Every night, same dream, Ben. It's pissing me right off!" moaned Ari with exasperation. "It's like this: I'm all alone in the desert. But it's not sunny and hot, like it's supposed to be. It's dark with heavy clouds. And it's raining this cold, hurtful, sort of sleet. It's pouring on me. And it's hitting me. Like pellets. Like bits of razor blades."

"Ouch," laughed Ben. "Sounds like what's happening out there today."

"But, this is Montreal, and we're in my room. Safe and dry. In my dream, I'm in the desert, I tell you. The sleet is clobbering me, but I just stand there. I don't move. Well, there is nowhere to move to. I don't try to defend myself. Nothing. Then it rips the clothes right off my back. I'm totally naked. And I still stand there. I'm bleeding. Like, all over. And still, I do nothing!"

"So, you die at the end, or what?" asked Ben, trying to seem sympathetic.

"No. I wake up. In horror. Like in the movies. Then, I kinda cry myself back to sleep. Which takes forever. It's terrible. And it's been happening every night, for weeks... ever since... you know... the thing in the rain, last time I was with her."

"Fu-uckin' in the rai-ay-ain," sang Ben, to the tune of *Singin'* in the same, accompanying himself on his electronic keyboard. He was finding it hard to concentrate on Ari's dream-problems. Today, he was elated. The CBC had just finished spotlighting him in the radio series *Impoverished Geniuses* which aired Saturdays at 6 am. He had played his music and was given ample time to ramble on about his philosophy of life-art — which he had never previously articulated. Invitation to this particular program tended to condemn its participants to lifelong failure and irrelevance, but it was Ben's very first public exposure and he was thrilled. That it might also be his last, did nothing to dampen his spirits, just as Ari's suffering couldn't. In any case, there was plenty for them to celebrate these days. *They Came From The North* was near completion, at the sound-syncing stage. Ben, normally critical of his own work, was quite pleased with the music he had written and performed for the film. Still, Ari's relentless harangue over his unrequited love-lust was beginning to get in the way of Ben's modest happiness. It wasn't that he didn't understand his friend's fixation. Ben himself had fallen in love with Arletty, albeit based on her two minute scene in the movie.

"So, why don't you break down and go knock on her door?" asked Ben innocently.

"So, why don't you take a shower once in a while?" snapped Ari.

"The plumbing. I told you. And my landlord... Hey, what do you mean by that?"

"I mean that I DID go back. I broke down. I couldn't help it. I parked near her house and I waited. But she never appeared. So finally, yesterday, I got out of the car, and I went up to her building. And I looked in her windows. Now, with the leaves off the bushes, you can see right in. And I looked. I sure did."

"Wow! You looked IN! What if she had been there with another guy?"

"Up yours, for even thinking that. But in fact, there was no other guy, there was no her, there was nothing. Zero. The place was cleaned out. I was, like, WHOA! WHAT'S goin' ON? Right? The dream every night, and now this! Over the top, or WHAT? So, I snapped. I phoned her mother. Even worse than hanging outside her door, is to call her mother. She absolutely forbade me to ever do that. But, I did. And do you know what her mother told me?" Ari was on the verge of tears. Again.

"No. Go on."

"She told me... that Arletty is in hiding. All her mother has is an e-mail address, and Arletty even threatened to cut her off from that, if she gave it to me. So, that's it, and that's all."

"Hey," laughed Ben, in an attempt to defuse the moment. "You're picking up *Joual.*"

"What do you mean?"

"What you just said. That's it, and that's all. That's a *Québecois* expression.

An hour or so later, now alone, having been abandoned by Ben, who was far too cheerful this day to put up with his pain, Ari did a routine check on his e-mail. There was one new item.

From: arleti@dynamo.que
To: arimac@aol.com
Date: Friday, Dec. 4th, 1998, 8:13 pm
Subject: you&me

I'm glad you gave my mother your e-mail co-ordinates, because I've been meaning to contact you, but as you know, I hate the phone. You didn't know? Well, I do. And funny thing is, that even e-mailing you is dangerous for me. There's too much going on between us. I'm sure you noticed. Keep your distance! Yes, this

makes me sad, too. But it is what it must be. Please
refrain from trying to find me. Instead, try to find
a wife: you need one.

From: arimac@aol.com
To: arleti@dynamo.que
Date: Friday, Dec. 4th, 1998, 8:17 pm
Subject: re: you&me

Always in my life I've wanted to quote great poetry at
the appropriate moment. Sadly, I have a terrible mem-
ory. That's why e-mail is great for me. I can just copy
out the passages directly from the book.
Here's some Marvell:

> *"Had we but world enough, and time,*
> *This coyness, Lady, were no crime."*

and also:

> *"... the Love which us doth bind,*
> *But Fate so enviously debars,*
> *Is the conjunction of the mind,*
> *And opposition of the Stars."*

From: arimac@aol.com
To: arleti@dynamo.com
Date: Saturday, Dec. 5th, 1998, 12:03 pm
Subject: re: you&me

Please reply. Why don't you reply? Did my quotations
offend you? — I take them back. Your friend for life.
                                                        Ari

From: arimac@aol.com
To: arleti@dynamo.que
Date: Sunday, Dec. 6th, 1998, 12:10 pm

Subject: re: you&me
Please write me. What can it hurt? It's digital. It's nothing.
It means nothing. Yet, for me, it's a great comfort. And a
reason to live. No, I don't mean that.. My reason to live is
that one day you might reconsider and let me see you
again. As always. Ari

From: arimac@aol.com
To: arleti@dynamo.que
Date: Monday, Dec. 7th, 1998, 3:17 am
Subject: re: you&me

Okay. You don't ever have to see me again. Just knowing
you're thinking of me will suffice. I swear. I await your
reply.

Ari

Three days after their last meeting, Maria and Josette once again found themselves seated across from each other at their usual indoor table by the window in *La Crevetterie*. The weather had relented, and bright sunlight was shining on the wet pavement: no Myconian spears or shooting stars bouncing off Mediterranean ripples, only a feeble, wintry respite, a faint reminder of kinder climes, no solace to Josette whatsoever.

"I'm happy you could come at such short notice. Today is my turn to need you," said Josette breathlessly, as soon as she had finished triple-kissing Maria.

"Nothing could've kept me away. You sounded terrible on the phone. What's wrong?"

"Everything. Absolutely everything. My trip to San Andres? Down the tubes. There is some kind of civil war threat, so they all canceled *en masse*. Are they crazy? There is always civil war in Colombia. So, what else is new? And the trip to Jamaica in February — also in doubt. There has been a rape in Montego Bay, and at least half of them are now afraid to go! Give me a break! There are always rapes in Montego Bay. Are they crazy? You just have to be careful, that's all. So, I'm stuck here all winter, and guess what? Louis-Marc is giving me the cold shoulder. There are two things that make winter bearable for me. My trips, and sex when I'm back home. Now, I have nothing."

"That's not exactly true. You have me. I'll take you to the sun. I could use a little vacation myself."

"No way. No, no. No one takes me to the sun. I sell my tickets, I earn my commission, and I take myself to the sun. Thank you very much."

"Alright. I won't take you to the sun. How about Belgium? There is no sun there, ever."

"Yeah. Or, Copenhagen. I made that mistake once. Never again!" Josette's sparkle was returning. They clinked glasses. *Yassou. Yassou.*

"This cold shoulder... Is it new?" Maria, tentatively.

Josette became agitated once again. "New? Brand new! Two months ago. Ever since our famous lunch with Ari. I guess I was too rough on Louis-Marc. But he can be such an idiot. Still, I suppose I should have shut up. He has been milling about like a wounded cat. He won't even look me in the face. He doesn't laugh at my jokes. He still cooks for me, but terrible, boring things. Hamburger steaks and chicken pot pies. Abominations. Insults to his ancestors. And in bed? Nothing. He always begs off when it's time to sleep, scurries off to his computer. Then he sneaks in, when I'm fast asleep, and settles in quietly. Careful not to touch me. It's torture. I want you to advise me. I know you have problems, too. How do you handle it? How do you get him in the mood?"

"I don't," said Maria matter-of-factly. "We don't even sleep in the same bed. Not since my mother died. And even before that, it was touch and go. Our real sex life lasted a very short time. Just until Ari was born."

Josette gulped down her *Pernod*. "Is this true?"

"Yes. It's my fault, really. I'm a neurotic mother now, you should have seen me when Ari was a baby. I used to stay awake all night, in case he sneezed, or cried. It was wrong, I know. But I couldn't help it. And I certainly couldn't concentrate on making love. I was so afraid something would go wrong with Ari, and I wouldn't be able to hear him, if I was, you know, passionate. I used to let Duncan do it to me, but my mind was always on Ari."

"Oh, brother!" exclaimed Josette.

Maria nodded in agreement. "This went on — it's crazy, I know — for many years. After he started growing up, then I would worry that he would hear us and get the wrong idea. Poor Duncan. I used to make him do his business as quietly as possible. Anyway, when my mother died, I blamed him for not summoning me back from Mykonos, as if it was his fault I went in the first place. And then I cried for six months. So, he moved out of our bedroom. Even so, he would come to me, I don't know, periodically, but I had lost the desire. So the visits got less and less frequent. And since my party in August, there hasn't been a peep."

"This is not good!"

"We're practically strangers now. I see him only at breakfast-time, and he tells me how much money he lost the previous day. He's on a losing cycle. For the first time ever. And he blames me. He claims I brought it on with my disregard for his money. You know, for giving Ari the money for his movie. So, Josette, I've decided to become a nun. Maybe, a Mother Superior." Maria lit a cigarette and coughed.

"No kidding," said Josette, doubly concerned that the same thing might happen to her. "We'll have to do something about all that."

From: arleti@dynamo.que
To: arimac@aol.com
Date: Wednesday, Dec. 9th, 1998, 3:01 am
Subject: Inflorescence

Think of each passing day as yet another bud on a floral axis. A cyme, a wave of flowers from a single stem. Our time together: just one of those flowers. Surrounded by all the other flowers. And in inflorescence, the flowers down below need to die, so that the new ones higher up get a chance to bloom. Let them bloom!

Chapter 16

Winter 1998-99. Cyberspace/Montreal.

Deep winter in Montreal freezes everything in its path except human turmoil. Things like love and discord, sadness and elation, the very desire to keep on living, or adversely, to give up and die, are all enhanced and accentuated by the overbearing weather. Blizzards of stiletto-sharp ice-shards, sub-sub-zero temperatures, winds from a desolate hell, suns that never rise, and stars too-bright on clear, Arctic nights. A never-ending cycle of unsurvivable cold, a numbing cold, a terminal cold which pierces the heart, in turn with salutary and destructive forces.

No one escapes the Montreal winter. Everyone is chastened. Loneliness is never lonelier, communion never more ardent, longing never more painful. This is the season of big emotions, the saltatory leaps of relationships, that can compromise the most faithful of couples while cementing the most unlikely allegiances.

Without any perceptible fidelity, and apparently not much of an allegiance, Ari and Arletty responded to the winter with a flood of reciprocal e-mails. They lived apart, ostensibly never to see each other again. They carried on their several pursuits — Arletty celibate and reclusive; Ari editing his movie, and cruising for sex — the two of them determined to overcome their need for each other. And yet, they tapped-out electronic messages endlessly, compulsively, often three or four times a day:

From arimac; To arleti
Dec. 23, 1998

Well, it's almost here. Never did ask you. How do you feel about Christmas?

From arleti; To arimac
Dec. 23, 1998

*I have only negative feelings for Christmas. The forced
cheer makes me very angry. It brings out the worst in
me. It makes me see myself as I really must be. It makes
me feel 100 years old. It deadens me. Am I making myself clear? Just what do you see in me? I'm a total grouch.
I hate people. Especially at Christmas. Never mention that
word to me again!*

From arimac; To arleti
Dec. 23, 1998

*I see in you an intelligence and a maturity I fear I shall
never possess. Okay, you're warped in some ways, but you
are independent. Me, I feel I'll always remain eight years
old, and oh so very dependent. Like my grandpa Ross.
Only, he enjoyed it. I do not. I want to be like you. Even
if it means I have to hate people — but I like people, except that they scare me — does this mean I can't send
you a present?*

From arleti; To arimac
Dec. 23, 1998

*I am NOT warped in any way whatsoever. And of course
you may NOT send me a present. Don't even think about
such a thing. I'd take it as a betrayal.*

From arimac; To arleti
Dec. 25, 1998

> *"Snow mountain fields*
> *seen thru transparent wings*
> *of a fly on the windowpane"*

> *— Allen Ginsberg*

I'm going to the Caribbean for a week. Wanna come?
From arlefti; To arimac
Dec. 25, 1998

No. I hope you're having a lovely holiday season.

From arimac; To arleti
Jan. 24, 1999

It's DONE! It's FINISHED! Our movie is ready for the au-
dience. I've been promising it forever, I know, but that
holiday you never want mentioned got in the way,
and tra-la, delay, delay, but who cares — it's DONE now.
It's in the CAN. It's even on CASSETTE. And guess what.
I HAVE A DISTRIBUTOR! Yes I do! A young guy, maybe
24, with a rich father — I asked, rich from what? And he,
Fred's his name, Fred kinda changed the subject— So I
guess it wasn't cast iron, or fine foods or anything like
that. Maybe it was the arms trade, or dope dealing. I
don't care. I should care, and tomorrow I promise to care;
right now, I'm in mid heaven. I CAN'T care about any-
thing negative. Because, BECAUSE, Fred gave me a
cheque! It's not the money, it's his commitment. It means
he's serious — Oh, what the hell. IT IS the money. This is
the first money I ever made on my own. It feels GREAT!
We all know I'm rich, but listen, I never admitted this
to you, the only money I ever see is what my mother slips
to me. And now after dad found out she gave me all that
money to make the movie, he checks her accounts very
closely. I used to have an allowance, but he cut it off on
my 18th birthday. Time to earn your own, he said. So I
did! It took me three years, but here it is. Ten thousand
dollars! No one knows I have it. Not even my mother.
Only you and me. And Fred, of course. So, Fred likes the
movie a lot. He thinks we have a hit. Obviously, he
especially likes your scene. But, I don't need to tell you
that. He has this huge office, with the biggest table I've

*ever seen, bigger than the one in The main dining room
at home, that seats 40. This one must sit about 80. And
he has all kinds of art, modern and old-style. The art
belongs to his father. It feels very adult to go there and
sign contracts and get a cheque. It's kinda like two kids
playing showbiz. But what the hell. Both he and I have
to start somewhere. Mine is the first movie he ever bought
international rights for. He's very excited. And me? I'm
soaring! But none of it will feel real until you've seen it
and tell me what you think. I gave a cassette to my mother
to give to your mother to give to you.*

*From arleti; To arimac
Jan. 25, 1999*

*Congratulations. You've made an indisputably Cana-
dian movie. It's a messy, perverted, terminally screwed-
up story about people too bored with their lives to ever
hope to be interesting, let alone relevant. I liked the music. Some of your shots are fine. The dialogue rings true,
at least to me, and no surprise since I also am bored and
terminally screwed-up, mired in a messy, perverted, utterly Canadian predicament of having absolutely no
relevance to anyone. Not even to me.You see: your movie
has had an influence on me. It increased my level of anxiety: no small feat. The scene that I played in the movie:
it embarrassed me, and I sped right through it on fast
forward.*

*From arimac; To arleti
Jan. 25, 1999*

> *"Winter hardens into stone the dew of heaven and
> the heart of man."*   Victor Hugo

*In your case, it's "the heart of woman." You hated my
movie because it's winter outside. I've never minded winter as I do today. It's killing my art. It's killing me. I wish*

*it were summer again. I wish we had just finished argu-
ing on Bernard Street and then we were back in your
little apartment. Making love. That's what I need today.
To make love with you. To make me happy. To console
me that you hate my movie. To plan our next movie.
Created by the two of us. A smart movie. Something so
much better than I could ever do on my own. You say
you liked my dialogue. That makes me so-o happy. xxoo*

*From arleti; To arimac
Jan. 25, 1999*

*The decisive moment of our relationship occurred exact-
ly during that summer afternoon you so callously recall.
That was my greatest mis-step with you. You had just met
my mother. There was electricity between you two. I was
very alarmed. I don't need my mother to be getting along
with my lovers. On top of that, I had barely finished des-
pising you for stalking me (stalking is a criminal offence,
by the way). I was perfectly happy to have nothing further
with you, ever. I should've stuck to my conviction. Instead,
I weakened, I caved in to temptation. I decided it couldn't
hurt to enjoy your sex just one more time. It was a grave
error. It has led to all manner of unhappiness and compli-
cations for both of us, ever since. That one steamy (and,
I must admit, highly enjoyable) roll-in-the-hay has been
our downfall. The first time we had sex was justified. The
heat of the moment, the headiness of working on the movie, the FIRST taste. Okay. But, that afternoon, our SE-
COND time was deadly. I wish there was some way to
erase its memory from both your mind and mine.*

*From arimac; To arleti
Jan. 25, 1999*

*"There is no mightier nor deeper pleasure than that
of bodily love; and none is more irrational."*

Plato

And none more impossible to forget...

Fred is opening doors for me. He's convinced we'll get it into Cannes. Apparently they love messy Canadian movies there. Fred is sleeping with a woman, who used to sleep with the programmer of The Director's Fortnight, and tra-la — This is my greatest dream. Next to making my next movie in partnership with you.

From arleti; To arimac
Feb. 20, 1999

This fake early Spring reminds me of New York. A warm chill, a chaud-froid that is neither winter nor summer, a translucent shield that tastily masks what is underneath. But, inadequately. It is brittle and perishable. It is easy to melt-off and thus penetrate the solid muck, at the heart of all things. What is missing is that special New York smell. A blending of gasoline and pizza sauce, with assorted garbage and human shit, just for spice. I miss New York, because there one is given full latitude to surrender to despair. Unrelieved, inexorable despair. Oh, don't fret!

This is exquisite despair, it's not mere boredom or depression. It's the core of human emotion, a mainstay of all the storytelling arts. And it's not pessimism. It's very far from nihilism. The contrary, actually. It is the immediate repercussion of taking one's life too seriously. It's real, and without it there is only self-delusion and tunnel vision.

Still interested in creating a movie with me?

From arimac; To arleti
Feb. 20, 1999

*You mirror my sentiments exactly. That's the movie I set
out to make with THEY CAME FROM THE NORTH, but I
ended up with (what was it ?) a messy, perverted story
of absolutely no relevance. That is because I didn't have
you to turn on the lights for me, and show me what's what.*

From arleti; To arimac
Feb. 20, 1999

*Your problem is that you think you can live in your ob-
livious castle, with me as your damsel in distress, and
still be able to deal with the true and the real. Your idea
of heaven is to make gritty movies, get the applause and
the money, and then retreat to the satin sheets of Redpath Crescent, cuddle with me, and bathe in the perfume
of your mother's gardenias. I can think of no sweeter hell,
but hell is hell, Ari, and I want no part of it.*

Ari stared at the screen for a long time. Another goodbye. One more
slap in the face of his desire. He dreaded that his response would
be crucial. One wrong word and he could become a non-person.
Deleted permanently from her contacts list. Cyber-nullified.

He attempted several replies, but rejected them. He went all the
way to Shakespeare for guidance — Romeo & Juliet for Christ's
sake! — but it all sounded hollow, or at least, pretentious. And
provocative. Was silence his best stance? That had been Arletty's
own advice to Duncan during the gardenia lunch.

An urgent and familiar tapping from outside the window
decided matters for him. He clicked off his letters page and
worked the casements and then the storm window, to create an
entry hole for Ben Cohen, who was arriving informally, as was his
custom. The about-to-be-lionized composer trundled in, electronic
keyboard first, wiggling body in tow. He tripped himself over his
two left feet, and landed upside down on the lush broadloom, the
keyboard securely over his head.

Ari laughed as he shut the windows. Ben grunted as he picked himself up. "You know, I resent more and more that I grew up so very clumsy, and with no native abilities at all. I've never been able to somersault, I can't make a loud whistle through my fingers, I can't spit with bullet-like precision, I can't throw a baseball, I run like a girl, and I can't fuck worth a diddle."

"Oh, fuck is it? That's new."

"Not as new as all that." Ben removed his disintegrating coat in pieces. The sleeves, which had been torn off last winter were peeled off first, so that he could more easily slip out of it. There were more threadbare patches on that coat than there were in Clinton's oral-sex defense. It was Ben's trademark apparel. He wore it winter and summer. He let its pieces fall in a heap on the floor. Ari picked it up and laid it to rest on a chair.

Ari, winking, "Sarah, the cellist?"

"Yes."

"Maybe she just doesn't know how to play your flute."

"Oh, she knows the flute, alright. It's just that I have no idea what to do with her cello."

"So, you're obviously gay, Ben. My father was right."

"I wouldn't mind. I wish I was something. Gay is better than nothing. I am nothing."

"You must be missing a gene. Maybe an entire DNA sequence. Maybe there's a cure."

"And maybe I'm better off this way. Look at you! You're a walking erection. You can't lay it to rest for one second. How are Cynthia, Jennifer and Lucie?"

"Gone. *Kaput.* That's ancient history as of last week, and they mean nothing to me," scoffed Ari.

"And this week?"

"No one. I'm depressed. I think Arletty is dumping me."

"No-o," smiled Ben.

"Cut it out! This is serious. Her last e-mail? Devastating. I think she wants to cut it off."

"You can always go back to Cynthia, Jennifer and Lucie," offered Ben.

"How can you put them in the same league as Arletty? There's no comparison. Anyway, Jennifer is out. Definitively."

"So, tell me. What happened when the two of them, you know...?" Ben was resigned to it, but it never ceased to embarrass him that listening to Ari's sexual exploits aroused him as nothing else could. Not even masturbation.

"You know, Cynthia was on her knees, like down-under, and Lucie was sitting on a bar-stool, not all that far from my face."

"Go on," said Ben, breathing a little hard.

"That's all. Figure it out. I'm not going into details."

"You always did before."

"Well, tonight I don't feel like it. I'm telling you. Arletty is dumping me. Again. I'm desperate."

"So, you ate out Lucie, while Cynthia blew you. But how does that work? How do you keep score? How do you know when everybody's happy?"

"When I come, everybody's happy."

"I see," sulked Ben, trying to imagine himself in that position, but failing.

There was a tapping at the door, followed by Duncan's authoritative: "Ari! Are you in there?"

All matters sexual suddenly vanished from the room. Ben was galvanized into action. He grabbed his coat and keyboard and jumped for the window, grappling with the hooks.

Duncan walked in without waiting for an answer. He shook his head at the sight of Ben, all in pieces and in a panic, while Ari stood helplessly immobilized off to the side.

"Relax, Ben. I'm not going to hurt you."

Ben finally managed to throw open the French casements and was now struggling with the catches on the outside pane.

"You're such a stupid boy. Do you think I don't know when you enter my home? I have a two million dollar surveillance system. I know when there's somebody within a hundred yards of this house."

Ben had succeeded in liberating his escape route, and exhibiting an agility he never knew he possessed, was already halfway out.

"Oh, don't do that," chuckled Duncan. "Go out the front door. You'll kill yourself, you idiot."

Ben's head disappeared into the void. A newly-risen, glacial wind was pouring into the room. Ari shut the windows. He turned to his father, and knees somewhat shaking, he tried to sound manly.

"Do I have to lock my door?" His voice came out self-righteous and whiney instead.

Duncan smiled humbly. "You're right. I shouldn't have barged

in. But I come in peace. I'm going to the hockey game. Want to join me? You used to be a fan."
"The Canadiens suck this year. It won't be fun."
"That's good, because then we won't have to watch. I need to talk to you. We'll talk as they lose. Okay?"
It was an order. Ari's knees shook to the point of rattling. Talk about what? This would come to no good. "Okay."
"Meet me downstairs in ten minutes," said Duncan, no longer smiling.

Chapter 17

Evening of February 20, 1999. At the hockey game.

After a mutually wordless limousine ride, during which Duncan continued his Tokyo stock exchange trading on a lap-top, and Ari stared at the dark, shining streets, thinking of Arletty, father and son arrived at the Molson Centre, newest home of the Montreal Canadiens.

The Canadiens are no mere hockey team. They are this wintry city's one great contribution to the pantheon of sport. The National Hockey League franchise, whose 1910 founding predates the existence of the league itself, is one of the two most celebrated squads — most championships, most cups — in the firmament of North American professional sport. Baseball's New York Yankees is the other.

More than that, *Les Canadiens* are the very pulse and soul of Montreal's cold months, one of the few viable reasons to remain loyal to the icy metropolis. The names and vital statistics — *goals-assists-penalties-sexual-rumours* — of the team's collection of thugs and toughs are the currency of city-wide discussions. School-children cut classes to go and stand for hours to watch them. Grown men and women have been known to cry when their beloved Habitants blow a two-goal lead.

Nothing can quite match Montreal's hockey-fever when the glorious Canadiens are winning; and conversely, nothing can quite relieve the frustration and deep sense of betrayal — not to mention homicidal anger — when *les Glorieux* are losing.

Sadly there had been little to cheer, and plenty to frustrate about the *Canadiens* throughout the '90s. Aside from the delirious surprise of 1993's *underdog-makes-good* Stanley Cup, the team was on a free-fall into oblivion. By Saturday, February 20th, 1999, a nationally televised *Hockey Night in Canada,* the *Canadiens* had become the most ex-illustrious of the league's bottom feeders. They displayed every sign of having suffered the unthinkable, being one of only twelve teams out of twenty eight to miss the playoffs. It was no shame to be eliminated in early rounds of the post-season; just awfully disappointing. But, to be blanked out of it, to finish the regular season in the cellar; that was ignominy itself. That was infamy, and had last occurred when most currently-rabid Canadiens' fans had yet to be born.

An ugly atmosphere greeted the MacLeods as they took their seats in their hereditary box, right next to the team-owning Molsons, behind the Canadiens' bench. The game was only three minutes underway, but the hapless home-team was already two goals down, to the almost-equally dismissable New York Islanders.

The arena was buzzing with a hatred that bordered on violence, peppered with vicious, anti-Canadiens cat-calls. Ari groaned, "I told you it would be horrible."

"And I told you it doesn't matter. If anything, it's more to the point. I invited you here to discuss your future."

"My future is making movies, dad. That's my only future," mumbled Ari.

"Then we have a real problem. I took a look at your so-called movie."

Ari gulped. It must have been the cassette he had given his mother to watch. Maria was notorious for forgetting tapes in the machine.

"It's not just bad, Ari. It's terrible. Like this Canadiens team. Worse. It's a discredit. It's not in the least what you intend it to be, a cherished stepping-stone to your imaginary career. If I were you, I'd burn every copy and torch the negative. The less people who see this movie, the better off you are."

Ari diverted his gaze to Svensenn, the Canadiens' pretty boy, Swedish superstar, as he flamboyantly carried the puck into the Islanders' zone, only to give it away in order to avoid a potentially painful body check by the visitors' defenseman.

"So you didn't like the movie. Is that it?"

Duncan sneered. "I wanted to spare your feelings, but no, I didn't exactly like it. No. I can't say I did."

"I'm sorry," said Ari as if he had inadvertently burped at the table.

Duncan did not acknowledge the apology, because just then Ryerson, the team's just-as-pretty, home-grown superstar was leading a charge, a clean three on one break towards the Islanders' goal. He then passed the puck directly onto the last Islander's stick, instead of his team-mate's. The reverse charge came within one centimeter of a third unanswered goal, when the visitor's shot beat the home-goalie and by sheer luck hit the inside of the goal post and bounced out, instead of going in.

"Pathetic!" shouted Duncan, adding his displeasure to the booing of the other 20,000 spectators. "Intolerable! These are not the Habs! They are impostors!" Duncan shuddered, as if warding off a disease. "No! No! This is ludicrous. And it's even worse because it echoes the miasma of this whole city. And the Province!"

"It's just a game, dad," added Ari lamely.

"But, that's just the point! It's so much more than a game. It's a way of life. It's a measure of our success, as a people. The Canadiens are a religion. I guess you were born too late to understand this. This team is the heart of Montreal. When the Habs lose, we all suffer. When they go beyond losing, and they disgrace themselves, then we wither."

A major fight had broken out on the ice. Hockey, originally a dexterous sport, a kind of virile ballet on skates, had transmogrified into a ruffian's field-day in the modern era. Punching, kicking, and maiming opponents became just as important as skillful skating and clever, labour-intensive play-making, especially in those sun-belt American localities into which the league's original six-team, snow-belt roster had expanded. The sport's brave new, non-ice-savvy fans in redneck Texas and blood-thirsty Southern California favoured it for its violence, rather than any of its finer points.

The players' benches had emptied and there were several half-hearted fights taking place all over the ice. The main event, between the proto-instigators — each of the two teams' opposing gorillas, whose sole function was to start fights — had deteriorated into a clumsy wrestling match. Both combatants were down on the ice, in a suspicious embrace, occasionally kneeing each other's heavily padded genitals. Duncan rolled his eyes, and turned to Ari.

"And the most offensive part of it was those excruciating two minutes with your scrawny girlfriend. It's an excellent idea to include near-naked young women in a movie, but you should've chosen someone who was pleasant to look at. And someone who bathes once in a while."

Ari bristled. This was no longer his dreaded father in the seat next to him. This was a lewd old man, insulting his goddess Arletty.

"It wasn't dirt. It was make-up."

"It was dirt. I know dirt when I see it."

"The dirt is all in your mind, sir!"

Duncan took pause to let his son's insolence hang in the air.

"Actually, Ari, I'd have been just as happy never to have seen your Arletty nude. I find her far more attractive clothed. But that's not what I wanted to discuss with you. You see, the reason this situation affects me and becomes my business, is that the repercussions of your actions, the embarrassment of it all, and judging by this movie, your certain failure is also my own failure. It means you'll end up on your ass, rolling around on the ice like those yo-yos out there, and my legacy, our family, our hard-earned place in society will amount to nothing. Less than nothing."

"My movie, like any movie, is a matter of personal taste. As it so happens, Arletty also disliked it."

"So, she's smarter than you make her out to be."

"But, Fred, the distributor—"

"Oh, Fred, the distributor—"

"He liked it so much, he gave me ten thousand dollars." Ari played and immediately regretted his only trump-card.

Peace had been restored on the ice. Now there remained the lengthy process of assessing penalties to the offenders, giving the TV audience a chance to relive the fights via instant-replay.

"Really? Fred Benoit gave you ten grand? I hope for Fred's sake that his father doesn't find out. And you, please write me a cheque for the full amount. Then you'd owe me only $347,500."

"I... I can't do that... I need the money."

"So do I, my boy. Your shenanigans have corrupted my relations with your mother, and they've clouded my judgment. I haven't had a winning day in the market ever since I found out that my wife gave you a sizeable fortune to indulge your childish whims. Your little flirt with show business is responsible for costing me well over a billion dollars, let alone my peace of mind. I can't stress this to you strongly enough, Ari. I HATE LOSING."

"I'm sorry. I'll give you my ten thousand."

"Oh, stuff your ten thousand! And listen to my proposal." Duncan peered at Ari. He saw only fear and revulsion, but decided to continue. "I've set up a job for you with an excellent European trading firm. It'll mean you'll live in comfort in not-at-all-shabby places like London, Paris and Amsterdam. And a bit of Frankfurt, which isn't much fun, I know, more a necessary evil. They'll train you to understand the market. They won't pay you, I will pay you, but they'll have the right to fire you, if you don't perform. You'll have to work hard, sometimes around the clock, but you'll do it with determination and ambition, and within a year to eighteen months, you'll be in a position to return home and work with me, en route to assuming your position as the future head of the MacLeods."

Ari stared at his father incredulously. He wanted very much to laugh, but wisely stifled the temptation.

"You want to laugh at me," continued Duncan, "I should have known. But beware. This is a one time offer, with countless rewards if you accept, and dire consequences if you refuse."

Cornered, Ari's mirth was erased by an overwhelming desire to flee. He stood up. He felt smothered, as if he was being choked.

"You give me no choice, but to refuse. I would have to refuse on principle."

"How like a MacLeod! Sit down, please," hissed Duncan, "people are beginning to notice us." Ari sat down and looked straight ahead. Play was about to resume. Both Duncan and Ari felt the visceral, birthright-Montreal arousal associated with watching the greatest team in hockey. They allowed this fantasy a few seconds' grace before the puck was dropped and the Islanders promptly took possession. Duncan turned to Ari, and continued as if there had been no interruption.

"Listen here, pal. If you don't buckle down and become a useful and responsible citizen you'll permanently remain a wannabe artist and a mama's boy. A useless man-boy etiolated in the brine of her protectiveness and shrouded in her fear of the real world."

Ari was flustered. I'm NOT ee-tye-olé-ted! Not in the least!" he blurted.

"You don't even know what the word means. And no wonder. You refused to go to a proper university. My year and a half of McGill is worth all four of your years at Sir George!"

"My grades weren't good enough for McGill."

"And whose fault was that, I wonder? In any case, they'd have embraced you at McGill. I give them enough money."

"I couldn't do that! We talked about that at the time."

"Yes, we did. And I still find it refreshing that someone of your generation could be so honourable, and stupid enough to end up at Sir George!"

"They call it Concordia now, and it has the best film-school!"

"Oh, FILM, again? It's an inferior institution, fit for minor intellects and immigrants."

"As it happens, I'm an immigrant, too. Half of me, anyway."

"You're every inch a MacLeod, buster," Duncan was desperately trying to control his anger.

"With about two feet eleven inches from Constantinople," sneered, Ari.

"If that's how you really see yourself, then I suggest you take both of your halves, and your mother too, while you're at it, and get out of my house."

Ari let out a bitter laugh. "So, unless I do as you say, you'll throw me and my mother out. Is that what I'm hearing?"

"Don't force me to become mean," said Duncan sharply and just a tad too loudly.

"I'll tell you what," started Ari seething, "let's bring this pimple to a head. Let me tell you outright, there's no chance in hell I'll ever agree to go to London and Paris and *tra-la-la,* to do your dirty work. And you won't have to throw me out. I'm MOVING out. Today!" Ari stood up. "I'll go home and pack right now."

"SIT DOWN!" hollered Duncan.

"Oh, what the FUCK for?" cried Ari, as he turned to leave. Duncan grabbed his arm and twirled him back. Ari tried to pull away, and Duncan tugged harder. And then, it happened.

Ari struck his father's hand to liberate his sleeve, but accidentally landed an open-fisted punch on Duncan's nose. Duncan reacted instinctively. He sprang out of his chair and slapped Ari ringingly across the face, twice. Ari reeled, and Duncan grabbed him by the collars, in order to break his fall, but to the onlookers it looked like he was about to conclude by strangling him.

The neighbouring spectators, including Senator Hartland Molson and his wife, all the nearby ushers-bodyguards-ice-cream vendors, as well as the entire Canadiens' bench of players, managers and stick-boys, stirred as one, got on their feet, shouted and swarmed the rowdy MacLeods to try and separate them.

This distraction directly behind the home team's bench was serious enough to cause a stoppage in play, and therefore become the highlight of the moment. The TV cameras — broadcasting tonight to the entire nation, several million viewers south of the border, and forty-four countries via satellite — like nothing better than capturing a fight in the stands. The prolonged image of Duncan throttling Ari, while the *Canadiens'* head-coach struggled to pry them apart, was flashed on the giant screens of the Molson Centre, as well as the homes of hockey fans worldwide.

It became front-page news, lavishly illustrated with a full-colour close-up of father and son *in extremis*. Firstly because it was the best off-ice, hockey-fight since 1995 when Patrick Roy, arguably the best goalie in all hockey at the time, publicly swore at then head-coach Mario Tremblay from exactly the same spot. He had left Montreal for Colorado the next day, dealing a death blow to the *Canadiens* from which they still hadn't recovered. Secondly, because viewers and observers now had irrefutable proof that the aged Senator Molson and his wife were not wax dummies but live humans. When the two of them jumped to their feet with alacrity, in order to avoid any bodily fluids that might gush from Ari or Duncan as a result of the fight.

Chapter 18

April 10, 1999. In Montreal

Ari, self-conscious and somewhat embarrassed, shuffled silently
beside Maria, outside the Greek Orthodox Cathedral on Cote Ste.
Catherine Road. It was near midnight on the Eve of Greek Easter,
and the Greeks had arrived for the announcement of *Anastasi,* the
Resurrection. Thus, an ordinary, seasonably chilly Saturday night —
Greek Easter is always a week or two after regular Easter — had
suddenly turned into a traffic-stopper.

Thousands of Hellenes bearing long, white candles, thronged
the front of the church to get the official news from the pulpit, that
Christ had indeed arisen, that life could begin once again, and that
they could finally break the forty-day Lenten fast: no flesh, no dairy,
no eggs, not even oil during the agonizing six-day stretch of Holy
Week. Few of them had strictly observed it, but all of them complained about the Fast. This was a vestige of the old days in the old
country, when the tail end of winter was a time of need, with precious little left in the larder save for "vegan" fare.

Truly fasting, or only pretending, whether in Montreal or in a
Peloponnesian village, Easter is the holiest holiday of the Greeks,
the most important day of the year. Easter's got it all. Pagan and
Christian, rebirth and resurrection, victory over death, blood and
suffering, divine intervention, and to top it all off, baby lamb, slow
charred on the spit, a festive table, good kefi, and lots of wine.

Maria, happy, squeezed Ari's arm affectionately. He hadn't
shown up for *Anastasi* since he was a pre-teen. She hadn't pres-
sured him, but she had sorely missed him. Attending alone meant
having to endure the smug sympathy of the community who didn't
have her money, but at least had their kids to share the *kiss of love.*
She had, with great regret, stopped coming altogether.

It had therefore felt like a miracle, and also a wonderful omen, when Ari himself suggested the excursion. It was even more gratifying to have actually made it, to be standing among the faithful, she in her most glamorous sable hat and coat. And he, head-to-toe in his new *auteur*-director look, designer everything, including a $3000 leather jacket. This was part of a whole new wardrobe she had bought him on impulse, during her recent weekend in London to see *Khovanshchina* from Sadler's Wells's well-worn seats (and would-they-PLEASE-hurry-up-and-finish-restoring-Covent-Garden!).

Ari was using *Anastasi* as a last resort. His life was in shambles after that incident at the hockey game, and he was here to appeal to the Easter genie. Of all Maria's superstitions and rituals, this one about Easter's light of truth, was the one that tolerated no detraction, and whose promise of good luck had thrilled Ari as a child.

At midnight sharp, the priests sing the resurrection psalm, and light the candles of those nearby with the holy flame from the altar. The yellow light is then passed backwards until every candle down to the corner of Wilderton is aflame. This is followed by a warm kiss to a loved one — *the kiss of love* — and then by somehow protecting the candle to bring it home alive, to let it burn out inside your house.

If observed to the letter, this ceremony ensures one year's worth, until the following Easter, of clarity in matters both financial and emotional. A cleansing lightness, which brings harmony, tolerance and self-fulfillment. Sometimes, even good luck.

Equipped with sturdy candles and metal cups inverted at the tips to counteract the nasty, little breeze, Maria and Ari heard the rousing call to *thevtai, lavaitai phos* ("come forward and receive the light"). The glow of the widening fire then spread to illuminate the street as multitudes of candles were lit, and the light, as well as a timeless truth passed from person to person, until it reached them.

Christos Anesti — Alithos Anesti ("Christ has Risen — Truly He has Risen").

Their candles alive, Ari and Maria hugged and kissed each other, bonding yet again, with the *all-is-forgiven-you-can-no-wrong-by-me* sort of love Greek mothers and sons have shared since Antiquity. Carefully shielding the flame, they boarded the waiting Bentley, Maria spitting three, genteel times to ward off the evil eye of any onlookers, and drove home by Holy candlelight.

Awaiting them in the floral solarium was Sophia, and a table set with the traditional, Resurrection-midnight meal. Red-dyed eggs, heavily yeasted Easter *tsoureki* bread, and *magiritsa,* the lavatorial soup of lamb's intestines and lungs, perfumed with copious amounts of dill and green onion. This was food designed to benevolently break the long fast, en route to the next day's major carnivory.

Magiritsa had never been a favourite soup of either mother or son, but they tasted it, "for the good of the season", and to help Maria break her mini, holy-week only, fast. They ate many slices of Sophia's heirloom *tsoureki,* and they cracked eggs — Sophia's egg proved the strongest. *Christos Anesti,* crack, *Alithos Anesti,* crack! After which they went to sleep, sacred candles melting slowly by each bedside.

Both candles burned perfectly, down to the last drop of wax, and both brought exaltation. For Ari, the good news was instantaneous. Fred Benoit's phone call rang at 6 am, while Ari was still asleep, and the candle had finished petering out. Cannes had called — *They Came From The North* had been accepted into *Director's Fortnight* — TWO screenings — BIG buzz — Fred rattled off the facts, let out a maniacal guffaw and hung up.

Ari's reaction was purely physical. His heart pounded mercilessly, quivering in his chest and shooting warm shivers to his extremities. Followed by a fierce erection that fired off a handful of come when he barely touched it. Finally, he let out a victory roar, that rang throughout the huge house, and was heard all the way down to Ste. Catherine Street. He hurried on-line and sent this e-mail:

From arimac; To arleti
April 11, 1999

We're in Cannes. You must come. I agree in advance to whatever rules you propose.

It was Maria's custom to rise very early on Easter morning and immediately get into the kitchen to cook. The ritual Easter lunch, meant to be served after the mid-day church service — the so-called second *Anastasi* — is the focal point of the orgiastic Holiday. It is an occasion for celebration with those closest and dearest. When she had been young, in Istanbul, this had meant a meal for only the five members of the nuclear family. The rest of the household, servants and support staff, being Moslem, were utterly distrustful of Christian holidays. In Montreal the tradition had been enlarged to include the staff and their families, none of whom would pass up one of Maria's meals for any reason whatsoever. This gave her a count between thirty-three and thirty-eight, depending on whether the chauffeur was back with his wife and four kids, or estranged.

This year, energized by Ari's desire to observe *Anastasi,* Maria had planned an extravaganza. She had taxed Sophia to help her concoct an ancient Constantinopolitan Easter-centerpiece: an entire lamb, de-boned and stuffed with a Byzantine-Armenian *farce* of rice, pine nuts, raisins, and pieces of liver, perfumed with cinnamon and cumin. It was a two-day ordeal, but Sophia and the kitchen crew worked without complaining, everyone somehow convinced that this was a special Easter, even more meaningful than usual, one that augured good tidings for the constrained household.

Ari's 6 a.m. scream of jubilation caught Maria as she was stepping into her shower. She threw on the first available but nevertheless stylish nightgown and rushed to Ari's room, alarmed. There, she found Duncan, also hastily robed, and, she was gratified to notice, equally alarmed. He had been wakened from a gruesome dream, in which he watched his ancestor Charlie MacLeod being gunned down in cold blood. On closer inspection, he had been horrified to discover that the victim was actually Ari.

Together, Maria and Duncan opened Ari's door and barged in. They found their son already on his computer, completing his triumphant but servile e-mail to Arletty. Ari turned around and with tears of joy melting his clear blue eyes, told them his good news.

Maria rushed over with a yelp and swooped down on her son, engulfing him. Ari found an unoccupied angle of vision through which to engage his father's eyes. Duncan, who had avoided his son like the plague ever since the fateful hockey game, smiled resignedly and muttered "Well done." He turned to leave mother and son to their embrace, but Maria disengaged and flirtatiously sang out after him, "Don't forget Easter lunch at 2:30, right after I come back from church!"

✳

At about the same early-morning hour, Josette stirred in her soft, Plateau bed. She instinctively threw her arms to Louis-Marc's side, so she could caress him and let him comfort her, but his side of the bed was ice-cold. It made her feel empty. It angered her. She could hear the *tap-tap-tap* of his computer from his office down the hall. It frustrated her. Finally it made her determined to take matters in hand and reverse this awful situation.

Maria, elated, almost buoyant, assembled her helpers and got to work by seven. She hadn't felt this Easter-happy since she was eight and had just noticed her body begin to shed its boyishness. Her brothers had been nice to her for a change, and her parents had actually been talking to each other instead of grunting, actually exchanging a semi-passionate *kiss of love* at midnight.

The first order of business in an Easter kitchen was the lamb. De-boned yesterday, it had been left to hang in the walk-in cooler, rubbed with lemon and oregano. Now it was brought out, and spread on the marble tabletop. It resembled a pink, fleshy throw-rug, all its bones carefully carved out and only its four shanks pro-truding, left in to preserve an illusion of its former self once it was stuffed and reshaped.

Maria and Sophia rubbed more lemon and oregano on both sides of the lamb, and added sprinklings of minced garlic to the interior, embedding it into the meat with their fingertips. They sliced excess meat from the fleshier parts and padded the skinnier sec-tions, to give it a uniform thickness. They turned their attention to the stuffing, arguing about the spicing, and the degree of the desired doneness of the rice. Finally they deemed it perfect, and spread it over the meat in an oblong mass. They flapped the flanks over the stuffing and stitched them in place. A few more pats and caresses, and it was ready. An elliptical meat-balloon, with four bony punctuations, pointing straight up towards the newly resurrected Christ, as if asking Him why He had particularly chosen it to become Maria MacLeod's sacrificial lamb.

The lamb, in its shallow bath of olive oil, meat broth and lemon

juice was placed into a moderate oven where it would slow bake for
more than five hours, requiring basting and turning once every
hour. So much more urbane and sophisticated, mused Maria, than
the barbarous, unappetizing habit of turning it on the spit, with its
head flopping from side to side and its legs dangling.

Their most pressing and lengthy process underway, the women
got busy with the thirty five other Easter courses, some of which,
like the bean dishes, the marinated fish appetizers, the oil-based,
rice-stuffed vegetables and all the desserts had been started the day
before. Today's chores involved last-minute touches: the various
potatoes — fried potato croquettes, garlic-heavy mashed potatoes,
oven-browned lemon-potatoes — the garnishing herbs, the onions,
the fried slices of zucchini and eggplant, the freshly whipped garlic-
cucumber tzatziki, the double-churned heavy cream of the *kaimaki*
for adorning the *ekmek kadayifi*. This was a dessert so syrupy, so
lethally rich, even without its cream topping, that Maria dared make
it only once a year at Easter, though Duncan, with his taste for all
things Levantine, would have it daily if it were available.

By noon, everything was underway, properly simmering, bak-
ing, chilling and tempering. Maria and Sophia, armed with several
of the housekeeping staff and boss Betty, trouped off to the master
dining room to set the table for thirty eight — the chauffeur and his
family were one happy group of campers again. Betty disapproved
heartily of Maria's obsession with feeding everyone in Greek-Easter
style, including the by-nature untrustworthy gardeners, but had had
to concede in view of her mistress's intractable position. And so, out
came the best: the most gilded china, the most glittering crystal, and
the most precious silver with the 18-carat gold handles, prompting
Betty's rule that everyone, especially the gardeners, and all children,
attend without bags of any sort, and be prepared to submit to body
searches on the way out.

As always, Maria slipped away just after one p.m., leaving Betty
and Sophia in charge so that she could go to church for the second
Anastasi, give her thanks to the All Powerful, and return to eat some
well-earned lamb.

✳

Josette stayed in bed until ten, as she did every Sunday morning, drifting off into her soundest sleep of the week. These were the sinful sleeping hours, which on weekdays, and even on Saturdays she spent at the office, already hard on the phone, juggling her clients' traveling whims. Louis-Marc had meanwhile come to bed, and was snoring softly, seemingly unperturbed by her intentionally-loud, morning sighs and cigarette-coughs.

She sensed that he was less asleep than he pretended to be, so she rolled close to him and gently ran her hand down his back. Reaching lower, she was gratified to discover that he was without underwear, like he always used to sleep prior to the disastrous Ari-lunch. She lightly cupped his buttocks, and he stretched his leg outward, freeing access to the rear of his crotch. She encouraged one of her fingertips to stray along his Great Divide, that thin braid of skin, which some godly stitcher had fused together to contain the base of a man's genitals. It was hard as a rock, which could only mean that he had an erection.

Josette smiled and withdrew her touch. She slipped out of bed and quietly left the bedroom. She showered giggling to herself, almost choking on the warm water. She hurriedly dressed and left the house on a mission of provisions for a festive occasion all her own. Nothing to compare with Maria's *bravura* performance for thirty-eight, more of an intimate brunch for two in bed. But just as important to the harmony and happiness of a household, exactly as momentous and celebratory.

The Easter lunch went off like a charm, with much lip-smacking and finger-licking, and a lamb so succulent and delicate it practically levitated. Maria was beaming the entire time, happy-happy, eating just a little herself, serving and prompting everyone, to gorge themselves; and so very content to have a satisfied, almost smug Duncan at the table. So pleased with himself, drinking and eating with gusto, relieved and re-empowered, having just finished a deliriously successful week of trading, on the e-business market, making big bucks and all the right decisions, his first winning spell since August a whole nine months ago.

And Ari, the entire orchard of her eye, the barometer of her well-being, who was smiling uncontrollably — CANNES, for Christ's sake! — and eating with great appetite, savouring the lamb, but exclaiming out loud at the buttery smooth *lakerda* (cured *bonito* tuna), which had been prepared from fresh fish flown in from Istanbul only yesterday.

The desserts appeared, more cracking of the traditional red-dyed eggs. Ari intentionally used a weakened egg when he cracked with Duncan — *Christos Anesti,* crack, *Alithos Anesti,* crack! — making sure his father won — "Hah, so you thought you could CRACK the old man!" — so that the MacLeod luck would flow, money would be made, and maybe the $375,000 would be less of a painful memory.

The lunch appeared to be all but finished and Duncan had downed two portions of ekmek with cream, and drank several glasses of sweet, dessert wine. Well beyond tipsy and a bit reckless, he surprise‡d Maria — as well as busybodies Sophia and Betty — by standing up and extending his hand to to her, in their old and nearly-abandoned signal to go up to bed and lie with each other.

Josette fussed over her breakfast tray, making sure everything was in place. The croissants with butter and jam, chunks of baguette, a dollop of rillettes with hot mustard and cornichons, a scoop of soft goat-cheese, a half bottle of Champagne, and a thermos-full of coffee with hot milk and sugar already added. All of Louis-Marc's favourites, plus the heirloom china and crystal flutes on a damask napkin, which she had had to iron at the last minute.

She entered the bedroom noiselessly and set her tray down near the bed. Louis-Marc heard her, but pretended he had not, though she knew he had, and he knew she knew he had. She slipped *The Godfather, Part 1* cassette into the VCR, and fast-forwarded the tape to the opening credits. The familiar theme in itself was normally sufficient to get Louis-Marc horny. She had in fact also rented *Part 2,* so determined was she to do whatever it took to arouse her husband, even sitting through seven hours of Mafia fiction she had already had to watch five times.

✳

Duncan shut the bedroom door with authority, even though he was very unsteady on his feet, and took Maria in his arms. Not having had time to bathe before lunch, nor having had a reason to have done so, she smelled of each and every dish she had cooked. This seemed to arouse Duncan all the more, and he deeply breathed her in as he undressed her. He stripped, almost ripped off his own clothing, almost tripping and falling down, just like he used to do when they were young.

Maria responding to his urgency, threw open the bed-covers and lay back, stretching luxuriously. She opened her arms to him and settled her matronly hips into the submissive position. He fell on her clumsily, hungry for her favours. He kissed her sloppily, repeatedly, and suddenly burped directly into her mouth. He blushed and rolled off to her side, until he was lying on his back, his erection pointing skyward like a flag post.

"Shorry, my beauty. You fed me too much. I want to very much, but I'm afraid I'd faint, or something—"

Maria cupped his manhood purposefully, before she put her ear to his stomach.

"Yes, it's full-up in there. It wouldn't be safe for you to move very much. You just lie back and leave everything to me." She rotated her body around, bringing her face into a region it had never approached before.

Duncan glared at her, surprised rather than shocked. "Seriously? You know how to do that?"

"My friend Josette, whom you must meet some day, explained it all to me. It'll be my first time, and hopefully it'll please you. But really, on a fine day like today, how can it fail?"

She took him in her mouth, and though it gagged and at first disgusted her, she persevered all the way to the gushing finale. The amazing thing was, she didn't mind it one bit, not even the numbing taste at the end.

Godfather, Part 2 turned out to be redundant. In fact, Louis-Marc ate his breakfast, accompanied by Josette's little pecks, drank the Champagne, and was all ready to boogie, before *Part 1* was a third of the way through. The horse's head bleeding on the satin sheets, his all-time favourite scene, propelled him into an ardour he had begun to think he had lost forever. He removed the tray to one side, and got deep inside the covers, drawing Josette in after him. He then buried himself in his wife's treasures, using tongue and nose and chin to give her sensations and titillations only a woman can feel.

From arleti; To arimac
April 11, 1999

I'd love to come to Cannes. I have no rules, and I make no promises.

From arimac; To arleti
April 11, 1999

> *"Would any thing, but a Madman, complain of Uncertainty?"*

> *William Congreve, Love for Love, Act IV, Sc. XX*

Chapter 19

May, 1999. On Mykonos.

Cannes had reeled off its usual, ineluctable torch-song to the rewards of celluloid. A wildly pulsating seductress, *Le Festival* sucks into its ravenous-cavernous void all the dreams and inventions of its willing victims, year after year. Churning them out the other end as hype, as accolade, as the kick-start to careers in film, and quite often as boots against the behinds of its supplicants.

Ari and Arletty had been entranced by the power of Cannes on contact. Gone was the chatty, tentative joy at being with each other again during the long airplane rides — upgraded to "business class" by Ari's MacLeod-style manoeuvering. Forgotten too was the giddiness of first entering the palatial MacLeod apartment: an eight room art-nouveau gem, right on the *Corniche* — purchased for peanuts by the forever clever, though underrated Ross MacLeod back in the '50s, when the festival was just being born.

They had felt dizzy, almost nauseous as soon as they had stepped out onto the bristling boulevards, to join the multitudes who come here to worship fame and beauty, not to mention money. A sick, hollow sensation, erect and incurable, the state of being of all cinéastes awaiting screenings of their *oeuvres,* had infected them and kept them on tenterhooks until the magic moment.

Ari had spent most of *They Came From The North*'s first screening in the toilet, vomiting. He needn't have, because Fred had done his job well, stacking the house with fellow Canadians. He had even managed to keep out some of the more acerbic critics by announcing contradictory screening times and locations. Very few of those who attended had walked out before the ending, since Fred had promised a lavish party with live movie stars, right after the screening. The audience had unanimously lauded Ben Cohen's sound-track, and were genuinely thrilled by Arletty's two-minute scene.

As a result, the movie had generated a good buzz, a buzz that wasn't even diminished by the paucity of stars at the post-screening bash — only Don McKellar and Jeremy Podeswa had bothered to show up. However, the Champagne and Russian caviar had been plentiful — courtesy of Benoit *père,* though he had no idea he was being so generous — as were the hyperboles for Arletty's short but unforgettable performance.

The significant second screening had been an unqualified success. Anyone who was anyone had fought their way in, including 800-pound gorilla movie-stars and all the most exacting critics. They had sat through to the trite ending, all because of Arletty and a scene that had been shot by sheer coincidence. Everyone but the critics gave the movie a standing ovation. The critics gave it sneers, unmistakably negative notices, though all of them gushed about Arletty, and several of them praised the music.

Ari had quit vomiting long enough to comprehend that he would have had no movie at all, were it not for his weird best-friend Ben, and his even weirder relationship with Arletty. Instead of being disheartened, he had telephoned his mother and gotten clearance to take Arletty to Mykonos. For leverage, as if he needed any with Maria, he had cited the standing ovation of the second screening, about which she had already read in the Montreal newspapers. Maria was so eager to have Ari enjoy her villa, she had ordered her agent on Mykonos to ask the holiday-makers renting it, to vacate. They had furiously refused to leave, and had to be forcibly ejected by the police, after Maria placed a sweet, little phone call to the mayor of the island,

Arletty had lost her awe of the festival directly after the first screening. She had become embarrassed by all the attention, unwilling as she was to submit to either lionization or to scorn, preferring at all times the safety of anonymity. She took instant refuge in Ari's suggestion that they escape to Greece.

And so, much to their own surprise, and Ari's reinstated expectations, they left Fred, the movie, and the chaos of Cannes behind. And here they were in Maria's villa on wildflower-swept Mykonos-in-May.

It was the evening of their third and last day on the island. A full moon shone majestically in a jet-black sky, shedding pearly light on the white villa, painting it a pale violet to match the fragrance of the blossoming lilacs on the lone tree near the fountain.

Ari leaned against the whitewashed stone parapet at the edge of the terrace. He was dressed in crease-free, creamy silk, an off-white, loosely tailored suit and a midnight-blue shirt, undone to its second button. His olive skin had turned a rich mocha from the last few days' sun, a textured contrast to the hues and the sheen of the silk. He was smoking a cigarette. A Cuban love song, steamy and distant, echoed from the sound system in the house.

He inhaled another puff, keeping the smoke in his lungs, enjoying the last smidgens of hashish embedded in it. The pre-rolled, customs-proof, cigarette-like joints had been a parting gift from Ben Cohen. Ari's mind reeled, trying to assess and rationalize the improbable sequence of events that had led to his standing where he was, looking like a young Mafia Don in pre-revolutionary Havana.

It was all so confusing, he made a conscious effort to empty his mind altogether. None of it had actually taken place. This, here, now was a clear and fresh moment. This was the start of the real romance. There was nothing but exquisite fun in store, nothing but promise. From the beginning of his life, this was the way things had evolved for Ari. An endless string of days, offering the most sumptuous promises.

The Cuban love song had played itself out. There was now only the night-music of the Cycladic springtime. The regeneration of the the ancient land, its cycle and its creatures. Not quite yet the tumult of full-blown summer with its crickets and its cicadas, its cacophony of earthy sounds, yet already vibrant, bolstered by the sprinkles of the fountain, and reinforced by the snippets of *bouzouki* music wafting in from town. Ari was transformed into an expectant groom, a Greek village boy, pimply and oversexed on the night before his wedding, his loins aching.

New music suddenly flowed through the sound system. It was lazy and upbeat, louder, more immediate. Louisiana blues from the sweaty swamp. Saxophones and trumpets and woodwinds made Ari turn around. His heart raced. Arletty was standing, framed by the terrace doors, cool as an iced drink on a sweltering evening. She wore a black, strapless dress with shiny fabric that slid down her body like running water, concealing nothing, accenting the whiteness of her arms and shoulders and neck.

Ari was no longer Cuban Mafioso or pimply groom. He was now a poet, a Southern gentleman hungering after a belle his manners had previously forbidden him to touch. He was desperate to possess her. To rush to her, to hug her, to fill her ears with flowery declarations of affection, to kiss her hand, her arm, the small of her neck, her ear, her cheek, her red-ripe lips. To abandon himself to her mercy, to fall at her feet, and never rise again unless she decreed it.

Yet he stood his ground. She came to him in slow motion, swaying to the music. She put her arms around his neck. She kissed his eager lips. She felt his back. The silky sensations. She caressed his firm buttocks. She moved her hands to his front. She teased his tumescent sex. She undid the zipper, and toyed with him flesh to flesh, skin to skin, lover to beloved.

They undressed each other, they linked their bodies in primordial embrace, they moved to the earthy rhythm. They made love standing up, much like their last time months and months ago, in a chilly, Montreal alley in October, when the rain came down in long, sobering sheets. This time there was no rain, only the perfume of the lilacs, the gentle murmur of the fountain, the reflection of moonrays on the Aegean like twinkling syncopations, or stardust falling off the heavens: a chimera concocted in part by the magical effects of nighttime, in part by the inexorable force of human desire.

Their sex act, an inflorescent function that gave rise to newer and deeper blooms as each final moment of it was fading, lasted many hours, maybe days. Its only nourishment: the bottle and a half of *ouzo* leftover from Maria and Josette's birthdays the previous October, several cigarette-joints from Ben's care package and unscheduled naps. All intended to relax and re-arouse exhausted bodies and insatiable libidos.

Finally, the *ouzo* ran out, the last joint was smoked, and their sexual organs, chafed and smarting, refused to cooperate any longer. Still they clung to each other, as if this were their final moment together on this earth. Intertwined on the ripe-smelling sheets, they were facing a sunset of heroic proportions. It made Arletty giggle.

"This is not real, is it? You arranged for those colours, didn't you? It's cinema, isn't it?"

"It's real, Arletty. All of it. And it's ours. No one can take it away."

"Except us."

"But we like it. Don't we?" asked Ari, groping.

"Like it?"

"This. US. The lovemaking. It's been to your taste. Hasn't it?"

Arletty engaged his eyes suggestively, sinuously. "We've been in this bed together for an eternity, Ari. How can it not have been to my taste? What a question."

"Me, too. It was incredible. Like my first time. Better. Like my first time should've been."

"Like your first twenty three times, don't you mean?" laughed Arletty, and kissed the pink tip of his sex.

"We did it twenty three times?" asked Ari, as he nibbled on her much-kissed nipple.

"Yes, we did," sighed Arletty, "and every single one a treat. Did you think so?"

"*Oh, Arletty. Je veux toutes tes fibres, tout tes pores. J'aimerais devenir liquide et penetrer chacun de tes orifices, et y vivre a jamais.*"

Arletty, wide eyed: "Why, Ari, did you memorize that just for little ol' me?"

"No, I've been learning French. How am I doing?"

"You sound like you're speaking English, with a lot of French words thrown in."

Ari sulked. "I've been studying all winter."

"My father would be proud of you."

"And you're not? All winter, all those hours I should've been with you, and weren't, I studied French instead."

Arletty hardened. "The less said of last winter, the better. Okay?" Then she softened. "Tell me again what he said. I need to hear it once more."

Ari feigned ignorance. "He, who?"

"*Cauchon!*" she pecked his cheek. "HE! Who else? Depardieu! Who else is there?"

"All of them. Every major star of France, Germany, Italy, several from Hollywood. Plus the Czechs, of course..."

"You didn't tell me that!" Arletty smacked Ari on a shapely buttock. "Turn, I must get the other one!" He complied, and she kissed his other buttock, instead of spanking it. "SO!? What did they say?"

"They all said the same things as Depardieu."

Arletty luxuriated. "Which is to say—?"

"Oh, you know. Nothing much." said Ari, and hid his face behind a pillow. Arletty wrestled the pillow from him and covered his face in kisses. Ari pretended he was being attacked by a slimy alien and panted as if he was being drowned, struggling to say: "Stop. Stop! I'll tell you."

"That's better," said Arletty primly, holding his sex hostage in her hand. "Proceed, and don't skip any words. And in English, please."

"He, Depardieu said, in his best, most Parisian French, that your one hundred twenty seconds in the film were the most *electrifying* event of this year's Cannes festival, AND that you cannot help but become a star. No. Make that, a GREAT star!"

Arletty smiled and released Ari's sex, to start playing with his dark-brown nipples instead. "That sounds good. That's all right, isn't it?"

Ari turned to face her. He cupped her breasts with both hands and fondled them gently. "Yes, that is very all right, Arletty. I wish somebody, anybody, had said even a hundredth a thing about my movie as all right as that."

Arletty held Ari's head in her palms. She looked straight into his eyes. She perceived traces of what could have easily turned to tears. *"Salop,"* she scolded him. "Anything, anyone has to say about me in your movie is because of you. I was on the screen because you put me there." She kissed him and he kissed her back gratefully. They didn't hold the kiss for long. Both their mouths were raw and tender from countless previous kisses. So they disengaged.

Wordlessly they washed, dressed, and went out to get a meal. They felt as if they hadn't eaten for days.

Chapter 20

Back to the beginning: June, 1999. At La Crevetterie.

"I'm hungry," muttered Arletty. She was determined to appear callous and unconcerned. She wanted Ari to leave this meeting absolutely convinced that she was serious. That this time she truly, irrevocably wanted no further contact of any sort, not even e-mail. Nothing. Ever.

Yes, Mykonos had been a pleasure. A storybook ecstasy. She had enjoyed it unreservedly. She had enjoyed it more than she had enjoyed anything in her entire life. But the trouble was, it wasn't real life. It was pretend-life. And she had regretted it the moment it was over. In the airplane on the way home, Ari had dozed off as peacefully as a well-fed baby, his head resting sweetly on her shoulder. His arm draped casually over her leg. She had regretted the whole thing, long before the plane touched down in Montreal. She refused Ari's offer of a lift in his limo. She then refused to reply to any of his endless e-mails. She tried to block him out of her mind. And she had almost succeeded. She deleted his e-mails unread. She refused to be seduced even by the possibility of him. And maybe soon, he'd understand as well. Already he was e-mailing only once every other day. This was down from once a day, and a steep descent from several times a day, when they had just returned. Maybe soon, he'd give up and stop altogether. Maybe Mykonos would remain their ultimate Paris, thus put the whole matter to rest. "Put paid to it," as her friend Anita from Bangalore liked to say. Maybe, maybe... Except that her pregnancy results had come back ruthlessly positive, and now here she was at her favourite table of *La Crevetterie,* arguably the best cafe-society table in all Montreal, listening to him sigh *I want to die.*

She replied "I'm hungry," not only to refute his sentiment and defuse the gravity of the moment, but also because she really was hungry. She was hungry all the time these days.

"Oh, yeah? *Poutine?*" he replied with venom.

She decided to ignore the venom. He was obviously in shock, if he dared to talk to her like that. "No! Don't even mention *poutine*. The thought of it disgusts me. What I crave now is *real* food. I knew something was wrong when *that* started. That's why I had the pregnancy test. My period has been late before, but the food thing was the clincher. I knew it was because..."

Ari banged the table with his fist. "Stop saying the word. Stop tormenting me. You never even gave me a chance to adjust to the PREGNANCY, before telling me to buzz off and never see you again. What the— what is this *really* all about? Tell me! TELL ME!"

"You know, Ari," she said icily. "You can fight with your father in public all you want, but not with me! I'll not have it. I am here to see you in person out of courtesy. I could have done this by e-mail."

"Yes, I know. You're *so-o* kind!"

"You're quite the angel yourself."

"My fight with my father is— over. Shit happens, and then it's erased."

"How very nice for you," said Arletty wryly. "For me it means *haute cuisine*. That's what I want now. The kind of stuff my father makes. No, no, not his *terroir* recipes. Nothing with gravies. I want fine sauces. I want gastronomic delicacies. Fine meats. Fragile fish. Rare vegetables. Freshly made noodles. Wild mushrooms. White truffles. Crayfish tails. Baby octopus. Things like that." She smacked her lips.

"Really?"

"Yes."

Ari summoned the waiter and ordered. Shrimps in butter and real garlic, a salad of fat-poached duck leg, mussels in white wine, sauteed snapper in saffron-lemon sauce, pistachio-stuffed rack of lamb, some French fries for old times' sake, a bottle of the best *Chablis,* and a couple of double *Calvados* to perk up his own appetite.

"Are we back to normal, then?" he asked meekly.

"What do you mean?"

"I mean, are you going to insist on paying for all this?"

She took the blow and smiled. "No. I'm broke. You can pay."

The thin victory failed to soothe Ari. When the *Calvados* arrived he slammed his down in one gulp, creating a little stomach-fire known as the *trou Normand*. It gyrated inside him, culminating in a painful hunger pang. Instead of easing him, it worsened his distress.

His gaze was riveted to her. He wished he could look away. He wished he could get up and leave. But he sat there, fixated, imploring, sad. She wanted to help him. To console him. But she was in enough trouble. She had no spare resources to deal with Ari's problems, especially since she had caused them. In any case, at this very moment, all she could think about was food.

The waiter passed their table hurriedly. By way of apology he threw a hand towards the kitchen, and then to the rest of the tables on the crowded terrace, Everyone was impatiently waiting for their food. There were faint but menacing screams from the kitchen. The chefs were having a panic attack. Most of the diners had arrived at once, creating a bottleneck. It would be a while.

Ari's hunger had subsided. Now the alcohol was evaporating into anger.

"You're *so-o* full of—"

"Shit? Yes. You told me."

"And what exactly do you want anyway? Do you know? What's it all about for you? You're so confused, it slays me."

"Talking to me?" asked Arletty. She had wandered off into a reverie of roast goose with red cabbage and potato dumplings, her father had cooked one Christmas, long ago. Maybe *terroir* recipes weren't so bad after all.

"No. I'm talking to myself. You're not really there, are you?"

"I wish I wasn't," said Arletty, in stale, flat tones. "I wish I was already fifty, or sixty, that all this was far behind me, and I was writing a wistful poem about it."

"Great way for a sixteen-year-old to feel. I mean seventeen. I guess you must be seventeen. You must have had a birthday. You didn't even let me wish you a happy birthday!"

"My birthday was years ago. And by the way, I'm not sixteen or seventeen. I'm twenty three."

"Yes," faltered Ari. "I knew that."

"Of course you did."

"Fine. I didn't. But, who cares! I'm happy you're twenty three. It means you can relate to me better."

Arletty smiled. "I understand you perfectly, Ari."

"The hell you do... Are you really twenty three? How old are you?"

"Twenty three. I swear."

"Well, it changes nothing."

"I agree."

A very loud silence followed. Ari was flabbergasted. She had made a joke about her age, and he had believed her. No wonder she had no respect for him. Meanwhile things were heating up on the terrace. The hungry clients were drinking on empty stomachs and getting rowdy. It encouraged Ari. He picked up his empty *Calvados* glass and threatened to smash it on the ground.

"I'm in love with you, goddamnit!"

"I thought you didn't believe in love," she said resignedly. She was queasy from hunger, but it was too good a point to pass up.

"I changed my mind. I'm Greek. We're allowed."

"Good for the Greeks. Personally, I'm not in the least bit in love with you." She said it. She wondered if it was true.

"Then why the fuck did you agree to come to Cannes with me and — and to MYKONOS! Why?" Ari cut his sentence short. The waiter had materialized with their wine, and some pitiful excuses for the delay.

All negotiations, even the most crucial, tend to take a pause when the refreshments arrive. It would seem from the beginning that the most important affairs of the human race have forever been hashed out in the brief intervals between between eating and drinking.

Arletty sipped on her wine. It tasted good, but it added to her nausea. She struggled to concentrate on Ari. She could have just got up and left, but she didn't want to leave anything dangling. No loose ends, no unanswered questions. This meeting had to really be the end. A clean break and then a return to her real life. Whatever she would decide that was.

"I came to Cannes because I missed you," she said. "I agreed to Mykonos because I wanted to get away from Cannes, but more than that, because I wanted to have sex with you..."

Ari was wide-eyed. "Sex? We had more than sex on Mykonos."

"I meant, to make love with you."

"You mean, to make a baby with me!"

"That was unintentional. I left my pills in Montreal, as a deterrent. To stop me from having sex, from making love with you. And then... I decided to take a chance, and it backfired."

"No, it did NOT," said Ari, slapping the table. "This was meant to happen. I went to midnight Easter, and lit a candle, and brought the flame home, just so it WOULD happen."

Arletty laughed. "What? No voodoo?"

"You missed ME! What about me? I've been dying for you."

Arletty shook her head dismissively. "Dying for me, while screwing everything on two female legs."

"Me? Never!" Ari blushed.

"Let's see now. Never with Lucie? Never with Cynthia? Never with... JENNIFER??" Arletty sneered.

"What did you do? Keep tabs on me?"

"Yes," said Arletty and downed her wine. Her stomach had settled down. Now her head was lazily spinning, like an overhead fan in a cheap hotel. "I had a terrible winter," she continued. "I'm pissed off as hell that you were having such a good time."

"I was NOT having a good time. I was TRYING to forget you."

"You had no right to forget me!"

"Well, I didn't. Did I?"

"You should have. You could have. It'd have been a favour to both of us."

"And what was wrong with you, anyway? Why did you have such a terrible winter? If you missed me so much, how come you didn't try to see me?"

Arletty took a deep breath, and refilled her glass with wine. She took a gulp. "I had a terrible winter because I thought of no one but you, I wanted no one but you, every night you came into my dreams, and you told me again and again how much you wanted me, even though you didn't know exactly why. Smothering me, nullifying me, fattening me up and grooming me, getting me ready to plant on your mantelpiece, until I became old news and you took me for granted, like your father takes your mother—"

"NEVER!"

"Of course NOT. Anyway, I had to find out. I had to see you again. I had to make sure... And now I am sure."

"Sure of fucking WHAT?"

"Sure that I probably do love you. That I'll probably never love anyone else. And surer than everything, that I must stay as far away from you as possible." Arletty was flushed. She pushed herself off her chair. She looked down at Ari, who had frozen. "That's it, Ari. I can't talk anymore. I don't feel well."

Lightening fast, he stood up and held her, to support her. She recoiled, shook off his touch and stared at him with loathing. "Let go of me!"

Ari glared at her. "I was TRYING to help you."

"DON'T try to help me." Arletty sat down again. The crisis had passed, but it had exhausted her.

Ari twirled on the spot. He finally realized what people meant when they said they saw red. Everything around him was awash in crimson fire. In scarlet. In vermilion.

"Well, you're STUCK with me, baby. I'm deep inside you, Arletty! I'm in there and I won't come out till I've sucked all your blood at least... TEN TIMES!"

"Shut *up*, Ari. Please," said Arletty. People in neighbouring tables had got wind of their fight, and were actively listening.

"Hah! Trapped you, didn't I? You *didn't* leave those pills behind. I found them in Cannes and threw them OUT!"

"You did not. I found them when I got back home. You did nothing."

"I got you PREGNANT!" Ari beamed. Several onlookers applauded.

Arletty glowered at him. "You want a fight? Is that it?"

Ari circled back to his seat unsteadily. He sat down heavily, and he burped. "I want you to get over whatever's bothering you, and GET REAL!" he shouted.

Suddenly, Arletty felt fine. Her hunger, her headache, her nausea, all subsided. "Fuck you," she whispered.

"What was that?"

"FUCK YOU!"

Ari let out a screech and took a sip of wine. "O-o-oh, *fuck* you, is it? It has such a nice sound to it, doesn't it? FUCK you! Fuck YOU! Nothing in French even comes close? DOES it? Nope. You're stuck with FUCK YOU, and if you think you can take my love and my baby and walk away from me, FUCK YOU, TOO!!!"

"Is this final, then? Can I go, now?"

"GO TO HELL!" screamed Ari.

Arletty stood up with some difficulty. "Have a nice time, Ari. It's been grand!"

Ari lunged for her arm. "Don't you DARE walk out on me!"

Arletty punched his hand, sending it off in a wide arch. She looked at him with pity. The entire terrace was quiet, hanging by every nuance of their scene.

"If you try to touch me again, I'll kill you," she hissed. She abruptly turned away, and was gone.

Ari was stunned. He wished he could act. Do something. Follow her. Throw himself at her. But he knew it was all useless. USELESS. Hopeless and desperate. At that very moment the waiter arrived with a large tray loaded with food. Ari let out a terrifying noise. He tensed his body and attacked the tray with all his might.

Plates of shrimps and mussels, *confit de canard* and pink lamb-chops, heaps of golden-fried potatoes flew up, came to a standstill in mid-air, and then came crashing messily down on the pavement. Ari fell on his knees, wailing loudly in a sea of grease and flesh and broken plates. He howled like a wounded animal.

Part Two:

The Pregnancy

Chapter 1

July 1999. In Montreal.

Like everyone else in this city of severe winters, Ari's favourite month was July. This year's July however, was hell. As each ponderous day passed distancing him yet farther from Arletty, the events of their fatal meeting on Bernard Street played and replayed in his mind like the death scene in a cheap melodrama.

He had failed. He felt ugly and scorned. He blamed himself, his father, and his whole slew of ancestors, for rendering him unacceptable to the one person who could have given meaning to his pampered, one-dimensional existence.

He now existed agoraphobically in his room. He had turned off his air-conditioning and kept the windows shut. The drapes were drawn except when Ben made his frequent, random appearances, up the trellis and through the window.

The room was stale and hot. Ari crawled around it like a sleepy iguana wrapped in self-loathing, taking refuge in endless naps on his greying sheets.

Maria regularly knocked on his door, sweet-talking him into letting her see him, console him, hug him, cure him, or at least, do his laundry and feed him. He would grunt at her from inside, whimpering, begging her to leave him alone but to send up a tray of food, and leave it — thank God, he was eating! — outside his door.

Ari's profound unhappiness cast a mighty pall over the MacLeod house. It infected everyone. Betty, Sophia, the whole staff, even the chauffeur — who was once again estranged from his wife — and most of all, OBVIOUSLY Maria, Mother of the Patient. Everyone was operating as if in a haze, sharing Ari's pain. Everyone, that is, except Duncan, who had decided to forget that Ari had ever been born.

The head of the household had other, far more important matters to occupy him. He had completely recovered from the malaise of the year's first quarter. He was back to trading and winning furiously. Several one-billion-dollar days, many brilliant moves, and to top it all off, continuously-improving relations with Maria. So many dexterous improvements, that Duncan no longer needed to waste time and money pursuing his pleasures elsewhere. Now, he could devote all his concentration to business, and still get laid when he felt like it, for free. Perfection.

Sadly, the sunshine of perfection never lasts: a black cloud inevitably drifts by to diminish the glow. In Duncan's case, this cloud took the shape of a woman in her seventies, disheveled, reeking of rot and malnutrition, making her way up Redpath Crescent towards a house that had once briefly been hers.

Cornelia MacLeod, née MacDermid, disowned wife of Ross MacLeod, mother of Duncan, grandmother of the suffering Ari; by marriage a Golden Mile dowager entitled to a soft old age, but in fact a forlorn drunk and a wastrel, had finally gathered the gumption to return to Redpath Crescent. One too many cat-food dinners, one too many pints of no-name alcohol, one too many pains she had no means to palliate, one too many years abandoned to abject poverty, one too many nights moaning herself to sleep, overcome by hate. Hate for the MacLeods, who had used and discarded her. Hate for her own family, who had embezzled every penny of her divorce money and left her destitute. Hate for a son who never tried to find her, nor even respond to her letters; and hate for her grandson, who had been told she had died decades before he was born.

Hatred can compel the most ugly confrontations, and hatred had fueled Cornelia's trudge across a line the law had barred her from ever crossing.

She turned the corner and she saw it. Suddenly, the oppressive heat, the arduous hike up from Sherbrooke Street, her rasping lungs, the daggers in her legs, all eased up and evaporated. There it was, all turrets and porticos, its long, hard steps to the impenetrable doors. Once you were out, you were out. Gigantic and atrocious, pretentious and melancholy, a citadel, a seat of power. A house but never ever a home.

She covered the last fifty yards with a lively gait. She was twenty again, walking up to the house for the first time beside her eager father, to meet her husband-to-be, a man much older than herself, but a lion, a god, a MaCLEOD! *Curses to you, Ross MacLeod, may you burn forever in your luxury grave.*

She rang the bell and followed its sound from room to room as it echoed through the vast house. There was no response of any kind for what felt like minutes, hours. Cornelia broke into a sweat. She felt very, very old and now, somewhat silly. She was regretting having come when she heard something. Steady, firm footsteps approaching the door. Louder, louder, and then she sensed being given the once-over through the spy-hole.

Cornelia peered into the reversed lens from her side of the door. It seemed very far away but she was certain that she was looking into the unmistakable grey-green eye of the girl who had started working for the family during Cornelia's limited season as wife. It had been fifty years, but she would never forget Betty's eyes, the mocking stare that had witnessed Cornelia's dishonourable exit. Her staying behind as Ross's housekeeper, and also, more than likely, his mistress.

Cornelia summoned all her diminished strength, and poured it into her voice. "Betty! Open this door immediately!" she yelled. She pressed on the bell again and again, until it sounded like a fire-engine.

Betty, ruffled, opened the door a crack. She intended to sound officious, but her voice sounded cowardly: "What do you want? Who are you?"

Cornelia was now unstoppable. She pushed on the door with enormous authority, causing Betty to trip backwards, parting the door just enough to enter the hallway.

"I am Cornelia MacLeod, and I have every right to enter my own house!" she exploded.

Betty's servility got the better of her. She found no voice. She was cowed by the woman who had been mistress of the house when she was first hired. Cornelia had dressed her down then, for the sake of training her. Half a century later, that protocol still held sway.

Betty returned to her senses just in time. Cornelia had already penetrated the multi-portrait lobby and was heading for the side stairway. The much more agile, vastly healthier housekeeper dashed past her onto the first step, and spread out her arms to block the passage of her former mistress. She was her current master's last defense against this most dangerous of intruders, Louis XVI's personal guard against all commoners who would invade the palace.

"No, ma'am. This hasn't been your house for a long time. You have no right to be here!" she said in a quivering tone.

Cornelia stopped and spat at Betty. "Move out of my way!"

"NO! You get out!" cried Betty, much more loudly than she had intended. She heard a stir from Duncan's office. Disturbing the boss while he was working was a capital offense.

"I want to see my son. I want my son to see me. I'm hungry. And I'm sick. I need a drink. I need help," Cornelia controlled her rage. "A bit of compassion..." She sighed and moaned as if she was choking.

Betty softened. But she was in charge again and knew what needed to be done. "Come with me to the kitchen, ma'am," she said firmly. "I'll give you lunch. I'll give you a drink," as she sniffed the fumes emanating from Cornelia. "Gin, if you like. A whole bottle. I wish I could give you cash, but—"

"Oh, shut up, Betty! Who do you think you're talking to!?" snapped Cornelia. Then she raised her voice to a pitch it hadn't reached in an eternity, since the day she had screamed at her father's grave when she discovered that he had spent every cent of her money. "I WANT TO SEE MY SON!" she yelled.

This time the response from upstairs was definitive. Duncan snapped angrily out of his office, Maria dashed out of her sewing room, and all manner of servants rushed towards the lobby. Even Ari heard the commotion, and sneaked onto the top landing of the opposite side stairs to watch.

Duncan was the first to reach the scene. He towered over the women, descending the master staircase in the middle of the atrium. Cornelia dashed out from the side, only to trip and fall on the rug in front of Duncan. Maria, who had run down the corridor, came to a dead stop at the top of the grand staircase, looking down at the fallen woman.

"What is it, Betty? What's this woman doing here?" Duncan quizzed his housekeeper, but kept his gaze nailed on Cornelia.

"She says she's y-y-your mother, sir..." stuttered Betty.

Duncan raised his eyebrows in a studied air of shock. As a child he had been told that his mother had died when he was a baby. Yet as an adult he had received a series of letters from Cornelia that had informed him otherwise. A tiny amount of sleuthing had quickly yielded the truth: she had not died, but had merely been bought-

out. The letters had ceased as suddenly as they had surfaced, and
he had laid the matter to rest, hoping never to have to meet her. If
Aunt Jaimie had seen fit to get rid of her, that was good enough for
him. Nevertheless, he had rehearsed a speech: "My mother passed
away tragically, when she was very young. How dare you play this
game with me! How cruel. Who sent you?"

"I am your mother," whimpered Cornelia.

There was a shuffle of anticipation in the foyer. The entire staff
had gathered around the principal players of this highly operatic
moment. Duncan, an obsessively private man, had no choice but to
continue his personal dilemma in front of an audience.

"You're lying," he said coolly.

"My name is Cornelia MacLeod," she said. "Look at my pension
card."

"It's a common enough name."

"Have mercy, my son!" screamed Cornelia.

"I am not your son!" shouted Duncan. He turned to Betty.
"Have her driven home, and give her some money. Give her a
hundred dollars."

"I am your mother," implored Cornelia. "I am. Ask her." She
pointed to Betty. "Ask her. She knows me. She was here."

Duncan sensed the trap. He peered at Betty, hoping she'd do the
right thing. Betty squirmed. "Speak!" ordered Duncan.

"I'm not sure. It's been so long..." hedged Betty.

"Tell him the truth, you miserable wretch!" barked Cornelia,
struggling to get up on her feet.

Betty's head throbbed as if a pair of boxers were using it as a
ring. However, being a devout Presbyterian she could not utter such
a monumental lie. She hung her head and, barely audibly, she said,
"I'm not altogether, not absolutely certain, but she could well be...
We can test her, if you like. If she knows the house... But, yes, I
think she is..."

This revelation galvanized the supernumeraries into stifling
silence. They stared at Cornelia, afraid to move a muscle. Maria drew
a deep breath and descended a step before she thought better of it
and came to a standstill. Ari's eyes bulged and he almost betrayed
his hiding post. For the first time in over a year he forgot all about
Arletty, he was so transfixed by the plight of his back-from-the-dead
grandmother.

Duncan's mind raced. He decided to gain time by showing no

emotion whatever, exactly as he would in a turbulent day at the stock market. His only hope was that this crisis would pass without any lasting damage. In fact, it would, but not before Cornelia had her turn on center-stage.

"God is meant to be kind and almighty. But not even God could have tamed master criminals like Jaimie and Ross. And now, it's obvious that God is no match for you, Duncan. My son! You are made of stone. A pillar with a hollow centre full of venom. You are vile. You are the chaos and the deluge. You are so evil that the Devil himself is afraid of you. At least your aunt and your father got to go to hell. You're not even fit for hell. You're going somewhere much more worse than that... You knew immediately that I'm your mother. Didn't you? But just as immediately, you wanted to see me disappear. *'Give her a hundred dollars, and get her away from me?'* For heavens sake. I am your mother! You came out of my body. You owe me your first breath. And every filthy, rotten breath you have taken since. A hundred dollars! For all those breaths? Shame on you. Shame on your family. Shame on the whole, stinking lot of you," sang Cornelia, by now addressing the entire assembly.

Her eyes perused the circularity of the room. Up and around the three-storey height of it. High up on the left staircase, she spotted Ari. Pale and wide-eyed, he met her gaze. She could tell he was scared. Shivering like a trapped, small, furry animal. She knew instinctively who he was. He looked exactly like her when she was his age. A male version of herself, indisputably a MacDermid, despite the olive skin and Grecian hair he had obviously inherited from his foreign mother.

Cornelia continued to circle the room. Her eye fell on Maria next. The Greek mother. But a mother, like herself. A mother who would have to live with the curses that Cornelia could justifiably hurl on Ari. She tried to open her mouth but the curses wouldn't come out. A clash of cymbals prevented it. Followed by dolorous music. Strings and harps wailing. Weeping, for her. It focused her grief and turned her torment into a lament. She gasped, as if her breath was giving out.

"Most of all, shame on me," she whispered hoarsely. She wanted to continue but all she could manage was spent air, the final note of a forfeited life.

She clutched her chest. Her eyes rolled aimlessly before she fell, loudly onto the floor. Maria quickly crossed herself three times as she flew down the stairs. Duncan moved more slowly, but they reached Cornelia at the same moment.

Duncan felt his mother's neck, then he held his hand over her mouth. He shook his head, and shut her eyelids. Opinion is divided on this, but most of the onlookers swear they saw a tear form in his eye, and discreetly roll down his cheek.

Chapter 7

Late July. In Montreal.

The funeral had been sumptuous. It bestowed on Cornelia all the honours and all the respect that had evaded her hapless life. Duncan had not dared spare any expense. His mother's death-rattling speech had filtered out almost verbatim — Duncan suspected the chauffeur — and a resounding rebuttal to the controversy was *de rigueur.*

She lay in state for three days at the extravagant *McGlinty & Jones* funeral home, in the heart of Westmount. The church service was held in St. Andrew & St. Paul's church, the Presbyterian jewel of Sherbrooke Street's millionaire-row, and attended by nearly two hundred heavy hitters. The departed one's skid-row buddies were not permitted into the church, but all of her relatives, and even their relatives were accorded places of honour, showing up in Cadillacs and Lincolns that were probably purchased with money that had been embezzled from her.

The interment took place in Cote des Neiges Cemetery, in a quickly erected, modest yet ample tomb, not far from the MacLeod family mausoleum. The entire church assembly followed the sad lady to her final resting place, not out of any sense of duty to her, but for the chance to connect with Duncan.

Ari skipped the church, but did climb Mount Royal to witness the burial, hidden behind a fat tree on an adjacent hill. He laughed aloud at all the hypocrisy, but his mirth flowed into tears when they started lowering the casket on its one-way descent into the ground.

This was Ari's third funeral. Each time for a grandparent: first Ross, then Eirini, and now Cornelia. One contented grandfather, and two utterly wronged grandmothers. He had cried lustily for Ross, on whose lap he had grown up; not at all for Eirini, who had in all her fury been unable to bond with him. And now for Cornelia, who had imploded in front of him, at this most twisted time in his own life, he cried his bitterest tears.

He walked out of the cemetery consumed with the poison of her profound hatred, sodden by the sudden downpour that had punctuated the funeral. Up summer rain-glistened paths that transect the mountain, past groping lovers poorly hidden in the bushes, past middle-aged joggers puffing and wheezing for health, past teenagers smoking pot and drinking beer, past gay cruisers too impatient to wait for the dark, until he reached the highest point looking south over the city, straight up from his own backyard.

He approached the house from the rear and climbed up the trellis in the manner of Ben Cohen, entering his room through the window he had left open. Once inside his cocoon he let loose, whimpering and moaning, not for the grandmother he had never known existed, but for his own sorry state.

Unexpectedly, entirely on its own, an idea came to him. He crossed the long corridor and sneaked into his mother's dressing room. He opened the huge closets with their hundreds of dresses, all hand-made by Maria, and the countless accessories. He selected things his mother hadn't worn in years, items she was not likely to miss. He grabbed a shawl, a pair of flaming-red shoes, black mesh stockings, a wig Maria kept for Mardi Gras parties, a fistful of costume jewelry, sundry makeup, and one extraordinarily long, rather twirlable string of pearls. He packed his haul into a laundry bag and returned stealthily to his room.

Ben Cohen thought he was hearing things. Disco music was pouring loudly out of Number One Redpath Crescent. The higher up the trellis he climbed, the louder it got. The next baffler was the open window, which had never before been open. The final shock of this very important visit was the sight that awaited Ben when he reached Ari's room.

A grotesquely made-up, pseudo-girl singer was lip syncing and dancing to the music in front of the floor-length mirror. Gyrating, throwing arms at imaginary fans, bump-and-grinding with awkward, boyish movements; a spectacle to be sure. Ben climbed quietly into the room, careful not to trip. He sat on a chair, trying hard not to giggle.

The song ended. Ari took several bows, accepting his ungiven applause with aplomb. Acknowledging Ben without turning around:

"Aah, my trusty Ben. Good of you to attend. This is the start of a new bend in my career."

"Oh, it's bent alright, ma'am," chuckled Ben

"Call me Gisella, okay fella?" winked Ari.

"The drag okay. But, what's with the rhymes?"

"That's how I talk now," sing-songed Ari, "so I can see out through the fog, you know?"

"That's nice," shrugged Ben, "but come back to Earth for a sec, okay? I've got unbelievable news."

"I want news of no kind. Not the true, nor the untrue, not the credible, and even less the incredible. But gladly I'd hear a song, be it *leider,* or even madrigal."

"How about some disco?"

"Ah, that. We'll return to that, and you'll see where I'm at!"

Ben grabbed Ari by his strapless shoulders. "Listen, you two-bit rhyming couplet. I saw her. I SAW Arletty!"

"In your dreams, little guy... Traitor! What gall! How dare you dream my girl?"

"Not dreams. Her! I was where she lives."

Ari took pause. He peered at Ben. He shivered. "Okay," he said in his best non-rhyming tone, "tell me."

Ben then told a tale, so fantastic, and with such a contrived coincidence at its core, that it could only have happened in real life, because in fiction it would have been dismissed as a facile plot device.

In brief, he had been in N.D.G. visiting his parents' alternative therapy clinic, a non-profit gig that involved a lot of massage, *Birkenstocks,* and a strange brew of herbal drinks. Being broke as usual, he had been slowly walking back downtown, looking needy, playing tunes on his keyboard. A beautiful woman, some Princess from the East, a vision in dark, flowing hair, peach-coloured silk saree, a milk chocolate face with flirtatious dark eyes, a ruby in her forehead, and one golden earring, had smiled at him. The next thing he knew, she was leading him home to feed him and mend his ills, as if he was some sort of homeless songbird. Ben had followed her willingly, unflinchingly, wholeheartedly. Thing was, he had fallen in love with her at first sight. Her name was Anita.

Her little house, the lower half of a respectable brick duplex, was one of many in a long similar row on an anonymous, tree-shaded street. With a love that grew after each mouthful of Anita's food — *samosas, tandoori,* chicken curry, all reheated but excellent on freshly made basmati rice, and priceless to ever hungry Ben — they had exchanged a slew of suggestive body language: unmistakable precursors to carnal intimacies Ben blanched to even imagine. At that point, another woman had entered through the kitchen door.

It was Arletty, a stale, exhausted, smelling-of-vomit Arletty, but with the same inalienably undaunted spirit, the same everyman's-wet-dream girl-woman as the Arletty in the movie. Ben's mouth had fallen open, bits of half-chewed *samosa* tumbling out of it. Arletty ignored him. She spoke to Anita, agitated. "It happened again. I'm disgusted. I'm sorry. I need some water to clean it up."

"Normal. Normal. I swear. The third month is the worst, and it's also the last one. No more vomit after this. Now, come inside and kip on a nice bed. We'll clean up later. I don't think so you want to be near this smell. Go on."

"Thank you, but no. I can't indoors. I feel trapped. I need to be outside."

"And with that, she went back to the garden, Ari," said Ben. "She has been camping out in a tent, in Anita's backyard. And she's having a really tough time. Vomiting. No sleep. But Anita assured me she's happy. I mean, she is well..."

"How did she end up at this Anita's?" asked Ari in a calculating tone.

"I don't know. It was all too intense. I stopped eating. I stopped flirting. All I wanted to do was get over here and tell you about it. Anyway, soon after she left the kitchen, Arletty started retching loudly, and Anita rushed to help her, so I left."

"What's the address? Where's this house?" Ari's stern look and forceful questions were undermined by his badly applied make-up, some of which was beginning to run, dissolved by his sweat.

"I don't think I should tell you. She would probably hate it. And Anita wouldn't like it either..." mumbled Ben, already weakening.

Ari, however, spared him. He nodded in agreement. "She wouldn't just hate it. She'd be furious."

"But, look," blurted Ben, relieved. "I'm inviting myself to go back and finish what didn't start with Anita. I can be, like, your spy. I can keep an eye on her for you."

"You keep your eyes away from her!" snapped Ari. "I don't want you near her. I want nothing to touch her, see her, feel her, speak to her, smell her. Nothing. Ever!"

"Okay, boss," gulped Ben. "Calm down. I'm on your side."

"Side? Which side? I have no sides. I am side-free. Now, it's only me. You hear? Only *me*. And for me, my presumptuous mate, it's all but too late!"

"Yeah, right, Ari. Whatever you say."

"I said it, and I meant it."

"Me, I'm in love," beamed Ben.

"Oh, yuck! You, in love? Double-yuck, and good luck to you, my dove," laughed Ari maliciously.

Chapter 3

First Saturday in August. On Redpath Crescent.

The party arrangements were in full flight. Maria's famous full-summer shindig on the first Saturday in August, which had all but been abandoned a mere two weeks ago because of the hostess's concerns for her son, had been resuscitated and scaled up, because of Ari himself.

In total contrast to last year, when a distracted Ari had refused to show up at all, this year the derailed scion had insisted that the party be held, not only because he wished to attend, but because he wanted to actually be part of the live entertainment. He had a surprise song and a new poem to deliver, with Ben Cohen as his sole accompanist. It occurred to Maria that Ari might have some subversive motive, but such was her relief to see him out of his cell — he had brought down his laundry and had started taking breakfast in the solarium, just like the old days — that she chased all suspicions out of her mind, and concentrated instead on planning and executing an extravaganza in short notice.

She chose a cinematic theme to reflect Ari's participation in Cannes, and assembled a guest list that would be the envy of the highest paid cinema-publicist. Every major entertainment journalist, from both French and English media, print-TV-radio; every major film personality within shooting distance of Montreal, including Jeremy Podeswa and Don McKellar to represent Atom Egoyan, who couldn't leave Toronto; but every inch of John Travolta, in town shooting some execrable Scientological epic; sundry other Hollywood stars also shooting in Montreal; the entirety of the cast of Cirque du Soleil; Margie Gillis with her hair in a mile-high bun; George Mihalka with Daniaile Jarry in fabulous tandem outfits; plus the principals of the Montreal Opera, *Là Là Human Steps*, *Carbone 14*, Jean Duceppe's theatrical company, and both Guy Sprung and Carolyn Guillet of InfiniTheatre. She vetoed Centaur's Gordon McCall for being too flabby, and Luc Plamondon for being too arrogant. At the same time, she failed to persuade Josette, who almost weakened in her resolve never to visit Redpath Crescent again. Josette finally persevered against coming, because there was an *Omerta* rerun on the tube that Saturday night and she had a hot date with Louis-Marc. All in all however, Maria had accounted for everybody else who happened to be anybody.

While Maria toiled, lobbied, and networked to stage the best-attended gathering in the annals of Montreal's social scene, the young people who influenced her life, both directly and by association, were having a summer to remember.

Arletty had finished with the vomiting, and was settling into the more meaningful phases of her pregnancy. More claustrophobic than ever, she spent her time entirely outdoors in the garden, entering her tent to sleep only if it rained, and Anita's house only to use the bathroom. The consistently warm but not hot, mostly dry, sweet-breezy weather was an ideal backdrop. She had become reflective, and secretly elated. Her initial confusion and discomfort had paved the way for the great paradox: she felt enslaved and liberated all at once. Vulnerable, yet empowered. She had lost control of her life and her body, her personal identity. But it didn't seem to matter. She was creating a new life. This excited her greatly.

In a parallel, but totally separate universe, and practically under Arletty's nose — actually just at the edge of the garden, inside the house — Anita and Ben were indulging in a torrid love affair. Ben had indeed returned to N.D.G., and had conquered his beloved within moments of his arrival — or, been conquered by his beloved, depending on whom you asked. Anita, six years older, but generations more mature than Ben, having been married off to a bully in Bangalore at the age of fourteen, having studied computer science in secret from both husband and family; and having fled India, penniless, literally with only the saree on her back, and the favour of a Bahrainee businessman with a private jet. She eventually arrived in Canada and worked her way up to her steady office job by the scruff of her neck and seemingly innate street-smarts. She had a weakness for the helpless. She had rescued Arletty from the brink of self-destruction, as well as two dogs from the pound; three fully-grown iguanas from acquaintances who had no room for them once they had grown, and a huge carp, which had been slowly expiring, unsold in a fishmonger's tank. And now she had adopted scrawny, little Ben as her love toy, or maybe her newest pet. Whatever his status, Ben was in ecstasy. Here, finally, was a woman of inestimable beauty who had the time to invest in his sexual education. And did she ever discover what a fast learner he could be.

Though consumed by this new-found aptitude and an inexhaustible appetite for sex and love, Ben tended to Ari during the day, when Anita was at the office. He refrained unhesitatingly from discussing his sex life, now that the tables had been reversed and he was getting laid nightly, while Ari was positively arid. In any case, Ari had other, far more urgent matters to attend to. He had a performance to rehearse, and every minute with Ben had to be spent on that.

The pair of them worked on the 'act' for the five days leading up to the party. Ben, who was at first leery, was soon swept up in Ari's obsessive enthusiasm. His only difficult task was to try and correct Ari's stage presence, a doubly tricky assignment considering his own lack of training as a director and Ari's erratic state of mind. Nevertheless, when Friday's rehearsal came to a close, both of them were confident they would be able to pull it off.

The night turned out to be magical. No bugs. No humidity. The steady seventy degrees and playful breeze was total bliss after last year's heat-wave, thought Maria, a monumentally-favourable omen that augured major good news. She was right, of course: there would be very wondrous news for her tonight, but of a nature she couldn't possibly have guessed. She thought, she hoped, for a positive turn-around involving Ari's recovery from his relentless love-sickness. Speaking of love, she also wished for a turn-around from Duncan.

Their renewed passion, which had begun during Greek Easter, and had gotten even better over the early summer, had signified a second honeymoon, as well a redefinition of their conjugal bed. Sadly the sex had come to a standstill following Duncan's consternation over his mother's dramatic, oh-so-public death.

Withdrawn and embarrassed, Duncan had retreated from all contact, burying himself in his computer. To his own surprise, Cornelia's words had struck deep, and not only was he unable to commune with his wife, but he had also lost his concentration and therefore his acuity in the marketplace. Every time he peered at the screen, it announced to him that he had made more wrong moves on the day, and lost even more money than the previous day.

This complete reversal of his luck on all fronts had quickly humbled Duncan. He decided to please Maria, and atone for whatever he had done to deserve this, by promising to stay at the party at least until midnight, and forego his usual retreat to the baccarat table, at which he'd surely lose during this ill-fated period, anyway.

That is why he found himself beside his wife — she, splendid in a black and silver Twenties' flapper-dress, and he, just as dazzling in a brand new, midnight-blue, *Ermenegildo Zegna* suit — when it came time for his son to take his turn on the stage. The party had been pleasant enough up to this point. Maria was showing him true warmth and compassion. The food was excellent, thanks to a new catering discovery, courtesy of Josette: some young gal from the Plateau, obviously headed for culinary greatness. Her signature lobster-stuffed brioche, a triumph.

Even the entertainment had pleased Duncan. Maria, extra-cautious after last year's abominable chain-masturbators, had chosen known quantities. The performers, pleased as hell to be appearing for such an august audience, while being paid top-dollar, had given from the heart. The emcee did irritate Duncan with some jagged anti-Anglo quips, but his routine had been meticulously pre-cleansed by his worried agent, and tonight he was harmless, almost benign. However, no amount of the emcee's naughtiness could have possibly prepared Duncan, or in fact, Maria, for the "surprise" Ari had in store for them.

"And now," teased the well-behaving, naughty emcee, "the heir to this conspicuously wonderful backyard, the apple of Maria MacLeod's eyes, the future master of the universe and king of the world, Mister Ari MacLeod. Ladies and gents, let's hear it for the young *scion!*"

Ben was already at the controls to the right of the stage, in a spot where only the beaming, bejeweled, flashy-saree'd Anita could see him — and beam. He waited for the emcee to relinquish the stage before he killed all the lights. The garden was now candlelit, its only noise the audience's anticipatory murmur.

A specially-rigged spotlight picked out Ari's exquisitely gowned figure at the rear of the garden. Meticulously maquillaged, wigged, the right amount of padding in the right places, Ari was a vision of womanhood. He was holding a mike in one hand, and gently twirling the pearl necklace with the other. After a couple of seconds the hormonally familiar, opening beat of Gloria Gaynor's *I'll Survive* gushed out of the sound system at club volume.

Ari held his pose, alluringly forlorn, sad but sexy, until his vocal kick-off. Lip-syncing Gaynor's life-affirming lyrics, he sang into his mike and showily walk-danced through the crowd, towards the stage, the spotlight alertly following his gyrations.

"Where's Ari?" Duncan shout-whispered into Maria's ear uneasily.

Maria giggled nervously. "I think that is Ari."

"For God's sake," spat Duncan.

"It's all in fun, darling, relax," smiled Maria, a bit queasy herself, yet flattered when she recognized Ari's dress as one of her own from a decade or so ago.

Ari reached the stage, and jumped onto it with ease. A cascade of lights greeted him, saturating him in multicoloured, flashing flames, animating the song's tumultuous ending. Here Ari sang along with Gloria on the open mike — not a bad voice, but who could really tell at that volume? — flat out, open-throttled, generous, vulnerable, explosive. It was as if disco had returned from obscurity for one more glorious moment, to take yet another stab at immortality.

The music wrapped its beefy, insistent loose ends into a repetitive conclusion, as Ari danced invitingly, infectiously, presiding over the collective swaying of the supportive crowd. Even Maria caught herself swinging to the beat, suggestively brushing against Duncan. Nauseated by this public display of debauchery, he endured the entirety of his son's gyrations, stonily immobile.

Gigantic applause punctuated the end of the song. It came suddenly, as both music and lights were extinguished simultaneously. While the cheering continued, a solitary spotlight returned in a tight frame around Ari's face. He did not react in any way to the crowd's approval, but he waited impassionately for the noise to subside. Then, in a time-honoured manoeuvre of cross-dressing performers, he removed his wig, and looked straight ahead. A heavily made-up female face, with a male haircut. But what really intrigued the audience was his demeanor. Unfeeling, unseeing, as if he was some-

Byron Ayanoglu 176

where else, somewhere profoundly disturbing.

A thin, melodic line from Ben's flute, ever so subtly amplified, otherworldly and distant, as if emanating from the star-lit, hilltop meadow of a Greek island, insinuated itself on the crowd's celebratory mood. Ari's face twisted in fear as he prepared to speak.

"Oh, no. The poem," whimpered Maria.

"The *what?*" muttered Duncan with dread, knowing there would be more. Ari was a MacLeod, and he would never abandon this big opportunity to go for the kill.

"So, you think I'm a wimp," chuckled Ari into his spotlight. "Well, fuck you, too." Isolated giggles from the insultees. "I'm trying to become adult. To grow up. It happens to be very difficult. Because, on the other hand I'm very grown up. The movie I produced is a huge hit. So it's not earning any money, like, it's a Canadian movie, but it's a huge success. It's going to show in Toronto. At the Carlton! They serve cappuccino in there. It's a good theatre. An adult theatre! And they're all sending me their scripts. They all want me to produce-direct their movies. That's grown up! I got a call from Hollywood two days ago. Hollywood stars want me to work with them! That's grown up. Arletty's pregnant, and she intends to have the baby. In five months... wait..." he counted on his fingers, "September, October, November, December, January, February... In six months I'm going to be a father. That's grown up! I haven't returned a single phone call to anyone. I'm pretending that no one outside of me and Arletty even exists. That's grown up! Arletty never wants to see me again. Arletty, whom I love above all else, and without whom I'll die, won't ever see me again, and therefore I'll never see my own child. Ever. That's grown up! I'm living a grown up situation, and I don't like it. And it hurts. And I'm confused and afraid. There! You can't get more grown up than that! CAN YOU?"

On a signal from Ari, Ben extinguished the spotlight. The garden was once again in candlelight, but this time there was no sound at all. No murmurs. No whispers. No loud breathing. And over this deafening silence, Ari threw in his exclamation point. A blood-curdling scream, delivered *in extremis* into the live mike.

It was a long note with a terrifying, precarious rise, followed by a zero-net, free-fall descent. A torturous arc of sheer pain. Toxic vapour. A loud, painful tumble onto the hardwood stage. Another moment's silence before the shouts of concern, the alarmed question marks, and above all, Maria's voice screaming *"Ar-r-r-i-i-i-i-i-i-i-i-i!"*

Chapter 4

Very early the next morning.

There is no known gauge with which to measure the intensity of human implosion. It's therefore impossible to determine which of them — Maria, Duncan, Josette, or Louis-Marc — experienced the greater seism upon being among the first few hundred, and eventually millions, via the media, to hear the news. Arletty was pregnant, and determined to have the child without Ari. But, to have the child! A gift of the gods. A miracle. A grandchild, a little touch of immortality for four individuals, all of whom had already resigned themselves to dying without it.

Josette and Louis-Marc got the word around one a.m., after Maria had tended to her wounded son. She was so full of concern she had no room for excitement until the doctor had sedated Ari and assured her he was okay. Only then had she allowed the grand-child-news to wash over her, and she picked up the phone. The Daoust-Tremblay household, now blissfully asleep after a long night of Montreal-Mafia and sex, reverberated and jarred by the relentless ringing. Josette grudgingly picked up, listened for thirty seconds, and caused enough of an emotional rocket to rip through the roof.

She banged down the phone and released an even louder yell of consummate elation. Louis-Marc had not even stirred. He was dreaming of a catastrophic, gangland shoot-out in the streets of Westmount, and was incorporating her screams into his dream. She shove-and-punched him not all that gently, so that he could discover that the best dreams sometimes continue after one has awakened.

His eyes had barely blinked open when she hugged him, almost suffocating him, and told him. She was giggling with glee as she spoke, but her words were precise.

"Oh, Josette," was all he could say, hugging and kissing her, slapping her back, as if they were at the racetrack and their $50 bet-to-win had romped home at thirty-to-one.

Josette squirmed out of his clutches, and jumped out of bed. "This is too good to be true!"

Louis-Marc also got out of bed. He put on his robe, and his glasses. He brushed back his unbound pony-tail with his fingers, and howled triumphantly. He did a side-kick and a heel-click. "Oh, baby," he danced around her, while she swished a caftan over her forever-inviting nakedness. "Oh, baby, this is— this is the greatest moment of our lives. Having Arletty was great. This is even better. This is monumental!"

Josette wiggled in tune to his imaginary dancing music. "Ever since she was fourteen. Always the same. 'Forget it, maman, never. Never. No kids from me. Period!' For eight years the same tune, rubbing out all my hope. And now! Oh, Louis-Marc, I am so happy..." She could cry.

"How di·d she sound? What a brat! Waiting for the middle of the night to call us. What a SWEETHEART!"

Josette shook her head. "Oh, that wasn't her."

"It wasn't?"

"It was Maria."

"Of course. Some Maria calls you after midnight to tell you your daughter's pregnant!"

"AND WILL have the baby!"

"Right. And this makes sense to you? Who is Maria?"

"Ari's mother."

"Oh, obviously. And Ari is the father, is that it? And why isn't our daughter speaking to us directly? There is obviously a big problem here." Louis-Marc sensed a dagger of some sort poised to puncture his balloon. "I thought you were in touch with her. Haven't you been speaking to her? Haven't you seen her? Couldn't you tell something was wrong?"

"To tell the truth, I haven't seen her for awhile. She calls me two-three times a week, but I haven't seen her, well, since June!" Josette felt sea-sick. "And true, she has been sounding strange. But, that's just Arletty, I thought. She told me she was tired because she was working, she didn't say at what, but long hours, and somewhere far out of town. In Hudson, or Pierrefonds. And, you know, I did press *69 to get the number she was calling from, but I couldn't get it. She must be pushing *67 to block it. I'll bet she s right here in Montreal, puking her guts out incognito! Oh, my baby..." This time Josette gave in to her tears, Louis-Marc massaging her shoulders to calm her.

Duncan paced up and down the sitting room, waiting for Maria to come down from Ari's sickroom. He had thrown off his jacket and tie, and rolled up his sleeves, looking even more elegant in the custom-made shirt and the slightly rumpled, well-cut pants. He could hardly contain himself. He wasn't agile enough to do a Louis-Marc style side-kick, but he was more than elated enough to break out in random giggles, whose origin might have just been the little nips of *primo* cognac he had been chain-sipping since the BIG moment a couple of hours earlier.

The information Ari had imparted during his histrionics, represented the prize piece of the MacLeod jigsaw puzzle. A grandson, a true heir, a second chance for the legacy to flourish as it could never flourish under someone like Ari. With a grandson in place, Ari could go on being the perennial teenager, while Duncan supervised the formation of the young one. Just as Aunt Jamie had done with him.

The child, whose embryonic stage Ari had so weepily announced, and whom he was willing to give up so pathetically — the sap — was the BIGGEST event in Duncan's recent memory. No breakthrough in the market, no amount of Maria's new passion for, and excellent delivery of blow-jobs, not even an offer to be dictator of Quebec, with a free hand to recoup its economy, which he knew he could do with one hand tied behind his back — none of that could even come close to the immensity of this glorious grandchild.

Duncan lit another cigar, his second this night and pointedly an indulgence. On the other hand, if you couldn't light a stogie to celebrate the upcoming birth of your family's saviour, what was the use of having one at all? He then refilled his snifter, noticing, just slightly out of focus, that the liquid in the bottle — which had started out full — was now below its midrib.

Finally Maria walked in. She had changed into a simple summer print with matching belt, and her diamond cross around her neck. She was exhausted, devastated, but strangely elated. Yes. Here was a baby that was being given a chance to be born. A grandchild to make up for the others, to make up for her own three miscarriages. God gave her only the one, and that one so sensitive, so fragile. The old concern returned and showed on her face.

"Aah, the worried *Grand*mother," intoned Duncan and raised his glass.

Maria shot him a growl and coughed. "I'm a mother first," she said.

"Of course. Ari. Or should I say, Arette? Aretha?" chuckled Duncan. "How's the poor dear?"

"He's fine now," replied Maria through his sarcasm. "The doctor gave him a shot. Sophia is with him."

"Yes, that is good. Let him sleep it off. He's done his bit. He has given us a grandchild! The rest is up to us. Some cognac?"

Maria refused the libation with a flick of her palm. "Up to *us?* Our grandchild is growing up in the belly of someone who wants to be a stranger. Someone who has pushed my son to a nervous collapse. I fear we may never get a chance to love this grandchild, maybe never even see it."

"Nonsense!" bellowed Duncan downing the rest of his drink. "I'll have this woman tracked down, and arrested if necessary. Then I'll chain her to a bed and force-feed her until she delivers a healthy, beautiful MacLeod. This I promise you, Maria. I'm not letting this baby get away. It is my last hope!"

"Really? Arrest her? Chain her? Take her baby and throw her out? And all that just to make you happy. What a great plan, Duncan!" Maria looked disgusted.

"We'll give her some money," laughed Duncan, holding his cigar towards her. "That was a joke!"

"But not far from the truth," sighed Maria.

"What would you rather I do?" asked Duncan annoyed. "I'm not Cupid. I can't charm her to fall in love with Ari and have a proper family with him. God, woman! Those two will have to sort themselves out by themselves. But, I won't sit by and watch them destroy my grandchild in the process. Oh, no. I want that child, and I'm going to have it!"

"Not by arresting her and chaining her, you won't!" declared Maria defiantly.

✳

The next few days were critical for all the protagonists of this situation, which was dangerously degenerating into a psychodrama. Ari, at the epicenter of mental turmoil, had composed himself sufficiently to avoid a spell at the Allan Institute. His doctors decided that a tranquilized, supervised rest-cure at the family chalet near Ste. Margarite, in the Laurentians, would do the trick.

The mountain air, the ripe August foliage, the cool-clean water of the private lake, and an enormous supply of little pills whose names were reminiscent of Star Trek's Romulans: all this was meant to normalize Ari, and restore him to a functioning human being. "Functional for Ari," Duncan couldn't help remarking when he heard the diagnosis.

In practice, the ancient, formerly volcanic landscape, with its magical forests, its sacred, spring-fed ponds, its animistic Amerindian inhabitants, its adulterated, but very lively and diverse spirituality, lifted Ari to ever higher levels of fantasy, as removed from functionality as possible.

He saw faces in everything. The rocks, the water, the placement of the trees, the clouds, the pointillist chimera created by rainstorm-droplets on the windowpane. He imagined similarities between disparate patterns, and found recurring images that became real entities, with identities and recognizable behaviour. He invented an operatic cast of characters, some heroic, others vile, all of them immensely powerful, all of them merciless. He found himself in a terrain where he was the only mortal, and therefore the sole butt of all malevolence, but also the only benefactor of any largesse.

In order to cope with his new world, Ari forged himself into a wizard, fighting the forces of evil by recruiting the forces of good. He was too spaced-out on pills and wonder to verbalize any of this, so he videotaped it endlessly on a small digital camera. Hours and hours of rock faces, water faces, tree faces, rainstorm faces, cloud faces. Boring in, penetrating the surface for the secrets within, the deep mysteries of life, about none of which he was exactly certain.

Arletty was entering the surprisingly uplifting stage of pregnancy. Now in her fourth month, she found herself more alive than she could remember. An appetite for food, an appetite for sex, an appetite for enjoyment, for walking in fields of wildflowers to the beat of flutes weaving willowy melodies.

However, being as obstinate as ever, she refused to renege on her original resolution to stay put in her little nest in Anita's backyard until the first snow of winter. Instead of willowy walks, she channeled her forces into writing. Among other, not-for-publication works, poems, and one-page stories, she wrote this letter to Ari. Naturally, she had no intention of mailing, or ever letting him see it.

Dear Ari,

Don't expect to see this letter ever, but truth is I still dream about you. Often. This is unbearably troublesome, even though these dreams are not as obsessive as the ones I used to have. The dreams I'm having now are beautiful. I see you like you were on Mykonos. Great clothes and no pennyloafers. Patent leather that your mother bought you in Milan. So smooth, I wanted to lick them. This is most disturbing to me. It is intrusive. I wish you'd stop coming into my dreams, however attractive your shoes are. You see, my dear, for me the only reality is the Now. This very moment. The past and the future are both illusions. The past becomes mythic and therefore unreliable, as soon as it has passed. The future is the unknown. No amount of planning or precautions can possibly ensure the future. All that is really left to us is the present. This very moment. This is the sum total of all existence. This is the inescapable truth. And this very moment is very much mine, entirely mine, unsharable, sacrosanct, forbidden-to-enter. That's the truth. On the other hand, I wish that we could have been two people with nothing more than the weather to discuss, with nothing more than sex to share. Then maybe I could see you once in a while, and then maybe, you'd quit invading my mind.

With Sophia and an army of guards, nurses, and staff in place, Maria felt she could absent herself for a few hours. So she took the limousine ride down from the Laurentians to the corner table at *La Crevetterie,* for her long overdue summit meeting with Josette. The two prospective grandmothers, each also a concerned mother, got emotional on first contact and shared salty tears, drenching their *Pernods* with maternal woe, while touching each other a lot.

The tears soon turned to laughter — after the third *Pernod* — and soon after that, the Plan was born: the obvious, and seemingly only solution to their dilemma. Josette called a lawyer friend on her cellular, and got confirmation that their deductions were correct. The Plan was workable, and legally sound. Self-satisfied, almost giddy with impending success, each repaired to her own husband to coax him into it.

Chapter 5

End of summer. In Montreal.

It took three weeks to pave the way for the big Meeting. The bringing together of opposing political factions is a thankless, near-impossible task, but Josette and Maria were highly-motivated arbitrators.

The campaign started directly after the mothers' boozy, conspiratorial meeting on the sidewalk of Bernard Street. Josette came home, as if straight from work, a bit late, a bit grouchy, hungry as always for Louis-Marc's cooking.

Inwardly moaning that he had allowed the *Gorgonzola* sauce to overly thicken and compromise the *gnocchi* into a gummy, unappetizing proposition, he greeted her with effusive kisses. He was distracted, it was true. A grandchild. A brand new *Québecois!* What good fortune. Born free in a freed country. There would be nothing to stop him from his loftiest goals. Nevertheless, the sauce was too thick and Louis-Marc's only recourse was to go on the offensive.

"Where is she? Why won't she come to us? Pregnant four months already, and I haven't laid eyes on her. Why is she punishing us? What have we done to her except to love her, and fret for her, and want the very best for her."

"I spoke to her today. She called," said Josette matter-of-factly, while pushing the plate of disagreeable *gnocchi* away. "She didn't seem surprised I knew about the baby. Well anyway, it's been in all the papers, right? She assured me she was alright, and warned me not to worry about her. And then she hung up."

"Just like that!" Louis-Marc discreetly took Josette's plate to the kitchen, and returned with his prepared platter of cheese and fruit.

"Pregnancy is a difficult time," mused Josette. "Well, it's a strange time. For someone like Arletty, it's probably a fascination and a nightmare rolled into one. If she doesn't want to see us just now, I'm happy to leave her alone."

"Well, I for one, am not!" exclaimed Louis-Marc. "I want her back with us. So we can... well, so she can get used to living here again. She'll need us when the baby is born. Won't she? And I don't care if she objects. I am her father, and I have a right to demand it. That's it and that's that. She must return to the *Plateau*. Even today!"

"What are you? Little Caesar? Listen to you! If she even got wind of what you were saying, if she even suspected that you were thinking this way, she'd never speak to you again." Josette grunted. "God, for a smart guy, you can be awfully thick sometime." She stared him down, while nibbling on an ideally matured, raw-milk *Saint-Marcellin* from Chaput's store on Bernard. It was one of her all-time favourite cheeses, one for which, to please her, Louis-Marc had made one of his rare sorties out of the *Plateau* and into Outremont.

"You talk as if all this is my fault," complained Louis-Marc, chastened.

Josette settled back with her wine, secure that she was within striking range of her goal. "Not all. Maybe not exactly the reason for this awful situation, but, yes, obviously you are at fault. From the beginning. You never liked that she wasn't born a boy. That she wasn't interested in your politics. That she wanted to be an actress —she is a child, she is ENTITLED to her fantasies — that... that she doesn't fall to the ground every time you walk into a room, and curl up by your feet to hear what you have to say. Why should she? Did we ever give a damn what our parents wanted from us? God, if it was up to my mother —may she rest in peace— I'd be living in Rosemont with a drunk plumber for a husband, and six children that hated me, not to mention spending all my Sundays in church, so that when I finally died for real, they'd let me into heaven, and I could have some fun for a change. You, mister, YOU personally drove Arletty out of this house, by being brutally insensitive to any of her wishes, her growing pains, her intelligence. You think you're so superior to her because you have all those degrees, and she refuses to even go to college. The very reason she refuses is you. Everything she's ever done, or not done, is because of you. And You want to know something? I'm really glad! Because by trying to oppose you and refute your approval, and to spite you, she has turned out pretty damn good. Pretty damn fantastic!"

Louis-Marc slunk back in his chair, crestfallen. She had spared him in the past. All of this was news to him. "I have no idea how to deal with children. Until I met you it never had even occurred to me that I might one day have one of my own. The whole prospect terrifies me. I'm not the 'family' type. Give me my books, a keyboard and a theory to work on, and I'm happy. It's all I need. And you changed all that for me. And now I find out that I've done nothing right. Not with Arletty, and probably not with you. I'm sorry... I'm very sorry..."

Josette chewed on a chunk of aromatic *chevre* with a crust of airy *baguette*. She shook her head, and then she smiled cheerfully. "Oh, baby," she cooed, "you're so cute when you're humble. But it doesn't really suit you, even though it makes me love you more." She had an empowering sip of the wine, and took the plunge: "And furthermore, I'm certain that your heart as always is in the right place. With her best interests. Which means that you won't give me any headaches about..." she hesitated. It was imperative that she got his cooperation.

"What?" asked Louis-Marc, alert and on the defensive.

"Well, it turns out that the only way we can have a legal stand, a strong legal position, is if all four parents are somewhat... in accord."

"What?"

"Maria and I are okay. You and I, obviously. Maria and Duncan, I hope so. You and Maria, if you only met her, you'd love her. What it leaves is... for you to make friends with—"

"That BLOODY cannibal, that FEDERALIST scum MacLeod!? We have been documenting his economic crimes against *Québec*. He is a monster! Never! Not even after I'm DEAD!"

Duncan expressed a fairly similar reaction when Maria confronted him over his lightly fried Dover sole with far-too-sour sauce — Maria's focus on cooking had been about as pronounced as Louis-Marc's — served cozily in the evening freshness of the solarium. "Meet that crazy, two-bit totalitarian? You're out of your mind. I've read his so-called essays in *Le Devoir*. The guy is rabid, and should be put out of his misery."

"What he is, is not the point. The *baby* is the point. We consulted a lawyer. If all four of us unite, it gives us power. Otherwise—"

"Oh, screw you and your otherwise-lawyer," fumed Duncan. He made an acid face as he tasted the sole. "I'm taking charge of this, I told you. I've already lined up the people I'll need."

"Well, you'll fail. Josette and her husband will oppose you, and they'll win because the courts will sympathize with them."

"They won't be able to oppose me if they don't know what I intend to do. By the time they find out, it'll be over."

Maria took a deep breath. "They already know. I told Josette."

"You did WHAT?!?" Duncan slammed his hand on the table menacingly. All the plates jumped up an inch, and noisily resettled.

Maria faced him unflinchingly. "As it happens, I oppose you, too. I will not stand by and watch you diminish Arletty into another Cornelia."

"You FUCK! You'd go against my wishes? You'd slap me in the face with my family history? You think you can thwart me? You stupid woman. You stupid—" he let the unsaid "bitch" drop.

Maria got up from her chair. She deliberately picked up her full plate and dropped it on the floor, ensuring that it broke neatly instead of flying all over the room. She spoke icily, seriously, forcefully, as if the future of her family depended on what she was saying:

"I wish you'd be more polite when you speak to me. Your great grandfather was a common thief in Scotland. Your father told me that. Well, my family go back to the eleventh century. I come from a long line of princes and lawgivers."

Duncan curbed her flow with a derisive snicker. Maria was suddenly furious.

"Stop that. Stop it immediately. You've dismissed my intelligence long enough, Sir. I really am not just some dummy you married on impulse while on holiday. If you wanted a souvenir of Constantinople you should've gone to the bazaar and bought a carpet. I've kept myself at your service only because of my breeding. Don't you for one moment delude yourself that I'm blind. I see everything, I know everything. I've kept my place and I've stayed out of your way, and I've kept your house, only because that is my duty. Also because once I left my home to come with you, I had no home to return to.

"The only thing about our marriage that I do not regret, that gives meaning to my life, is Ari. I've turned him into a mama's boy, as you call it, but what choice did I have? There was no one else to take care of him, was there? You? You hated him from the start. Too dark. Not blond. Too small. Not tall. Too shy. Not a killer. Not a MacLeod! You used to torture him. He was three years old, for God's sake. You screamed at him and would have hit him, because he lost the quarter you gave him to buy ice cream. He was a baby! Why couldn't you get the ice cream for him? Or let me? Well, this time, you *will*. You *will* meet with Louis-Marc. And you *will* be polite to him! And you *will* help me to save Ari, by saving his child!"

"You've used Ari to do battle with me ever since he was born. There was never anything I could do for him, because you always did it first. And this time, especially this time, I'll do nothing of the sort," sulked Duncan, as he sat back down to give the acidic sole another stab. "Over my dead body!"

From this rocky first round, to the day of the meeting an agonizing twenty one days later, the two couples were immersed in unceasing conjugal bickering, soul-searching, and quite often shades of all-out war, until the husbands capitulated.

Doing battle with Duncan was such an overwhelming task, Maria found little time to tend to Ari. Fortunately for her, he had soon tired of the Laurentians and his search for wizardly faces, and had come back to Redpath Crescent, still demonstrably disturbed, but calmer and far more manageable. He continued to act dopey and sedated, but it was a front. He had quit taking his medication, but pretended that he hadn't so that they'd leave him alone. He had decided to find his cure in poetry. A self-prescribed regimen of seeking the eternal truths in the words of the great bards.

He gave his unused pills to Ben, who was able to sell them for extra money. This was the first time that Ben had showed any undue interest in money, beyond the few survival bucks he earned by selling joints. Ben now wanted the funds so that he could buy presents for Anita. Poor sap. So in love.

Ari had removed himself as far as possible from all notions of love. He felt more comfortable with hate, with states of lost grace, with sins, and with punishments. He studied Milton's *Paradise Lost, Books I and II,* and he tried his hand at versifying, devoting minute care to punctuation, and usage of the upper case, as well as internal rhymes, altering meters, and naturally, blank verse:

> *Demons, DESPERATE Demons; pecking my*
> *Fallen flesh — EONS, Centuries, MILLENNIA —*
> *Hungry chunks of my Genitalia; my*
> *Angry rendition; my forgotten fury; my recognition,*
> *My delusions, my affections, my pubescent happiness;*
> *My hate, my loveless attachment; my boredom;*
> *My Freedom; all is blood, all is gore,*
> *All is Futile.*

Chapter 6

Film Festival time. In Montreal.

In Montreal, summer is open season for huge indoor-outdoor festivals. One after another — Formula One, Jazz, Comedy, French-language song, Tennis, and all manner of ethnicity are celebrated enthusiastically, Streets are closed off, creating traffic havoc and delighting the tourists. The whole shebang culminates in an orgy of cinema with the Film Festival. Not quite Cannes or even Toronto, but a noisy, crowded, self-hyping movie-party that spans the bridge between August and Autumn, one last fling for the populace to dress sexy and strut their stuff.

They Came From The North had been included in the official competition, after much lobbying by Fred Benoit. The critics had given it no chance for any laurels whatsoever, but the Festival had accorded it a splashy *Place des Arts* gala screening, stacked with supporters, friends, crew members, and their families — an occasion which was guaranteed to be uplifting, complete with home-team lionizations of Ari, Ben, and most decidedly, Arletty.

Pouting and severely sequestered, both Ari and Arletty resisted the respective coaxings of Ben and Anita, and refused to attend. This left Ben and Anita no alternative but to go and represent them. At the appointed hour, Ben appeared in a used tuxedo jacket, t-shirt, worn jeans, and his overused, discoloured sneakers; and on his arm Anita, in a most splendid, sapphire-coloured, silk saree, with matching jewelry and forehead gemstone, waltzed up the red-carpeted staircase of the sweeping, *Salle Wilfrid Pelletier* lobby, en route to their seats in the opera-sized auditorium.

At exactly the same moment, Louis-Marc got out of his costly taxi at One Redpath Crescent. He was royally annoyed — fighting mad actually, having ultimately conceded to Josette that he would meet Duncan, promising NOTHING, as nothing good could possibly come from such a meeting — but, in Westmount, not in the *Plateau*. He'd be too horrified that someone might witness Villain MacLeod entering Patriot Daoust's home, and how could he ever explain that?

The clincher for Louis-Marc was his discovery that Duncan liked to gamble. Silly baccarat, instead of noble poker, but cards were cards and Louis-Marc dug out several books to read up on the game, which had obviously been designed for the brainless rich. It was a cinch if one had mastered poker, and he was bound to win because he had arrived fully-motivated to humiliate this infamous anti-*Québecois*. Luckily, he was also able to come equipped.

He had already been predisposed to be disgusted by the conspicuous privilege of the bastard's house. He took a sneering look at the actual building. What silliness. How many turrets did one house need, anyway? How could anyone feel at home in a monstrosity like this? What bad taste! Hah. This guy would be easy pickings. Louis-Marc took a deep breath and rang the bell, which tolled and echoed throughout the building, as if out of some funny horror movie, like *Young Frankenstein*.

His smirk widened when Betty, the next best thing to Cloris Leachman, opened for him, and stood aside unsmiling to let him pass. He couldn't help but allow himself a couple of seconds to be dazzled by the sunset colours that filtered in like rainbows through the stained glass onto the back wall and the dome. Then he resumed his original stance, getting angrier and angrier with each softly-carpeted stair, with every sleek step across mirror-like glossy corridors. By the time Betty knocked on Duncan's office door and opened it without waiting for a reply, Louis-Marc was angry enough to punch Duncan on contact.

Duncan sprang out of his chair when he heard the door opening. He walked to Louis-Marc with a major smile on his lips. Maria had insisted on *politesse,* but had she figured on murderously jovial? He even tried to place a chummy hand on Louis-Marc's shoulder but withdrew it when his guest shrugged it away wincing. Duncan extended his hand to shake.

"Come in, come in, Monsieur Daoust. Please."

Louis-Marc ignored the offered handshake and walked brusquely to stand dead centre in the room. His eye caught the panoramic view of Montreal from Duncan's generous windows. He hardened

his gaze, and turned to face his host head-on. "I did not come here
to be friends with you. That is not even to be imagined," he said
with equal measures of stiffness and exaggerated pity.

Duncan laughed merrily, and slapped his forehead. "That's
where I saw you! Yes. I never forget a face and yours was instantly
familiar. God. I must have been fourteen. We met, believe it or not,
when we were fourteen. *Jeez,* that's amazing! Don't you remember?"

Louis-Marc, caught unawares, looked blank.

Duncan continued jovially. "You were delivering an order of my
father's from your grandfather's store! I opened the door. Why I was
the one to open the door, beats me, but there I was, and there you
were, with a parcel, salmon and beluga, I believe, and a few slices
of your grandpa's home-smoked country ham for Aunt Jamie. It was
only a two second transaction, but I remember you clearly. I believe
we smiled at each other."

Louis-Marc peered at Duncan with suspicion. "I never worked, I
mean, except very briefly... and I'd have remembered—"

"Look. There's no shame in working. I started going to the office
before my teens. And it was well-known that all the Daoust grand-
kids had to work in the store in the summers." Duncan smiled
benignly, thankful for the gossip he had been able to dig up about
the Daousts. He had already dazed his opponent, who was busily
searching his memories to remember a delivery that he had never
in fact made.

"And your family home," continued Duncan, "not far from here.
A handsome, solid building, if I'm not mistaken. We could've easily
met in the streets, not that I was given leave to walk the streets
when I was a kid. My Aunt Jamie was one strict task-master, like
those boot-camp sergeants in the comic strips," concluded Duncan
with a guffaw.

Louis-Marc looked down at Duncan, and raised his eyebrows.
He began to see through the tactic. He approached the nearest chair
and purposefully sat down on it. "We're longer helpless out on the
Plateau, you know," he said in measured tones. "You're not the only
ones who can afford lawyers."

Duncan manoeuvered his lanky frame behind the desk and into
his power seat. Louis-Marc had sat precisely where Duncan would
have wanted him: in the light, while he was in partial shadow. "My
dear man," he objected, as he sat.

"I'm not your dear man."

"Fine. My un-dear man," Duncan chuckled. "Obviously, we can all afford lawyers. They're a dime a dozen. The point of this meeting—"

"The POINT of this meeting," interrupted Louis-Marc, "is that it has no point. It's pointless. I'm only here because my dear wife wished me to come, and I love her too much to refuse her anything. Otherwise, it's a done deal. Arletty, my daughter, is going to have a baby. She wants to have it out of wedlock, away from your son. This means that your son, despite his brief role in the pregnancy, has dubious rights over this baby. As for you, you have no rights. None. Zero. So, can I go now?" Louis-Marc flashed a victory smile, but made no move to get up.

"That is one way to look at it, and I'm glad you see it that way, because it means we'll have an all-out, gang-bang battle over this kid, and nothing excites me better than a good battle. Now, listen to me, if you don't mind, so that you'll have no unpleasant surprises later," said Duncan, without altering the grin he had sported throughout Louis-Marc's attack.

"Speak, Sir. Me, I'll admire your extraordinary view of my favourite city. One of the best views of the best city on earth." Louis-Marc turned three-quarters towards the window.

Duncan spoke to his guest's remaining quarter: "Your daughter is exhibiting erratic behaviour. She could, COULD I say, be proven to be endangering the life of her baby, and therefore to be an unfit mother. In which case, my son, as the biological father, has the right to intervene and fight her, as well as you, for custody."

Louis-Marc, without turning around: "Well, he would lose. He is a casual one-night stand. He has no rights."

Duncan toughened his voice. "Except that we are willing to spend five, ten, fifteen million to prove that he does. And the mother's side?"

Louis-Marc grudgingly swiveled himself away from the view. He spoke as if to one of his thicker students: "The mother's side is *Québec,* monsieur. *Québec* fulfills all the conditions necessary to obtain international ratification as a sovereign state. And therefore, *la decision democratique du peuple du Québec d'acceder à la souveraineté constituerait le fondement legitime d'une reconnaissance international.*"

"I'm sorry," said Duncan gingerly, "you've lost me."

"You should open your ears and listen to what the people are saying. That was the finding of *La Commission Belanger-Campeau* on the feasibility of a liberated *Québec*," said Louis-Marc dismissively. "And my point is, that the law is on our side."

Duncan raised bittersweet eyebrows. *"Monsieur* Louis-Marc, I hear you are a highly educated man, and I bow to your superior knowledge. But, kindly do not be naive. I don't have any college degrees, and the law is not conclusively on my side, but, you see, I have... money."

"I'll fight you to my dying day. To my last penny," promised Louis-Marc icily.

Duncan nodded appreciatively. "That's the spirit, Sir. It has been proven repeatedly that all-out war always results in benefits for the human race. Well, for those who survive the war, that is."

Louis-Marc shrugged. "You are being boring. There's no war here. Just a miserable, insulated, rich guy, who wants something he can never have: a happy family. As for the actual war raging around us, I for one, will not rest until a sovereign *Québec* can proudly kick your *maudit-Anglais* behind, and take back everything you stole from us. This is my dream. A dream shared by all combatants of all histories. I want victory in my lifetime, and fuck the world, if I won't have it!"

"I wish you luck," responded Duncan offhandedly. "Meanwhile, my grandson, if lucky enough to be born, will become the plaything of a stubborn, irrational girl, who thinks she can support herself and him by cleaning houses, and end up ruining his life before it can begin. I cannot sit by and let that happen. And it appears that I don't have to. The best lawyers in the Province assure me that if all four of us band together, and we have Ari's endorsement, not to mention my deep pockets, then we have the means to make her cooperate. Legally. In court, if necessary. And at the end of it all, you and your wife will have equal rights as us to care for the child. Fifty-fifty profits, but you won't have to lay out a penny. I'd call that a good deal."

Louis-Marc resumed his professorial tone: "When the enemy begins to negotiate, he has already lost."

"Who said that? Cardinal Richelieu?"

"No. Me. And the answer is no. I'd never take my daughter to court. What an outrage! And especially not, when it involves your deep pockets. No!"

Duncan retrieved a set of papers and pushed them over to Louis-Marc. "These are the papers. Please read them through. I'm sure you'll find the arrangement generous to a fault. Get smart. You're acting like a petulant child."

"Yes, I suppose I am. While you are acting like a perfectly toilet-trained adult."

"*Touché,*" said Duncan insincerely. "And the matter need never go anywhere near a court. These papers are our leverage. First however, we'll try love, presents, inducements, whatever it takes."

"You don't have what it takes to win over my daughter, Sir. My daughter is even tougher to negotiate with than me. You're wasting everyone's time."

"Time means nothing to me," spat out Duncan. "Nothing means anything, except this grandson. Your refusal means nothing. I'll go at this all on my own if I have to. Do you understand?"

"What's not to understand? It's exactly the same as I feel. Except that I don't need you nearly as much as you need me. I'm sure your lawyers have apprised you of this," said Louis-Marc, particularly pleased with his usage of the word *apprised.*

Duncan weighed the situation. He felt he was losing. He needed to change his tack. He opted for the apologetic-dilatory technique. "You are obviously unhappy to be at my house. We should've met on neutral ground. However, please take these papers with you, and who knows, you might reconsider and decide to peruse them." He pushed the papers closer to his guest.

Louis-Marc grabbed the papers carelessly, and shoved them into the pocket of his sport coat. "I'm not at all unhappy to be here," he said. "I'm too busy to get away from my desk much. I enjoy an outing."

Duncan eyed him suspiciously. "Well... you are welcome anytime."

"I don't think so," replied Louis-Marc, deflating his opponent yet again. Now this is where I want him, he thought. Aloud he said: "But now that I'm already here, maybe we can get better acquainted. I thought that maybe we should play cards, or something. How do you say? Put our 'dicks' on the table and compete? I brought money." Louis-Marc whipped out an envelope from his inside pocket. He neatly slid a cheque out of it, and laid it on the desk. "It's from my trust fund. Twenty grand. I get one every two weeks. I thought it'd be fun to double it here, today. Dig into those deep pockets of yours, so to speak."

Duncan laughed out loud. "Or, make them even deeper," he

said. "I only play baccarat, and only for real stakes. At least... a hundred dollar minimum."

Louis-Marc laughed in return. "A hundred? I don't have all day. Just a short game. Thousand-dollar minimum, and we only play for twenty thousand each. If I double my money I leave, if I lose my twenty I leave. Agreed?"

"Anything you say," agreed Duncan accommodatingly.

Louis-Marc uncapped his fountain pen to endorse the cheque. Duncan motioned him to stop. "You don't have to sign it yet, monsieur. Wait till I've won it," he said convivially, scoring a point and sending little shivers down Louis-Marc's back.

The shivers were redoubled, registering distinct alarms in the challenger's mind, when Duncan proceeded to transform his office into a gambling den by pressing two buttons. The first button caused heavy curtains to draw speedily across the windows cutting off all outside light while simultaneously re-adjusting the room lights to a soft glow, with a strong beam on the centre of the desk. The second button opened a trap-door on the side of the desk, out of which rose a tray with two unopened decks of cards, a dealing shoe, and a rack of antique chips, at one time the property of the *Société des Bains Casino* in Monte Carlo.

"I use my office for head-to-head baccarat whenever I get the chance," smiled Duncan in explanation.

Louis-Marc drew his chair closer to the desk, trying desperately to master the new conditions, no longer so sure of himself. Duncan lifted the cheque with a feathery touch and placed it in the slot of the chips' rack. He gave Louis-Marc twenty chips before opening his desk drawer and withdrawing a stack of thousand-dollar bills. He carefully counted twenty and replaced the rest in the drawer. He put his cash into the slot beside the cheque and counted twenty chips for himself.

"We'll deal *chemin-de-fer* style, if you like," he said. "You keep dealing as long as you keep winning." He broke the seal of one deck, flipping the other to Louis-Marc so that he could do the same.

Duncan seized both decks and shuffled them nimbly together several times. He offered Louis-Marc a cut, marked off the top half of the cards, and fitted them into the shoe. "We play with half of the combined two decks. To avoid counters. We used to play with only one deck, and down to the last card, but we once caught someone counting the cards. Apparently black-jack isn't the only game where one can be too clever."

Louis-Marc slapped a pure-ivory chip on the desk's glassy surface. "You deal first," he said tersely.

"We should spin for the deal," countered Duncan. "It's an advantage to deal, the other player gets to draw first." He pointed to a tiny arrow free-floating on a swivel on top of the dealing shoe.

Louis-Marc was flustered by his second blunder and made things worse by trying to save face. "You deal," he insisted. "I'll win the first hand, and you'll never deal again."

Brave words, but it was he who would never get to deal. Duncan won the opening hand solely because Louis-Marc had to draw first, and ruined what would have been the winning hand had he not drawn a card. After this lucky break, Duncan won the next nine hands in a row at least twice because the slowly unhinging Louis-Marc drew on borderline fives that would've been winners had they been left alone.

"You're having terrible luck, Monsieur Daoust," said Duncan solicitously, but with no trace of a smile or a smirk. "Maybe we should stop and continue on another day."

Louis-Marc, now intensely challenged, made his third and fatal error. "No bad luck lasts forever. This next one is mine," he said with bravado, and slapped down all of his remaining ten chips.

"A ten-thousand dollar hand. Are you sure?"

"I put my money down, didn't I? Deal the cards."

Louis-Marc's heart beat wildly. Duncan had dealt him an eight. A hand with which to recoup his losses and get the hell out of this game. He flipped his cards over triumphantly. His glee was short-lived. Duncan opened his cards to reveal a nine. Louis-Marc groaned and uttered a *Québecois* obscenity.

"Ouch," sympathized Duncan. "Well, I guess it means no caviar for you for the next couple of weeks, but we can always re-meet for your revenge." He was unable to control a smirk at this juncture.

"Fuck you," muttered Louis-Marc, snatching his cheque from its slot, signing it on the back, and flinging it at Duncan, all in one fluid motion.

"I'm sorry," replied Duncan stiffly, "I thought we were having a friendly game."

"Friendly? With you? Rather impossible, don't you think?" hissed Louis-Marc in a venomous tone. His chair made scratching sounds as he pushed it back and unsteadily got to his feet.

Duncan took the cheque in hand, and extended it to him. "Please take this back. We can settle after the return match."

Louis-Marc, now master of his posture once again, even if minus twenty big ones, a nest egg that normally paid for an entire year's worth of necessities, pulled the legal papers out of his pocket. "Shove it right up your Anglo ass, you pig! I wouldn't touch that money, if it was the last money on earth. As for your papers? Those too! Right up your ass."

He flipped the papers violently at Duncan and walked out of the dreaded man's office, and then his house, into the sweet August air of early evening. He was in the darkest mood he had been in since the early 1980s, when the Federalist Liberals had, for a God-awful spell, dislodged the Separatist *Parti Québecois* from the Provincial leadership.

Chapter 7

The next morning. On Redpath Crescent.

Josette couldn't help smiling, even though she was on a messy, highly distressing mission. She was cavalierly speeding her way to Redpath Crescent, with the roof of the *Beemer* down, a soft, late-summer breeze through her hair, the Gallic rock-&-roll of *Beau Domage* blaring a bit too loudly from the radio. She was feeling distressed, yes, but also oh-so-proud. Arletty's two minute performance in the movie had gotten glowing reviews in the morning papers.

All of them. "Leaps off the screen," "a *Québecoise* star is born," "grippingly talented," in two languages, even in the stringent *Le Devoir* — which hated the movie otherwise. In the populist *La Presse* — which didn't take it seriously, but recommended it anyway. And most enthusiastically in the Anglo-partisan *Gazette,* where an English language movie that is set in Montreal and made by locals is such a rare occurrence, the rave notice almost wrote itself.

This was extremely good. A little insurance policy, in case the Plan didn't work. The unstinting accolades would surely please Arletty, maybe even encourage her to crawl out of her shell and let Josette shower her with some motherly care. Going through her first pregnancy on her own, living in a tent in N.D.G. God help us! Well, at least she wasn't working as a maid in Hudson.

Thank God, Maria had gotten the information about her whereabouts. And thank God again, Maria had found out about the baccarat game so quickly. Thank God, Duncan was such a braggart, he had told Maria every detail of his stupid victory. It's not always best to be right, Duncan! Thank God, Josette had no fear of confrontation. If anything, she was aroused by the prospect of it.

As per their arrangement, Maria met her at the corner and let her in through the backyard, along a path beyond the surveillance system's reach. Once inside, they quietly walked to Duncan's office. The idea was to barge in on him, thus never give him a chance to refuse her entrance. What the mothers neglected to take into account was that Duncan was armed.

He reached for his gun — a functional Magnum-44 — when his door-handle was turning, an action that automatically engaged a discreet alarm, while releasing the drawer containing the gun. The idea was to give Duncan time to train a gun on the door before an intruder actually barged in. And so, by the time Josette appeared in the doorway, the Magnum was focused at her chest, both of Duncan's hands hoisting it at arms' length, à la Dirty Harry.

"STOP!" he yelled. "Or, I'll shoot!"

Josette stopped in her tracks, while Maria, just to the side of the door, gasped. Josette stared beyond the nose of the gun, into Duncan's angry face. "If you shoot, you'll kill me, which means I'll never get my husband's cheque out of you, which would then make me really, REALLY mad!" she said patiently, as she took a bold step into the room.

"Oh, I see. You are the redoubtable Josette," said Duncan, holding the gun steady and poised. He simultaneously touched a foot pedal which shut the door behind her with a smart click, like the shutter of a Leica.

"Whatever you said, yes, I am she," replied Josette, steadily walking into the room towards Duncan's desk, aware of the gun, never releasing her hold on his gaze, staring right into his pupils, commanding his attention. Unexpectedly, in a lightening fast move she had picked up in martial-arts class, she struck Duncan's wrist with her left fist and grabbed the gun with her right hand.

She let it dangle by her fingertip, eyeballing it distastefully. Duncan stared at her in shock. Josette tossed the gun into a corner of the room, where it landed with a thud, like deadweight. "Disgusting appliances... Aren't you a bit too old to be playing with fire?" she asked winking. She daintily seated herself on the Queen Anne chair to Duncan's left, the phantasmagoric view of Montreal behind her.

Duncan settled into his chair and pushed it away from the desk, placing himself completely in shadow. "You be thankful I didn't shoot you the moment you barged in. I have the right, you know."

"Yes, you think you have all the rights. *Le cheque!*" demanded

Josette, with hand extended.

"That cheque is mine. I won it fair and square."

"The fuck you did!" hissed Josette, springing to her feet, and leaning on the desk menacingly. An intoxicating smell of female sweat mixed with some expensive French perfume emanated from her agitated cleavage and penetrated Duncan's nostrils, sending shivers of arousal down his spine. He hadn't had sex for weeks, what with Cornelia, Ari, the matter of his grandson, and Maria's hostility. He lacked even the gumption to look up any of his old regulars.

Duncan pulled away from her, on the pretext of searching for the cheque. He located it easily, as it was sitting at the very top of his 'out' tray. He extended it to her. She snapped it from his grasp, took a quick look, and stashed it in her shoulder bag.

"I was intending to return it to him. I wasn't going to cash it."

"Well, you were very stupid to have won it from him in the first place. You have caused irreparable damage to the Plan," admonished Josette, sitting back down on her chair.

"You mean I should have lost to him on purpose? You're mad!" Duncan laughed. "He's a player. He would've been outraged if I let him win unfairly."

"So, what's the story, mister big-shot? All this money, all this house, and you can't even offer a lady a drink?"

Duncan sprang to his feet in mock contriteness. "I'm dreadfully sorry," he said, as he touched a button on the wall. Magically the bookcase parted to reveal a fully equipped bar. "What'll you have?"

Josette spotted the *Napoleon* shining brightest in a constellation of bottles, each one filled with a rare potion. "A finger of the cognac, if you please," she smiled. Duncan poured her cognac, noticeably more than a finger, into a sheer snifter. He fixed a single-malt on ice for himself.

"My husband is a winner. In his own mind, anyway. If you had made sure he won, he'd have walked out of here feeling your equal, and signed the papers. For only twenty grand we'd have won our position — to help Arletty and the baby. To make things right. We need all FOUR signatures, or we cannot proceed. Do you see now?"

Duncan waltzed past her and deposited her drink on a coaster on the desk. He took a stiff gulp of his own. "I suppose I should be sorry," he said ungraciously.

Josette sipped her cognac. She waited a moment for its kindness to spread through her head. "Not as sorry as you will be, my friend. Trust me. The price of his signature is sky-high now, and you won't like it a bit. Not a bit." She sipped again.

"Price?"

Josette's eye caught a bronze baby bootie. "This is fun. Is it yours?"

Duncan offhandedly: "It's my son's. His umbilical cord is sealed inside. One of my wife's many barbarisms."

Josette cut him off: "Don't you mock Maria. She is a saint. And you are the luckiest man on earth that she is your wife, and not me!"

Duncan polished off his scotch. "I'll drink to that!" Then he got up to fix himself another. On the return he brought the bottle of cognac to top up Josette's glass. While pouring, his hand brushed against her bare arm. Instead of pulling it away, Duncan let it rest there. Josette giggled, and slapped his hand off, as if he was a little boy who was reaching for the cookies just before dinner.

"But, no problem, right?" she laughed at him. "You'd never marry someone like me. You'd go slumming in the East End to fuck someone like me. But marriage? No way. Am I right?"

Duncan, blushing, retreated to his shadows, behind his desk. "First your karate chop, and now your candor. You've entirely disarmed me, madame."

"C'est quoi, 'candor'?"

"C'est la franchise', la sincérité'," informed Duncan in his fluent, but heavily accented French.

"Ah, yes," smirked Josette. "I am famous for my candor... So let me ask you, do you really give a good-goddamn for this kid? This half-breed, future grandchild? Or, is it all only a game for you?"

"Frankly and sincerely. From the bottom of my heart. Absolutely and certainly. Yes, I give a great, big good-goddamn for this grandchild."

"Why? It's really like, almost an accident. Okay, it's your first, but Ari and Arletty are so. out of sorts with each other, that the baby is far removed from you. Ari is very young. Eventually he'll grow out of his obsession with my daughter, he'll marry, he'll give you grandchildren right in your house."

"Or, he won't," sighed Duncan. "For me, it's a miracle that an actual child of my bloodline is going to be born for this house. We've had several false alarms. There were Maria's miscarriages after Ari, three of them..."

"Oh, the sweet lady. She never mentioned them."

"It's not her favourite subject. But save your sympathy, because she has found it in her heart to pay for five of Ari's indiscretions. For Ari, she'll do anything. Five of my grandchildren, at the cost of two thousand each, ended up in some abortionist's trash can." Duncan shuddered.

"*S'il-vous-plait! Je suis Catholique!*"

"I'm not, but it wounds me deeply. I have nightmares. I see myself playing with all five of them in the garden. And then a killer appears out of nowhere and hacks them to pieces. I want a grand-child!"

"Well, there is a price," said Josette flatly.

"How much?"

"Not how much, it's more like what. After I found out what happened here yesterday, I spoke to Louis-Marc. You might say he wasn't in the best of moods. But me, I can always get him to smile. And to talk things through. So, we talked and talked, and finally he named his terms. He said, he'd go along with us and sign those papers, but only after you pass a test on *Québec,* in French, answering questions of his choosing. The testing to be conducted by telephone."

Duncan cringed. "That's the silliest thing I ever heard."

"It gets sillier," laughed Josette. "He intends to drill you worse than the nuns did him. You'll have to memorize a whole lot of history, including the parts of the history of France that relate to Canada. You'll have to read many, far too many, of our literary heroes. Emile Nelligan, Honoré Beaugrand, Phillipe-Aubert de Gaspé, Felix-Antoine Savard, Louis Frechette, Germaine Guevremont, who knows, all of them. Poor you! Plus all the political writers, especially the Separatists. He'll test you on *Québec* geography, all those lovely saints we named towns after. Oh, you won't have fun!"

Duncan downed his drink. "He's crazy."

"All you had to do was to let him win. Or, to come out of here even-Stephen. All you had to do really, was to say you win, when he showed you his eight, and throw your nine away. You could have then refused to continue, and let him go home with some dignity. And his twenty thousand dollars. That cheque represents three-quarters of his annual income. You had no right to take it from him, you macho man, you!"

Duncan peered at her out of weary eyes. He was cornered.

Either he could wage bloody war on his own, against an enemy who possessed knowledge of his every move from his own wife. Or, concede the point, align himself with the women, and try to win over that aggressive little prick, Louis-Marc. Talk about a rock and a hard place. "All right," he said unhappily. "I'll do it. I'll surrender to Louis-Marc."

"Really?"

"Yes."

"You're far more macho than I imagined," said Josette approvingly.

"Actually, it's all a front. In reality, I'm scared senseless. I'm beside myself with fear and apprehension. I dread the fact that all the work, all the great expectations, all the glory, has come down to this. A useless compromise, an ignominious capitulation, an infamous and reprehensible surrender. Suddenly, everything I've ever believed in and lived by must go down the drain of subterfuge and appeasement, so that I can have the ghost of a chance of ever seeing my grandson, of watching him grow, caring for him, and protecting him, and giving him the advantages he'll need to survive. This little game that I need to play with your husband makes my whole life worthless, Madame Josette. But, I'll do it, so that I don't die a lonely death. I've already discounted my son. He'll never amount to anything I can appreciate. With this grandson, the hope begins all over again. The candle flickers. My own life is a waste. At this time, a publicly-documented waste — in the papers with yet another scandal every other week. But, my legacy must continue..." Duncan closed his eyes, as if in prayer.

Josette applauded him. "You use beautiful words, *Monsieur* Duncan. Just like my Louis-Marc. Only he does it in French."

Duncan opened his eyes. There were traces of unshed tears. "Please help me, Madame Josette. Please tell me what to do."

Josette was satisfied. Maybe everything would work out after all. "Well, for starters," she chuckled, "stop calling the kid a 'he.' There hasn't been a boy in our family since 1648. We all give birth to girls, and so will Arletty, you watch."

Chapter 8

The October 4th joint-birthdays. In Montreal.

There was to be no opera for Maria, and no mid-Fall Mykonos. This year her birthday season belonged to Ari, who needed her more than ever. Her particular motivation in trying to secure rights to the grandchild was rooted in somehow snaring both baby and Arletty, and reuniting them with her son. She had had to rule out the possibility that Ari would snap out of his ailment unscathed. She feared that unless he could have his Arletty, her sensitive, sweet son might be disabled forever.

She loved him with a passion that bordered on the unnatural. She understood this, yet proceeded full-force without embarrassment or hesitation. She had known from the moment he was born,that the only way he'd survive was through her unswerving devotion.

He was all dark, when he was born. Dark hair, dark eyes — which would turn blue later on — and tiny. A little, brown baby. Not at all like the the ultra-fair skinned, long-limbed MacLeods. Duncan had disowned him on first glimpse. He failed to recognize his fragile Levantine beauty, a delightful victory over multiple layers of Scots blood. Ari had always been hers, never Duncan's. A *Constantinopoletes,* not a Highlander.

Sadly, tragically for Duncan, all three of her miscarriages, six- and seven-month-old fetuses, would have become true MacLeods, tall and fair. But they were not to be. Ari was it, and Ari was ill. Ari could die from this terrible situation. Unless she could prevent it.

There would be no out-of-town celebration for Josette's birthday either, this year. She was far too preoccupied with her own pregnant daughter Arletty, to consider any frivolity such as a trip away. In any case, she had been given a chore, a sacred trust: Arletty had put her in charge of feeding her and by association, of feeding the unborn Tremblay inside her.

The pregnant one's defection to gastronomy, which had been significantly hampered during the nauseous months, had now, in mid-term, returned with great gusto. She loved Anita's Indian cookery, but didn't want to restrict herself to it day after day. Gourmet, or not, *samosas* and *jalfrazees* do not a rounded Cyrenaic diet make. Arletty wanted, nay, craved, the specialties of France, and Italy, and even cuisines with which she was not much familiar — Thai, Japanese, Moroccan — to supplement the Indian staples. She wanted to sample foods she had only read about and never even seen. She wanted it all. *Mangosteens* and *porcini* mushrooms, crayfish and lemongrass-infused coconut-milk soups.

The obstacle to her pervasive gastronomy was money. Not exactly eager to clean people's toilets in her condition, she was living on the last of her meager savings and Anita's generosity. She therefore ate her pride — a grand appetite will do that — and called her mother. This call filled Josette with great contentment, as she'd get to see Arletty on a regular basis.

They arranged for Arletty to pass by Josette's office twice a week, and pick up a care-package stocked with enough delicacies to last two days for herself and Anita. Thus, four days of each week were accounted for, the balance happily rounded off with Indian cooking. Such was Arletty's fervour for fine dining, that she found herself planning her meals days in advance.

Arletty would place a carefully-structured order, say on a Monday. On Tuesday she'd come by to pick up things like a tray of sushi from *Maiko,* a few cheeses from *Chaput,* garlic shrimps from *La Crevetterie,* croissants and pastries from the *Belge,* bread from *Première Moisson* — either a fesse, or a parisien — *rilletes* from *Anjou* — a real extravagance, but they were the best — and whatever *Cinq Saisons'* vegetables and fruits looked appealing.

Josette did as she was told, dutifully risking parking tickets to stop at each specified store. She religiously collected the cash receipts, as per Arletty's insistence that the tab be strictly maintained, to be paid, with interest, when she started working again.

Further, Josette had to agree to keep these arrangements secret from Louis-Marc. Although she loved him, Arletty flatly refused to see him until after the baby was born. She explained that she was in no shape to undergo any lectures from him on the nationalist importance of her baby. She was having the baby for herself, no one else. "That's all and that's that."

Josette agreed to everything, because this way she got what she really desired, which was to see and to touch and to hug her pregnant daughter. And what a sight. Forever skinny, a little gaunt, determinedly alabaster Arletty, had colour from living outside. And from being pregnant, she had bigger breasts, though surely highly sensitive by now, the beginning of a belly, and an indefinable joy that made her cheeks glow. Bliss to witness.

The meetings were brief. Arletty declined to discuss anything of importance: not her stupendous reviews, nor her possible career as an actress, an old dream of hers. Nor her current living conditions. Nor absolutely anything to do with Ari, the future, or how she intended to raise the baby. If for no other reason than the huge food-parcel her mother had assembled, which was now sitting alluringly on the desk, and it was all she could think about. She couldn't wait to grab it, jump into Anita's waiting car, race back to N.D.G., and tear it open.

Josette was inwardly happy that Arletty had shut her out. Because this way, she was free to feel even less conflict between her duty to the flesh of her flesh, and her conspiracy with the MacLeods to undermine her and compromise her authority over her own baby. For Josette the whole business, the food parcels, the legal papers, all of it put together was tied to the combined effort needed to protect her young, and her young's young.

It was moot if Arletty would have given up her gourmet packages from Josette, had she known of the Plan that was being concocted behind her back. These days she found herself being motivated strictly by bodily desires. Eating was foremost, but sex was not far behind.

In truth, she had had only two lovers before Ari, and neither of them had gotten to bed her more than once. Her sex drive had forever been an annoyance, because she had deduced early that sex necessarily meant having to share not only your body, but also your time. It meant having to compromise and accommodate. These states of being repelled her absolutely.

Therefore the sex drives of other men who would ogle her, and if cheeky, proposition her, she considered an intolerable intrusion on her privacy. All of this was, however, in the past. Now in her fifth month, hormones raging, her core chemistry recalibrating itself hourly, her entire outlook on life palpably altering into a physical world, where corporeal pleasures were all that counted, the idea of lying in someone's arms was no longer such a painful concept.

She found herself craving sex. This was confusing enough, but what had happened the other night was downright shattering. A colleague of Anita's was visiting. Handsome, shy, compact, wearing lime-green sneakers, very much her type. He had thrown sparks at her all evening, and when Anita had retired to her bedroom to sleep and it was time to go home, he had instead followed her out to the garden, unencouraged. He had sat down very close to her, just outside the tent, and engaged her in inane conversation, transparently attempting to seduce her.

It was her reaction to his foreplay that was shattering. She found herself in a serious conflict. On the one hand she was hungry to have him, to tell him to just shut up and get undressed, already. On the other hand, her mind was exploding with images of Ari. Here he was, invading her waking hours too. She saw Ari when she looked at this man. She imagined Ari when she imagined making love to this man. And finally she had to make an excuse and asked him to leave, because she saw Ari weeping, begging her not to spend another minute with this man.

She slept very badly that night, and the next morning it took her two *pains au chocolat* from *Duc de Lorraine,* a St-Viateur street bagel with cream cheese and lox, and one of Anita's home-made *massala dosas* to calm her down.

A storm was raging between Louis-Marc and Duncan. Humbled and committed as he was to cooperating, Duncan teetered between states of homicidal anger and unmitigated harassment. Louis-Marc was systematically and gleefully whittling away at his opponent's self-importance and money-based superiority.

The quiz questions on Duncan's assigned reading list were designed to trip up the student. It was obvious that Duncan couldn't possibly read the absurd amount of the material on the list, forcing him to hire others to read and review for him.

Most of the telephone-testing sessions ended badly, with asinine remarks by the tester, like "Oh. you'll have to do a lot better than that, if you're going to be a useful minority in my homeland," followed by Duncan's tooth-grinding and half-uttered profanities. Ironically, the only tests that Duncan passed involved books written by extremist *Québecois* nationalists he had already read cover to cover, being from the school that believes it's imperative to know what the enemy is thinking.

The most grating thing for Louis-Marc was Duncan's incorrigible, Anglo-studded French pronunciation. Duncan reached the end of his patience several times, but Maria would presciently arrange for one of her dinners, followed by a session of their renewed sexlife. During these trysts she would appease him, stroke his ego. She would also relate exaggerated reports from Josette about how Louis-Marc was growing more impressed with Duncan's diligence every day, and was actually on the brink of signing the papers.

In reality, Louis-Marc was farther away from signing than ever, as peeved with Duncan when he passed, as when he flunked the tests. It was also becoming obvious that no number of nice meals, nor loving, increasingly proficient blow-jobs would contain Duncan much longer.

Therefore, when October Fourth rolled along, the mothers made a date to meet, not so much to toast their universally-ignored birthdays, as to conduct an emergency brainstorm, and find a more operatic denouement to their predicament.

The venue for such a crucial get-together had to be something special, and just the right item had appeared in Maria's mail. An invitation to the opening of *Ancestral Iceberg* at the *Musée du Vanguard,* whose honorary chairperson she happened to be, and sole Westmount heavy hitter on its board.

The *Musée* specialized in state-subsidized, ever-baffling installation art, which had no historical foundation and therefore no guidelines, no discipline. This art form was born during the government-grant environment of the 1970s and '80s, and was, according to Duncan, a Canado-Dutch conspiracy to terminate western art. As such, the *Musée's* openings were amusing and outrageous, always chock-full of Canada Council artists being intentionally eccentric, while loading up on the free plonk and party sandwiches with both hands.

The energized crowd and special attention *Musée* sycophants

were prone to accord Maria, promised to bring the birthday girls as
close as Montreal could get them to Mykonos-style *kefi*. There was
no doubt in either one's mind that last year's joint birthday on that
debauched island had been the most remarkable of their lives.

They had arranged to meet outside the *Musée,* which sat on a
dreary, industrial strip of Beaubien Street, just west of St. Lawrence,
an area famous for its cut-rate automotive repair shops. Maria's
chauffeur-driven *Bentley,* a car that would blanch at the mere mention of ever being serviced on this street, slid into an open space,
right in front of the *Musée,* a utilitarian building, barely retouched
since its earlier incarnation as a cheap furniture sweatshop. It was a
sort of installation itself: art conquers worker exploitation, or something to that effect.

Josette was waiting outside as promised, but surprisingly, so
were another two hundred souls. Judging by their arty outfits, Maria
could tell that they comprised the rest of the party guests. Seeping
from the building's front doors were two steady streams of murky
water. Central to this tableau were two protagonists: the harassed,
pony-tailed, and bespectacled museum curator, and a tall, handsome
Cree woman in her early fifties with artist-trademark crazed eyes
and a scowl that was heavy enough to melt any iceberg, ancestral
or otherwise.

And that, apparently, was exactly what had happened. Her art-
piece, a huge chunk of ice transported from her tundra homeland,
had melted due to a fault in the refrigeration unit.

"It's not my fault," wailed the curator. "The transformer, I mean
the generator, well, we did not, we could not, take this into
account."

"Why not?" demanded the artist icily.

"Because refrigerators are machines. They break down," whimpered the curator, close to a breakdown himself.

"That ice comes from the holy glacier. It is, it WAS, sacred ice. I
have transported that ice, unscathed, all over Holland and all over
Canada, for ten years!" she yelled. "That ice is the heart and soul of
my art. Of my life. It is the essence of my people. The source of our
history. And now it has melted into the sewers of Montreal." She
would have been in tears, had she not been so furious. "This is a terrible omen, and it'll bring great misfortune on you, on everyone
here, and on everyone in this city, for at least TEN generations!"

Maria shut her ears against the curses, spit three times, and crossed herself another three. She quickly swooped up Josette by the arm, and scooped her into the *Bentley*.

"But I have my car here," objected Josette.

"We'll come back for it later," urged Maria. "We must get away from this place instantly. I can't afford anyone else's bad luck at this point in my life." The big car was already shifting gears to put distance between them and the ill-omened spot.

"And now, captain?" enquired Josette, amused.

"Now, admiral, we do what we did last year. We drink, and we talk," winked Maria. "Instead of the villa, we ride around in this car. It's almost as big as a villa, don't you find?" She laughed, and then flicked open the car-bar. In it, a full bottle of *ouzo,* a bucket of unmelted ice cubes, and two tumblers. Beside the drinks set-up, a plate of feta cheese, black olives, and sourdough bread.

"You came prepared," said Josette, impressed.

"I've been to *Musée Vanguard* parties before. They don't always pan out. Know what I mean?" laughed Maria, as she poured two stiff drinks, and plunked ice into each one. She handed one to Josette, they clinked and drank to their special day, and then they hugged. With no further provocation than this both succumbed to loud tears.

The weeping was brief. It was followed by another, even stiffer drink, then giggles, and finally a *eureka* scream from Maria. She tested the soundproof barrier between the cabin and the driver, to make sure it was all the way up, but whispered to Josette, just to be safe:

"Her ice melting might be a bad omen for others, but for us it signifies a cleansing. Our problems are about to dissolve, Josette. I have just this minute made a Revised Plan. It 's a devilish notion, and I hope you have the stomach for it."

"Oh, I have a good stomach," laughed Josette. "You're the fragile one, remember?"

Maria belched lady-like, into her palm, and gave the Greek hand-wave that means "Don't worry about me!" She blushed and choked, and crossed herself three times — Orthodox-style, from right to left — and got it out quickly. It was an audacious plan, rather embarrassing to talk about, but she did it, slamming down her empty glass like a warrior.

"Like *Tosca,*" laughed Josette.

"I suppose it is," mused Maria. "So, do you approve?"

"If you can carry it off, I couldn't approve more. Not only

approve, but I know exactly what to do. I am well acquainted with this particular *Scarpia,* and I know his limits. Give me ten days, and I'll have him primed for your entrance."

Now that it had been spoken, both women knew there was no turning back. They poured each other triple *ouzos,* skipping the ice and downing them Greek-style, *aspro pato:* straight down the hatch in one swig. Then they hugged each other desperately, and burst into fresh tears mixed with boozy laughter.

At the same moment, over on Redpath Crescent, Ari was putting the finishing touches on his latest poem. This was influenced by e.e. cummings — or was it T.S. Elliott? He couldn't decide. He read it aloud to himself:

> *spirits and shamans*
> > *faces on old rocks*
>
> *the dead the undead*
> > *the living the rest*
>
> *and culture and art*
> > *what about all that*
>
> > > *Just Wandering*

Chapter 9

Ten days later. On the Plateau.

Arletty composed a second letter to Ari, without intending to ever show it to him. Ever.

> *Listen Ari. I must get away. I've made up my mind. It hurts, but it's the only way. It's the only solution. I was a bit confused for a few months. The nausea. It wasn't fun. But it's gone now. I'm better now. I can think clearly again. It's obviously the right decision, because I made it. It's my life, and no one, NO one is allowed to meddle, to dictate, to destroy, or to help: nothing. I didn't make up these rules. They are obvious. They are natural. They are the rules of nature, and the only criteria for a life of dignity. I'll never bow. I'll never be conquered. And I'll not be dissuaded. I'm doing it. I'm going, and that's that. I can't continue as is. I love you too much. I love that you can be so childish, and get away with it. I couldn't. Never. I love you so much, that it'd kill me to live with you. Or even to see you. To capitulate to your childishness? Never! To be happy, just because? Why? No. No! My decision is taken. It hurts like hell, but that's the way it must be.*

Josette had said, "Take a taxi. Don't bring the limo to our house. Louis-Marc would be mortified." And so, Maria had taken what she considered to be an even more discreet route. She had left her taxi at the corner, and walked down the street to the house.There was a mid-October chill in the sunny lunchtime air, and Maria had worn her black sable with matching hat, her black, patent-leather, high-heeled, Cossack boots, and an equally shiny black handbag that was attached to her kid-gloved hand. To complete the ensemble, she had chosen her wide framed, *Sophia Loren Collection* sunglasses.

She looked like a Hollywood star lost in the Plateau and thus turned many heads in that neighbourhood, as many as would have noticed the *Bentley*. She walked fast, breathing in the unseasonably Arctic air that smelled of ozone and sea salt, a throwback to the wintry northerlies that used to blow down from Russia, unabated across the Black Sea, to ice the citizens of the imperial City on the southern tips of the Bhosphorus.

She located the address and climbed the exterior staircase to the second floor. She hesitated for a long second before ringing the bell.

It took an eternity for Louis-Marc to open the door. He had been furiously typing away on his computer. He had awakened late, with a clever idea that would provide a definitive *side bar* to his latest thesis. He hadn't bothered to wash. Josette was already gone to work, so he had brewed a pot of strong coffee, bypassing all other morning activities to jump right onto the keyboard.

He had on yesterday's frayed shirt and a pair of snugly threadbare jeans, his favourites, but permanently smelly because he dared not launder them too often, they were so fragile. He had no shoes on, not even slippers. He faced his unexpected guest and figured out who she was. He felt naked, unprepared to meet her, and annoyed to be interrupted.

"Josette's not he-e-re," was all he managed to stutter.

Maria was sympathetic to his plight, but she was pleased that he was unwittingly putting her in control. This would be far easier than she had feared. "She said she might be a little late. Do you mind if I wait for her?" She sang her question in her carefully accented French. "I'm Maria MacLeod," she added redundantly.

Louis-Marc reacted in slow motion. He shut his hanging mouth wishing he had showered and finely-dressed to receive this goddess. Then he collected his wits. "Please come in," he said. "I'm Louis-Marc," extending his hand, and as she walked in, "You must excuse me. I'm a mess. I was working."

Maria removed her sunglasses and hat, holding them with one

hand and fixing her hair with her free hand. She said contritely:
"You must excuse me. I've barged in on you. I've also entered your
house under false pretenses. I didn't come for Josette. I came here
to see you."

Louis-Marc was intrigued. "I'm glad you came. I've been wanting to meet you," he said flatly, as he led her into the parlour, which
was welcoming and orderly thanks to Josette's unscheduled house-
work the previous night.

Maria wafted in. What she had to do was staring her in the face.
She was so focused she failed to notice anything about the room.
Not the Louis XV furniture, shiny and bright in aquamarine damask
and sky-blue; not the embossed details; not the player-piano with its
disk of *Québec* folk-songs ready to come to life at the touch of the
pedals; not the imitation Persian rug — Turkish, actually — not the
ornate lamps with the tear-drop crystal hangings; none of the details
that would've reminded her of her mother's parlour back in Istanbul, and that would've made her feel instantly at home.

She deposited her hat, gloves, sunglasses, and handbag on a
meticulously-restored, Lower Canada writing desk. She let her coat
fall off her shoulders, and didn't make an attempt to catch it. One
hundred thousand dollars worth of sable pelts hit the rug, and
slumped into a jet-black mound of untended luxury.

Under the coat, Maria was dressed in a clinging, low-cut, silk
dress she had designed and hand-sewn just for this occasion. It was
a bright red, almost vermilion, like a tropical sunset. She wore no
jewelry to speak of, just gold earrings, one ring with a humongous
ruby on the same finger as her wedding band, and a diamond-crust-
ed *Constantin Vacheron* watch.

"I came here to make a personal plea, on my knees if I have to,
to persuade you to forgive my husband his trespasses and sign
those papers." That is what Josette had instructed: Come right to the
point, and work up from there.

"Won't you take a seat... Can I get you a drink?" Louis-Marc
could have kicked himself. He was letting her fluster him. By all
rights he should ask her to leave. But she smelled so wonderful, a
combination of the night flowers that had enchanted him in
Tangiers, and the unmistakable scent of a woman in her prime. Try
as he might, he was unable to look away from her cleavage: erect
globes with a gap between them. Tits like these are the kind that
cannot tolerate a bra. They spring out in opposite directions, with

big, dark nipples, that harden at will.

Louis-Marc summoned all his reserves to override his desire. He had felt the old, dangerous stirring in his crotch. He was rightfully horny. Josette had asked him to sleep alone for the last ten days. Something to do with hot flashes. But, surely this was excessive. Getting hot and bothered for the wife of his enemy, and his own wife's newly closest friend. This was a formula for disaster.

Maria sat down on the elegant sofa, sideways, aiming her best profile towards Louis-Marc. "A *Pernod*, if you have it," she said. "Otherwise, a beer."

"A beer, really?" chuckled Louis-Marc. The notion of this noble creature guzzling beer lightened his stress. "A beer it'll have to be." He left the parlour, and returned in no time with two bottles of beer and two glasses. Maria refused the glass. She twisted off the beer-top, and extended it for a clink.

Louis-Marc clinked, and watched in amazement as Maria took a rather long draught and burped politely. She giggled. "My secret vice, beer straight from the bottle. It's so bubbly, it rises right to your head," she confided. "Now what were we talking about?"

"Your husband's trespasses against me, and against *Québec*," laughed Louis-Marc, treating himself to a sizable gulp of beer, full of bubbles straight from the bottle. His burp was altogether too loud. He blushed, and giggled.

"Oh, yes," said Maria earnestly, her free hand caressing the silky texture of the upholstery.

"The man is impossible," started Louis-Marc, as if to console her. "He refuses to bend in the slightest. He doesn't even pronounce *Québec* correctly, even when speaking his so-called French. He says Cue-back, as if it was someone's backside!"

"That is just bad habit. It's the way he learned it."

"Well, it's non-stop. He says *Sant-Vee-Ay-tor*, instead of Saint-Viateur, Sant-LAW-rence, instead of Saint-Laurent, he even says Dorchester instead of René Lévesque. We threw out that coloniser's name and replaced it with the name of our national hero two decades ago!"

Maria brought the bottle back to her lips. This time she took a small sip. "But really, what purpose is it serving to humiliate him? And treat him like an errant schoolchild?"

"He and his kind have robbed us of our national dignity for centuries. It's time he was humbled. But never fear, I don't think he'll give in."

And what does that have to do with the baby?"

"The baby, madame, must grow up as a *Québecois*. It is my inalienable duty to do whatever it takes to keep the baby as far away from Westmount, and from MacLeod, as possible."

Maria engaged his gaze away from her cleavage. "When I was small, my mother used to take me for walks along the main street of Moda, always ripe with the smell of magnolias, and down to the the *peer*. There, close to the sea, we had a tiny chapel, Aghia *Aikaterene,* Saint Catherine. It was just big enough for two people to pray in it at once. It was a miraculous chapel, and if you prayed with faith, your prayers would come true. Moda is too far for me to go, so I pray to Saint Catherine every night. To help me find a way to be a grandmother to my grandchild."

"You're not in Istanbul anymore, Madame," shrugged Louis-Marc insensitively.

"Oh, but you are wrong. Where you are born and brought up is always with you. How can I erase it? I love Montreal, but it lacks the Anatolian breezes that smell of jasmine and honeysuckle. It doesn't turn pink in February from early cherry blossoms that will be laced with frost at dawn. It doesn't have bonito tuna that melts in your mouth fried in olive oil and smothered in sweet onions from Bursa."

Louis-Marc looked down at her professorially — the better to admire her bust. "Claude Carbo said... Do you know Claude Carbo? A great man and an immigrant, like yourself... He said, well, he DEMANDED that Immigrants integrate themselves into *Québec,* and join the struggle to preserve *Québecois* cultural specificity!' Why? *Because, the democratic values of Québec guarantee immigrants' security, liberty, and prosperity.'* Can nostalgia be any match for such a rich tapestry of opportunity, Madame?"

Maria made a Greek hand-gesture that means I understand all that. "You've been fighting each other for a thousand years. You English and French. Always wanting what the other one has. Always trying to prove that one is better than the other. But really, you are the same people, aren't you? You even share common ethnic roots. The fighting is a game, isn't it? A game no one knows how to play. And a game that threatens me in the worst possible way. A game that will destroy all of us, Monsieur Daoust. Please, please, reconsider, and sign the papers."

Louis-Marc looked away. "I cannot," he said firmly.

Maria stole a glance at her watch. It was one minute to two. Josette had said to start it around two, and keep it going for five minutes. She moaned loudly, and brought herself to the point of tears. She stood up as if possessed. She whirled around to face him squarely, and with no further warning, she fell prostate in front of him, burying her face on his feet, whimpering through painful tears. "Please, oh, please... I implore you... Don't be so heartless... It'd kill me... It'd kill my son!"

Maria's nose took the brunt of Louis-Marc's foot odour. Like *feta* and *brie* put together, but mild. For him the sensation was one of warm tears on his feet, bringing an arousing whiff of Maria to his nostrils. Like magnolia, and jasmine, and honeysuckle, as well as night flowers. A composite Anatolian breeze that was driving him to the brink of recklessness.

"Madame, please," he said breathlessly. "This is not an opera." He bent down and placed his hands under her armpits, in an effort to help her up. His fingertips melted into the softly shaved flesh, giving him a jolt. He tried to move his fingers away from the danger spot, but they settled near her breasts. The stirring in his crotch was turbulent. She reached and found his hands. She held onto them, and slowly pulled herself up, rubbing against the length of his body as she did so. She sensed his erection. She stole another glance at her watch. One minute past two. She needed four more minutes.

She was now on her feet, being supported by his arms, which had somehow encircled her. Their lips were very close to meeting. She placed her hands lightly on his shoulders, pretending to be faint. Her hair smelled of magnolia and jasmine. Her body, of night flowers. Her breath was honeysuckle. Her nipples were erect and were pressing against his chest. He was at her mercy.

His lips brushed against hers with understated passion. She didn't kiss back, but she parted her lips. His tongue darted into her mouth, he could control himself no longer. One of his hands cupped her buttocks while the other caressed her breast. He kissed her again. Four minutes past two. She had no idea whether she could hold on. He was arousing her as Duncan could never bring himself to do.

Louis-Marc was panting now. He was kissing her on the face, on the ears, the shoulders, the fingertips, the breasts. His hand clumsily found the zipper in the back of her dress. His other hand was raising her skirt. This was getting serious. It was nearly seven minutes past two, and still no Josette. Something must have happened. This thing had to stop, because she was reaching the point of no return, while he had obviously gone well beyond it.

At eight minutes past two, with one tit jutting out of her dress and her underwear half off under her skirt, Maria let out an urgent cry, and went completely limp. Louis-Marc jolted by the cry, and panicked by Maria's sudden fainting, was struggling to keep her from falling to the ground. Just at that merciless moment, he heard the key turning in the door, and he froze. His erection vanished. The blood drained from his brain. His arms, temporarily paralyzed, could no longer support Maria's weight, and she plummeted to the floor with a thud.

Josette entered with fury. She glanced down at Maria, and snapped her fingers impatiently. "Okay, gorgeous one. You can get up now." She didn't bother looking at Louis-Marc, whose only recourse at this juncture would have been an earthquake or some other act of God.

Maria got off the floor with as much elegance as she could muster. She repaired the disorder Louis-Marc had caused her clothing and reclaimed her seat on the silky sofa. She picked up her beer, looking somewhat guilty.

Josette finally addressed her husband. "Well? Did she make you sign, or what?"

Louis-Marc had been granted his act of God. The seduction was planned by his wife. He was not to blame. "I'm never going to sign," he said smugly.

Maria smiled sweetly at Josette. "I am not responsible for what happened after five minutes past two," she purred. "What kept you?"

"What kept me," began Josette with agitation, "and why, you mister, WILL sign the goddamn papers, is that I was busy finding out Arletty is going to India, to have the baby over there!"

"*Quoi?*" snapped Louis-Marc, as Maria screamed, "Oh, NO!"

"That's right," yelled Josette. "I can barely breath, I'm so upset. I was leaving the office to come here, when Duncan called me."

Louis-Marc groaned.

"That's right, Duncan. He has had a private detective on the case, and they've been watching her. Well, not her. They've been watching her friend Anita. There's been a lot of travel agency action. And phone calls. Thank God, they didn't use the Internet or it would've been harder to trace. Anyway, I used my favour bank with the airlines, and THERE she was. Booked on a flight to Bombay, and then to Bangalore, on November FIFTEENTH!!!"

Maria had no more tears left in her. "We're done for," she gasped. "We've lost her!"

"No, we have not! On the contrary. This action of hers will furnish us with the requisite conditions. Duncan's lawyer explained it to me. Once she has her boarding pass, and she clears security, she gives proof that she intends to proceed with the irresponsible, endangering action, and can therefore be declared an... unfit mother. Then we can stop her, and I can finally take care of her." Josette was flushed with this dubious victory.

Louis-Marc listened to her angrily. Anger was his only weapon against this new twist. *Damn Arletty.* "Why couldn't she have stayed put?" He lashed out at Josette. "Josette, the master conspirator. Bravo! It's like I'm seeing the real you for the first time."

"I'll do whatever it takes to save my daughter," hissed Josette through clenched teeth. "I'm not like you, content to see her dead, as long as your ego doesn't suffer."

"What are you talking about? Dead? For God's sake. She wants to go to India. What's the big deal?"

"SHUT UP, Louis-Marc," bellowed Josette. "Stop torturing me. It's not my fault you lost your money to Duncan, and I was the one who had to go and get it back for you. It's not my fault that Louis XIV made a deal with the English king, all that time ago, and gave away *Québec.* It's not my fault Parizeau was too stupid to win the referendum. You are a great man. A man of the people. Duncan is an animal. No offense," she made an aside to Maria before turning back to her husband: "Why do you descend to his level? Why can't you show me your compassion and your intelligence? Why can't you show Arletty some love? This is not a game of cards. This is not a political manifesto. This is the life of my baby, and the life of her baby..." Josette continued with a slight quiver in her voice: "She's going to India without a penny. She's going to give birth in India, without a PENNY. Do you know how many penniless babies are born every year in India? More than twice the population of all *Québec!* And do you know how many of those babies, AND their mothers, are better off dead? At least half of them. You'd abandon Arletty into a situation where she'd have a fifty-fifty chance of survival? I don't think so. I don't think you could be that mean." Josette, in exquisite control of her emotions, dug the famous papers out of her shoulder bag, and slapped them down on the heritage desk, which creaked from the force. She held out a pen, and glowered at Louis-Marc.

He uttered an obscenity, signed, and promptly left the room. Maria was far too preoccupied to be joyful that the signing ordeal was over. She was still trying to fathom the significance of those crazed eight minutes in Louis-Marc's embrace.

True, she had done it so that Josette could catch them. But, she had certainly been swept away by it. And had she not used her last ounce of will-power to fake the fainting, she could easily have gone all the way with him, despite Josette, despite the compromise to the Plan, despite, therefore Ari, and Arletty, and the grandchild. Despite — or, maybe in spite of — Duncan, despite all the ruling principles of her life, and her dedication to monogamy. It had taken Louis-Marc only eight minutes to prove to her that there was life beyond the marriage bed and beyond the reticent, Presbyterian love-making of her workaholic husband.

Chapter 10

November 15th. At the airport.

It had sounded like a simple, fail-proof plan. But no one had counted on just how feisty Arletty was capable of being, and no one, not even the lawyers were able to stop the parents from showing up at the airport. It was Louis-Marc who had once again upset the balance. He had refused to stay away from the scene and leave his daughter entirely at the mercy of the barbarians. Josette, who had tried to talk him out of it, did so halfheartedly, because in fact, nothing would have kept her away from Dorval Airport that evening. Learning that the Daoust-Tremblays would be in attendance, Duncan dragged Maria, so that they would not be left out.

The legal mechanism was in place. There was a court order in the hands of a senior, rather famous lawyer, with half an alphabet of degrees and distinctions to his name. He would accompany a pre-instructed police officer, who would formally charge and arrest Arletty at the moment she cleared airport security on her way to her gate. The lawyer would accompany the accused to the police station, witness her booking, and then take her into his recognizance. He would then turn her over to the custody of the parents.

Arletty, now in her sixth month, with a fetus that had taken to performing somersaults inside her, was developing a belly that had begun to noticeably protrude from her slender frame. She was dressed in one of Anita's more subdued sarees — brown, with gold highlights — to hide her new girth. She had darkened her eyes with kohl, and stuck a topaz on her forehead. She had dyed her hair very black. She looked Indian, not because she could've foreseen any reason to disguise herself, but to begin melding with her destination.

This would be a winter away from the snow, enabling her to complete her term outdoors far away from her meddlesome parents, but mostly away from Ari. As far away from Ari as she could go. Anita had organized things very well. Friends to meet Arletty at the Bangalore airport, friends to set her up in a tent — "Just wait till you see an Indian tent! I don't think so you've ever seen a tent like an Indian tent!" She had even arranged for an excellent midwife to deliver the baby in a reputable *Ayurvedic* clinic.

Arletty looked so very different from her image in the provided photograph, that she was able to pass directly beneath the noses of the waiting posse, with neither policeman nor lawyer able to recognize her.

It was Josette who knew right away that the Indian girl in black hair and gold-highlighted saree was her flesh and blood. She watched in agitation as Arletty ambled away towards her plane. She briefly considered just letting her go, since she had beaten the watchdogs — but she couldn't. Her maternal instincts persevered, screaming at her to do something to prevent Arletty from hurtling herself into danger. To keep her safe.

Josette broke from the ranks and emerged from the hiding place behind the pillar that had been assigned for the parents. They had been warned not to interfere. But this was an emergency. She ran to the policeman and told him, a tad too loudly, that the girl in the saree was HER. It was Arletty.

Arletty, many paces ahead and surrounded by airport din, isolated the sound of her mother's voice saying her name. She turned, and she saw Josette, the policeman, the ominous old man with the scowl and the black briefcase. She knew immediately that she was in trouble. When in doubt, RUN, was one of her mottoes. It had served her well all her life, and it would have to do now.

She ran, weaving in and out of shocked passengers, alarmed security guards, and emergency-minded airline personnel. She sneaked a look over her shoulder, and saw a number of pursuers. The surprisingly nimble lawyer, her parents, the MacLeods, the whole pack of them led by the original policeman, plus several of his colleagues who had joined the chase in progress.

It all was happening a bit too fast to allow thought, any kind of clear plan. So, Arletty ran faster, ran breathlessly, though it should have been obvious to her, to anyone, that there was not a chance in hell she could escape. There was a closed door up ahead. She could see a stairway beyond its meshed window. There was a large, *Authorized Personnel Only* notice on the door. She reached the forbidden portal and kicked it open. She flung herself down the metal staircase. She was a couple of steps down, when she heard the door behind her open noisily. She turned her head to the shouts of the pursuers, while continuing to fly down the stairs. She lost her footing, and tumbled down the stairs, like a rag doll, falling backwards, like Scarlet O'Hara after her big fight with Clark Gable.

She was in danger of losing her baby for three long days and nights. Her own body came out of it fine, bruised, angry, betrayed, but nothing that couldn't be mended. Doctors' tests had shown that the baby had not suffered any real damage either, however, that it had misread the tumble as a signal to be born. At twenty six weeks far too premature to guarantee its chances for survival.

For three days and three nights, Josette, Louis-Marc, Maria, Ben, and Anita kept vigil in the corridor outside Arletty's room. Missing principal cast members included Duncan, who had departed after Louis-Marc had threatened to chop off his testicles and stuff them in his mouth; and Ari, who had countered Ben's and Maria's urgings to come to the hospital, with an irrefutable, *I don't think she'd like it.*

Arletty would have actually welcomed a visit from Ari, if only for the opportunity to tell him to go to hell. Louis-Marc could blame Duncan, and also Josette and Maria, all he wanted. Arletty was convinced that the real source of her misery, her pain, the possible loss of her baby, was Ari. With his sexy body and the luscious lips, and all that pathetic helplessness. And now the baby would die, or it would grow up impaired, possibly disabled, and she would have to bear the pain all on her own.

Happily, the baby didn't die. And it wasn't born prematurely. It had settled back into the womb, shocked, but no worse for wear. It had responded well to all the treatments, and the doctors had declared it totally out of danger. There was a loud cheer from the gallery out in the corridor, from Duncan in his office, and from Ari in his room. The baby was also decidedly a girl, as the doctors had determined during all the tests — a very loud cheer from Josette. Yes, the baby was fine but Arletty was hereafter to become a prisoner.

Chapter II

Mid-December. In the Tower.

There were a full dozen shopping days to go until Christmas, but it was not coming up fast enough for Arletty. Christmas would arrive today, even if she had to push it.

It had been hell. And, now that she had managed to convince herself, now that she was ready to take the ultimate plunge and reverse all of her previous convictions, now that she had tasted hell, Christmas would put an end to all her suffering.

There was no other word for it. Arletty was a prisoner. Directly from the hospital, she was driven to a hyper deluxe apartment. It was located in one of the towers of The Trafalgar, the tightly secure, old-world condo-fortress that perches inaccessibly to all but the very rich, on the crest of Cote des Neiges. This mega-structure boasts comprehensive views of Montreal, along with total immunity from all ills that might result from contact with the less fortunate.

The apartment, one of the many reminders of Ross MacLeod's seemingly random, frivolous purchases, was a gem. A split-level penthouse with windows galore and a wrap-around terrace for walking, it was decorated in Monet-esque pastels, *Provençal* furniture, and a varnished flagstone floor softened by thick, cuddly area rugs. Several fireplaces, state-of-the-art audio-visual systems, a jacuzzi, as well as an indoor pool, and a full library. It was a home for all seasons, a complete universe onto itself. Josette had approved it instantly, as a neutral location ideally suited for Arletty's legally-stipulated, last-trimester confinement.

Arletty was already hating it on the way up in the elevator. They were demented! They really believed they could shut her up in a tower, like some Medieval damsel in distress — so where was her conical hat with the tulle flying off its tip? — with a nurse, a house-keeper, and twenty-four hour guards posted outside the door. And get away with it? They were crazy all of them. Her mother had actually tried to come and visit her. Arletty couldn't believe it. Speechless, she threw some priceless vases at her, and pointed to the elevator. The nerve! Shortly thereafter Josette had telephoned her. This time it was purposeless to break any more vases, and being far less speechless, Arletty let her have it:

"You are no longer my mother. You're no better than my worst enemy. I hate you with all my heart. If you dare to ever call me again, I'll find you, I'll kill you, and then I'll kill myself. Okay? NOW GET THE FUCK OUT OF MY LIFE!"

Topping off the shackles of her imprisonment was the day-to-day grind of her advancing pregnancy. She had entered that bizarre, late-pregnancy state when one seems to exist in a bubble, when that which is growing inside lays claim to its host, and when just about anything jarring takes its toll on one's ability to cope.

Arletty's only pleasure during her interminable month since the airport incident, had been the endless supply of freshly-delivered gourmet creations by Montreal's finest restaurants, as well as the air-freighted specialties of places as far away as Paris and even Sydney, Australia.

Her only solace as well as the anchor to her real life, was of the loyal Anita, the only visitor Arletty had authorized, and who came to see her at odd times, juggling the hours between her job, her ever growing involvement with Ben Cohen, and her duty to her besieged friend.

It was Anita who had arrived early this morning, on the way to work, to provide her with just the little tidbit that would make Christmas come soon. She provided the perfect pretext Arletty need-ed to call Ari, and justifiably ask him to come see her. She needed to speak to him in person. She worried about being overheard. The phone, as she had correctly deduced, was bugged.

A piece of voice-mail concerning her was left on Ari's answer-ing machine. Ari had told Ben about it and Ben had rushed the news to Anita. Now Arletty knew about it, and she barely waited for Anita to leave before she dialed Ari's number.

Ari had also correctly deduced that once Arletty knew about it, she would call him. And yet he found it difficult to be coherent or to concentrate on what she was saying when he picked up the phone, and encountered the real, live Arletty's sweet voice at the other end. He mumbled that he could send the cassette — with its earth-shattering message — to her via Ben and Anita. She agreed at first, so as not to scare him. She gained time by chatting about her predicament, laughing about it, being in jail inside some multi-million dollar pad. Yet, she only gained his interest when she talked to him about the baby and its continuous calisthenics inside her belly. She snared him.

He came to see her that same afternoon, dressed once again as if he just stepped out of the L. L. Bean catalogue, complete with pennyloafers. This was obviously some form of perverted revenge, and Arletty ignored the gesture, kissing him warmly three times. She led him into her luxury jail, ordering the nurse and the housekeeper into the kitchen with a glower, so that she could be alone with Ari.

Ari hadn't said a word since he had walked in. She had confused him outright with her friendliness. He supposed she was excited about the message. He took out a small tape-player, which was already loaded with the cassette in question, and flicked a button. Gérard Depardieu's unmistakable falsetto-baritone thundered from the tiny speaker:

"*Fantastique Arletty. Arletty seconde. Je vous laisse ce message sur l'engin répondeur de votre preux chevalier, le splendid Aristos. Vous êtes une Star. Alors, parée pour un autre role? Nous débutons le premier janvier, et nous aurons besoin de vous au moins quinze jours. Vous serez royalement traitée et payée. Je m'en occupe personnellement. Putain, j'espère que vous êtes libre entre le premier et le quinze janvier. On a déjà repoussé les dates deux fois, mais la c'est bon, on est fixé. Petit détail: vous devrez m'embrasser. Une seul fois. Et pas trop profondément. Alors Aristos, relaxe. Le rôle est juteux, drôle, et touchant. Vous aller bien vous amuser. J'vous DHL le scénar. On s'voit le premier de l'an. Ou avant, si vous voulez.*"

Arletty pursed her lips, and sighed. "I'll be eight months pregnant in January. They'll have to rewrite the part."

"For you, they'll do it. I'm sure they will."

"Well, I wouldn't go even if they did. I'm no actress, Ari. For me it's bad enough to have to live through anything once. To have it on film, and let it play itself out time after time, that's torture. To let any stranger into my deepest emotions is an abomination to me. I did it for you, but that's it and that's all."

"Thank you," said Ari, sensing some kind of compliment.

Arletty made a face, and uttered a little groan. Ari looked at her alarmed. "No, no. It's nothing," she said. "The baby moved." She held her belly, as if to keep the baby from escaping.

"Oh, yeah," said Ari. "You told me over the phone that it moves. I didn't know babies did that."

"Oh, they do! Aah, I think it's going to do it again. Come, come," she beckoned him. He rushed to her, and she put his head against her belly.

He listened in wonder. He could hear the rumblings, and then he felt it. An actual kick. He pulled back instinctively. "He kicked. And he smiled at me. I know he did," he said emotionally.

"It's a she, Ari. We found out after the accident. And she kicks at will... I think she'll be a ballerina."

"Yes! A girl... I always wanted... Maybe she'll be a soccer player. Women's soccer is getting... is getting very..." Ari didn't finish his sentence. He remembered his position with Arletty. He glumly returned to his seat.

Arletty got up and seated herself in an upright chair. "I can't sit in one position for too long," she explained.

"It hasn't exactly been a picnic for me, either," replied Ari in a stale, flat tone.

"I'd love it, if you don't mind," started Arletty cheerily, "for us to forget about the past for a minute, and deal with the present."

"Right. I've been trying to. I've been writing poetry."

"Can I see it? I love poetry."

"No, you CANNOT," Ari raised his voice, but regretted it immediately. "It's not any good. I tore it all up."

"Were they poems about me?"

"Yes. They were."

"I wrote you a couple of letters. But, I tore those up, too."

"Better that way." Ari was suddenly very angry. "And I don't know why I came today. I don't think I want to see you again. I should've sent the tape with Ben. I have no interest in anything anymore, you know."

"You were interested in the baby."

"Of course I'M INTERESTED IN THE BABY. It's MY baby," he was shouting again.

Arletty came over to sit beside him. She took his head in her palms, and kissed his lips. "Shshsh... Be gentle. It's a tiny baby, and loud noises frighten it."

Ari stroked her belly. Then he laid his head on her shoulder. He closed his eyes, and would have wept, if he hadn't been so confused.

"Has anyone told you what our adorable parents intend to do with our baby?" she asked him as she ran her fingers through his thick hair.

"Ben told me things. They're keeping you here till you give birth. I know that."

"Actually their plans extend to infinity. It's all legal, and court-approved. After I give birth, I lose custody of my own child, unless I live at home. And I have a choice: either with my folks in the Plateau, or with yours in Westmount. And wherever it is, there will be a guard posted outside the door, around the clock, so that I cannot kidnap her. If I refuse, and want to live on my own, then all I get is scheduled, chaperoned visiting rights."

Ari was no longer confused. Now, he was bewildered. "Can they do this?"

"Who the fuck knows? They're doing it."

"That's incredible."

Arletty brought her lips to his ear. She whispered into it, tickling it: "There is a way we can fight them."

"What is it?" asked Ari loudly.

"Keep your voice really low. I think the room is bugged."

"Really?"

"Just to be safe."

Her breath tickling his ear sent shivers up and down his loins. He decided to fight off his desire. Arletty obviously had something up her sleeve, and it wasn't necessarily going to be pleasant for him. But, then she whispered again, and stunned him. She said: "We must get married."

She hadn't been able to guess what his reaction would be. She knew that she would have to improvise, and took his total lack of response to mean that he needed an explanation. "I spoke to a lawyer. He said, that the only way I can fight them, is by getting married. Preferably to you. And don't get me wrong here, but I think I can manage you much better than I can manage their court order." Ari saw the ruse. She wanted to use and discard him. "If I married you," he whispered forcefully, "it would mean we would live together. As a family."

"Oh, yes. Naturally," whispered Arletty earnestly.

"I see," said Ari, but he didn't really.

"So? What's the answer?"

Ari squirmed. "I... I need time... to think."

"Sorry. There's no time." Arletty sensed victory.

"What'd it be like? Our marriage?"

Arletty shrugged. "*Ouf*, I don't know. I don't intend to change. You can't change. So, it'll probably be hell. But we have to. Otherwise we lose our kid."

"Our kid! Sounds good, Arletty."

"So? Will you do it?"

Ari narrowed his eyes, and then he smiled broadly. He took her face in his hands, and kissed her lustily. She had the good sense to kiss back.

"Okay, then," she whispered. "It has to be tomorrow, and it has to be done to the letter, or we'll fail. Here, I have written it all down," she pressed a sheet of paper in his hand. "Read it carefully."

Arletty's plan was worthy of a master tactician. Ari was to return the next day, accompanied by Ben. Ben was to be dressed in a heavy overcoat, a large tuque to cover most of his face, and oversized jeans. During the visit, Ben would strip and let Arletty dress in his clothes. Ari and the fake Ben were then to leave, having informed the nurse that Arletty was napping, and didn't want to be disturbed. Ben, as the fake Arletty, was to be in her bed, covered up to his neck should the nurse decide to look in. Ben and Arletty were the same height, and except for the belly, shared about the same size of frame.

After their escape, they would rush to City Hall to meet Anita with Arletty's paperwork. Ari was to bring his own documents. The lawyer, a very loyal client of Arletty's house-cleaning service, was to join them, and they would be married, with proper witnesses, the official seal, and everything.

From City Hall, they would be driven to Anita's house for ninety minutes' worth of honeymoon. Some careful, long overdue sex in Anita's spare bedroom, where she kept some of her homeless animals, like the iguanas, the six lame pigeons, and the family of tortoises she hadn't been able to resist rescuing from a pet store, where they were squished all together in a crowded plastic basin of water. Anita had built them a handsome, Styrofoam-based pond, which the pigeons had immediately adopted as their toilet.

When it was all over, they would return to Trafalgar during the early afternoon and rescue the patient Ben from his too-long nap. And Arletty would bluff the whole thing off, as a caprice, a little adventure, a break from her confinement. It was important to her that no one found out anything until she was ready to tell them.

The plan, with its myriad pitfalls, worked precisely, beginning with a very easy escape from *Trafalgar.* Dressed as Ben, Arletty giggled along in Ari's big car all the way to City Hall. Ari, still not convinced that they were really going through with it, grinned until it hurt. The ceremony was brief. The sex in Anita's spare room was guarded, with each partner trying unsuccessfully to pretend nothing was out of the ordinary. Nevertheless, it left them giddy and persuaded them beyond any doubt that at least sexually, whatever the conditions, they were compatible. Even the pigeons behaved themselves, resisting the temptation to shit on them instead of the tortoise-pond.

The transition back to Trafalgar went as smoothly as it could, except that the guards were fired, and new ones hired. Although the nurse and the housekeeper were spared being harder to replace, they were nonetheless read the riot act, and put on probation.

Arletty slept well that night, even though she woke up many times reaching for Ari and discovering that he wasn't there. Now it was a matter of waiting for ten days to get her hands on her own court order, as promised by the lawyer. Which meant she would be having her second Christmas in a row, exactly during real Christmas. She'd be free.

"Why, that calls for a party," she exclaimed aloud when she woke up in the morning. A wonderfully wicked, little plan had come to her in a dream. A dilly of a plan, that ensured sweet revenge.

Chapter 12

Christmas Eve, 1999. In the Plateau.

Arletty must have been living right, because her second devious
plot in a row worked out in as charmed a way as the first. This
time her plan involved the unwitting participation of a number of
at-risk personages, as well as the resolution of a tricky legal matter
within a narrow time-limit.

The first hurdle involved assembling the cast all in one place on
Christmas Eve. It was essential that the boil be lanced exactly on
that day so that she could fully celebrate Christmas as a free woman.
A holiday, which in the past she had regarded strictly as a vestigial,
winter solstice rite, sanitized of its original orgies and end-of-the-
world frenzy, had taken on new meaning for her. She could now
appreciate a world-wide birthday party for a little baby, because
soon she would have one of her own.

She started the ball rolling by calling her mother. Josette's initial
elation turned instantly to panic. "What is it? Is something WRONG?"
she shrieked. She had become a touch manic about Arletty, having
had many nightmares since the airport incident.

Arletty laughed off her concerns, and stated her own. The idea
of spending Christmas Eve at Trafalgar was too depressing for her.
And could she come home and spend the holiday with her and
Louis-Marc?

Josette had to bite her tongue, so she wouldn't scream for joy
and make Arletty change her mind. But Arletty wasn't finished. Her
next request was that Ari should be there. She wanted to see him,
and make Christmas peace with him. Even though: "NATURALLY, I
don't want to have anything more to do with him again. EVER!"

Josette, her heart beating wildly, took a few seconds to smoke a cigarette and calm her nerves, before dialing Ari. Already primed by Arletty, he hedged at first. He finally agreed to come to the *Plateau* on Christmas Eve, but only if he could bring his mother. Josette, too over the top to analyze the request, agreed on the spot. Maria almost swooned as she accepted the invitation. That left Duncan, who insisted that he must come as well, if everyone else would be there. So far, everything had worked out pretty much as Arletty had divined it would.

The only loose cannon was, of course, Louis-Marc. Arletty had hoped to count on the persuasive powers of Josette, but they proved unnecessary. Louis-Marc welcomed the opportunity to host Duncan, a little too quickly and too eagerly. He appeared to have a secret agenda, but Josette had far too much else on her mind to worry about that.

On the sacred evening, Josette and Louis-Marc, dressed in silks and fine wools, fussed endlessly with their festive decor, and their vast, labour-intensive meal, redolent of holiday recipes made famous by Louis-Marc's grandfather. Duck *rilletes,* lobster *quenelles,* onion pies, wild mushroom soup, baked grapefruits, roast goose with kumquat and oyster stuffing on a bed of red cabbage, potato and Brie puffs, white asparagus with *Parma* ham in champagne sauce. Then five desserts, from a simple fresh raspberry sorbet to the ultra-Christmas-y Mont-Blanc, a hill of feathered *marons-glacés,* decorated as a mountain, with melted-chocolate trees, and whipped-cream snow. Maria had offered to bring the booze, but Josette had bought four hefty bottles, a magnum of champagne, and a litre of *Pernod,* just to be on the safe side. Total tab for groceries, alcohol, and frills: $1,700. Thanks to the improving economy, she had had a nicely lucrative Christmas-travel season.

Everything was in readiness as the two of them sat on the Louis XV, holding hands, listening to the crackles of the fire in the fireplace, watching its flickering reflections in the Christmas tree decorations. They sighed in unison, with the unspoken, mutual wish, that maybe, just maybe, the smoke would clear on this special day, and Arletty would once again be their friend.

Arletty was the first to arrive, radiant, positively pregnant, and seemingly ready to grant them their wish. She walked in effusively, kissing them both as if nothing untoward had ever come between them. She hugged her father, told him how much she missed him, enchanting him even as he was signing the bodyguard's release, so the guy could go home, and have a Christmas with his own family.

She sat down between them on the sofa, touching them, and luxuriating in their caresses, talking and talking, about the thrill of being pregnant, and how much she was looking forward to the baby. The baby! The clothes for the baby, the toys, the cute prams she was perusing on the Internet, and so forth. Finally the bell rang and rescued her from having to continue.

The MacLeods had arrived. Duncan and Maria were dressed as the possibly exiled king and queen of a fashionable kingdom. Ari, beautiful in the exact same outfit he had used for his Mykonos seduction, fell short of sartorial kudos, because of the pennyloafers he had slipped into. This was probably due to his excitement — Arletty nearly fainted when she spotted the offensive footwear. Right behind the masters was the liveried chauffeur armed with two boxes of wines and champagnes of mythical vintages, as well as a few bottles of the *Napoleon* Josette liked so much. Total tab, if one could locate the auctions and bid on these bottles, was in excess of $180,000.

The chauffeur deposited his boxes in the kitchen and exited. Josette and Maria embraced warmly. Duncan shook Josette's hand as that of a fellow player. Maria and Louis-Marc kissed each other on the cheek, politely, almost shyly. Duncan and Louis-Marc nodded to each other with a distinctly anti-Christmas mixture of disdain and contempt.

They were all so busy encapsulating their various relationships into their greetings no one noticed what Ari and Arletty were doing. When the four parents turned to enter the parlour, they all stopped in their tracks, and performed a chorus-line of simultaneous double-takes.

Ari and Arletty were relaxed and cozy on the old Louis XV, with Arletty's head in the nook of Ari's shoulder, both of her legs jauntily across his lap, while he whispered nothings into her ear, making her giggle. Maria's heart jumped for joy. She crossed herself. Somehow, somehow, her prayers were being answered, and her Ari had been reunited with his Arletty. Could it be some kind of a trick, an illusion?

The other three didn't know what to make of the tableau the lovers had choreographed for them. Before they could collect their thoughts and properly react, the doorbell rang. Still perplexed, neither Josette nor Louis-Marc made a move to answer it. The bell rang again. This time louder, and punctuated by a baritone voice booming out: "Open up. POLICE!"

Louis-Marc opened the door to find not one, but two of Montreal's finest, tallest, and most muscle-bound, dressed in recently ironed uniforms. They parted to allow passage for Arletty's lawyer, in tuxedo and cashmere overcoat, obviously on his way to a fancy party. He walked in, brandishing two copies of a voluminous, legal document with an impressive red seal. The ink was still wet as he had managed to obtain it just before the court was to shut down for the Christmas break.

Following behind were Ben, looking ragged, even though he was wearing the new clothes Anita had bought him, and Anita herself, once again in a spectacular saree and matching jewelry, glowing with renewed optimism, having just received positive results from her pregnancy test. The policemen stayed posted outside the door, which they kept open, in case they were needed.

In the discomfort of the cold air pouring through the open door, the lawyer dropped a copy of the documents on the heirloom, lovingly restored, hall table. He then informed the parents that Arletty, now legally married to Ari, was no longer bound by the judgments of the previous court order, having been entrusted to the custody of her husband, and that she was free to walk out with him, as she pleased.

On this cue, Arletty sprung to her feet, and took Ari by the hand. The two of them dodged the disempowered parents, and flew into the arms of Ben and Anita. They were almost out the door, but Arletty couldn't resist a final stab:

"So long, suckers," she sneered relishing it, "and Merry Christmas!"

Arletty laughed the kind of infectious laugh Josette remembered having heard at the end of particularly risqué *doubles-entendres* on cafe tables. She stepped out the door. It had started to snow, and the cops made a cradle for her with their arms, and carried her down the slippery stairs, followed by the entourage. They got into shiny police cars, and sped off with sirens wailing.

The parents were left behind, agape, all four in a row, their mouths hanging open. In shock. In disarray. At first, in denial. Followed closely by anger. Denial. Anger. At having been fully and royally taken-for-a-ride. Cheated out of their Christmas. Rebuffed in their efforts to dictate the destiny of their grandchild. Cheated. And *agape*, which happens to be the English spelling of the Greek word for love.

Louis-Marc was the first to return to reality. It was the matter of the heating bill, one of the household expenses he had assumed. The door was still wide open, and it was chilling the whole house. He hurried to shut it and turned to the others, vexed. "The ingrates! After all I've done for them! All the concessions. The humiliation. Dealing with the enemy. And for what? It's all your fault, Josette."

"She had hate in her eyes. For all of us. Even me!"

"She had a right to hate you, Josette. You were the mastermind."

"I did all I could for her. I'd die for her, you know that!"

"You'd also take over her baby. And she out-tricked you. You lost, sweetheart, admit it."

"We all lost," sighed Josette, chastened.

Duncan grunted irritably. "You're both being stupid. This changes nothing. Those two married! Hah! What a joke. A nightmare. So, the battle really begins. And I have the money. And I... and we will win!"

Louis-Marc banged his fist on the wall, outraged. "Hold on, Mister! What do you think is going on here? You think you can fight a married couple, and take away their kid? This is unheard of, except, I suppose, in the wilds of Scotland. In civilized societies—"

"Oh, shut UP," snapped Duncan.

"Really? Shut UP? In my own house?"

"In your own house! Exactly! This is the final humiliation. Being screwed by my son in Louis-Marc's own house. That's IT! He's disowned. I never want to see that puny prick again," hissed Duncan.

"And what's wrong with our house?" asked Josette icily.

"Nothing at all, except that it is your house," said Duncan, just as icily.

Louis-Marc laughed derisively. "Well, take a good look, buster. Because this is the last time you'll ever see it."

"You can bet on that," muttered Duncan, looking around for Maria. "*Maria-a-a*," he called with impatience. "Maria! Come on. We're leaving!"

Maria was not in the hall. During the bickering, she had wandered into the parlour, sat down by the fireplace, and was leaning on an overstuffed cushion. The snow was falling in puffy, Christmas handfuls on the other side of the bay windows. It added just the right touch to the warmth of the fire, to the cheer she felt inside her. Yes, her baby had fled the nest. But he seemed so happy as he stepped out of her life, clutching Arletty's hand. As if he had just won the lottery. Which meant, that she too had won the lottery. The greatest lottery of all.

"Maria! Where are you? Let's go," echoed Duncan exasperated, but unwilling to roam through Louis-Marc's house to look for her.

"Yes. Go. get the hell out of here. Just to look at you makes me want to vomit," instigated Louis-Marc.

Duncan addressed him, as if from a great height. "What you do is irrelevant, sir. Little people do not count. Their actions go by unnoticed. It's as if you don't exist."

Louis-Marc laughed out loud. "Your problem is that I do exist. And it's little fellows like me that have you big guys, great-grand-sons of thieves and criminals, on the run. You've had a cushy, cozy time of it, my DEAR man, all those centuries when you bullied and shoved your way into our home, and expropriated whatever struck your fancy. But then, when little guys like me, guys even littler than me, found the courage to say *boo,* go home, get outta here, boy did you run for cover, or what! Straight down the 401 highway. Didn't you? All we had to do was say BOO, and your team just turned around and ran like so many yellow-bellied rats. Didn't you?"

"Are you quite finished?"

"No. Not yet. I won't be finished till every LAST one of you gets the hell out of here, and moves to Toronto."

"Fine state you'd be in then! Don't you see the writing on the wall, you myopic, navel-gazing parasite? How do you think you could ever survive without the capital, and the know-how, and the centuries' worth of international networking that we created and very much control? How?"

Josette had heard enough rhetoric for one night. She left the two of them to their debate with a *Bof!* and a lewd hand gesture. She walked into the parlour, looking for Maria. She saw her by the fireplace, and fixed two *Pernods* on ice. She lowered herself onto the floor, opposite her soul-mate, and handed her one of the drinks.

"And I had such nice plans," said Josette. "The side room, Arletty's old room. I have the colours picked out. Bright pink, and canary yellow. And a vermilion crib. A lovely mobile of twinkling baby-angels to amuse her."

"Me, too. I was getting ready for the new baby that I never managed to have myself. I was thinking of the room over the solarium. Looking out at the rose garden. With the blue jays, and the cardinals, and the acacia tree with the fragrant white flowers in August. Muted colours on the walls, but a golden, shiny crib, and an army of big stuffed animal cartoon characters, all female. To keep her company."

"And now, it's a big mystery if we'll ever get to even see the little one."

"Don't be silly. Of course we'll see her, and we'll babysit for her, and we'll love her to bits. I don't know about you, but I'm proceeding with my plans for the baby room, for when she comes to visit... Oh, Josette," Maria was bursting, "I'm so... SO... happy."

"Happy! Are you crazy?"

"Yes! Crazy... with happiness."

Josette reflected on this, and finally she threw up her hands in surrender: "You mean, because the kids are married and Ari will get healthy, and Arletty will be taken care of, she'll have the baby in a clean *Montréal* clinic, and our lives will improve one hundred percent? Is that, why you're happy?" Josette hugged Maria with a little yelp of happiness.

"Also," added Maria, "because you and me are now closer than ever... we're like... sisters. Officially!" They hugged each other, in earnest, in great relief, with love, and a common purpose, finally, a truly positive, direct, uncompromised, common purpose.

Meanwhile, out in the hall, the Duncan — Louis-Marc situation was reaching new lows:

"The English," spat Louis-Marc, "with their Trudeau, and Lalonde, and Chretien, are wasting their time trying to make us disappear. *Québec* is having its day as a distinct national entity. It is surviving, and it is here to stay. So said François Shirm, one of the founders of the F.L.Q."

"Oh, the genius spokesman, of a charming, terrorist organization," sneered Duncan. "All I know is that as things get tighter and tighter economically, you guys will all eat more *tourtière* pies, and drink more cheap beer, and fart louder and louder, until your balloon bursts right in your face!"

"Too bad you won't be around to enjoy the spectacle!"

"Oh, but you are wrong. My family helped to build this city. I never intend to leave Montreal, and I will do everything in my considerable power to foil your every plan."

"You'd like to do that. But, you'll fail, and eventually you'll get the fuck out. And then I and my Josette will move into your family house, and shit on every branch of your *arbre généalogique.*"

"Over my dead body," said Duncan matter-of-factly.

"That too can be arranged," Louis-Marc shot back.

Despite themselves, as if reliving childhood scraps neither of them had ever been left unsupervised long enough to have, they started circling each other.

"You're an imperialist son-of-a-bitch, Duncan."

"You're a low-down, toothless *Pepsi* scum," countered Duncan. This was too much, even for a pacifist-at-heart like Louis-Marc. The next moment they were on each other, grabbing, pushing, grunting. Fighting like two men who had no idea how to fight.

Josette and Maria, hearing the violent noises, rushed out to the hall, just in time to witness Duncan land a minor jab on Louis-Marc's jaw. Louis-Marc had ducked for no reason, and placed his head in the way of Duncan's flailing fist. Louis-Marc reeled back with a cry of horror, and fell onto the floor. Josette ran to solace her wounded husband.

"You BRUTE!" she yelled at Duncan, who was nursing his fist. "You... you ADULTERER!"

"What did you say?" Duncan was taken by surprise. He turned to Maria. "What did she say?"

Louis-Marc had recovered from his knock-down, which was caused more by the shock of being jabbed, rather than its force. He shook away Josette's protective arms and leaped to his feet, screaming: "I'll KILL you!" He charged at Duncan, grabbing a chair on the way and running for him, intent on maiming him. Duncan retreated, but he was backing into a wall. He tripped and fell to the floor. Louis-Marc skidded to a stop in front of him and raised the chair over his head, poised to crush Duncan. He held the pose, waiting for the women to come and restrain him.

And they did come, and led him away from the fallen Duncan, into a neutral corner. He seethed for them. Breathing fire, throwing Duncan poison glares. Duncan stood up, and brushed down his handmade London suit. He looked at Maria, searchingly. "It's not true, you know. Whatever you're thinking."

"I'm not blind, Duncan. I've even flipped through your little black book, which you used to leave for me to find."

"That's right. So you would know you could lose me, and come back to me all those years you were rejecting me. For any reason at all. For Ari, who might wake up and hear us. For being depressed over the miscarriages. For blaming me for your mother's death. For whatever the fuck reason." Duncan looked around for his coat. "I'm going home. Come on!"

Maria smiled apologetically. "You're right, Duncan. I'll try to be a better wife for you from now on. But, tonight, sorry. I'm staying here."

"What?"

"We have nothing ready to eat at home. I've been dreaming of that goose. Can't you smell it?"

"Get your coat, We're going home."

"We can't. Tonight our home belongs to Sophia. She has started an affair with the chauffeur."

"I thought he had a wife and many kids."

"And tonight, he has Sophia."

"Get your coat!" Duncan was angry. "And we'll send for our wines later," he shot at Louis-Marc.

"I'm staying, Duncan. I want to have Christmas."

"Christmas in this house? With this ruffian?"

"You hit me!" hollered Louis-Marc. "You made me fall to the ground."

"You attacked me," said Duncan indifferently.

"I attacked AFTER you hit me."

"Oh, sorry. I forgot. The bloodless revolution," sneered Duncan.

"You apologize to me right now!"

"Why not?" smiled Duncan. "I apologize. There! You happy?" Turning to Maria: "So, can we go now?"

"Nothing has changed for me," winked Maria. "I still want to eat the goose." To Josette: "Do you think it's ready?"

"Of course it's ready. It smells ready," said Josette, joining Maria, in support against Duncan.

"We brought good wines," said Maria.

"We won't drink Duncan's wines in this house,' replied Josette. "I have wine too."

"Oh, I don't know. I've been looking forward to the *Romanée Conti* with the goose. And the *Chateau d'Yqem* with dessert..."

"*Romanée Conti, Chateau d'Yqem,*" echoed Louis-Marc dreami-
ly, suddenly remembering that he was really, really angry.
"Come on," coaxed Maria. "Let's go and lay things out for din-
ner."
"And leave them alone? They'll kill each other."
"Oh, they'll be alright," shrugged Maria, and let Josette lead her
into the kitchen.
Left on their own, the two accidental pugilists eyeballed each
other wearily. "Aren't you supposed to be leaving?" snapped Louis-
Marc.
"And leave my wife here? I don't think so!"
Louis-Marc nodded, but he was still angry. "You hurt me, you
know. I can't ever forgive you."
"It was an accident. And I already apologized."
"No-oh-no. You meant to hit me. I saw it in your eyes."
"You started it."
"You provoked me."
"You insulted me first."
"You revolt me!"
"I can't help that!"
Louis-Marc rubbed his jaw. "I think you broke my jaw."
"Maybe we should take you for an x-ray."
"Thank you. No."
Another standstill. Some shuffling. A posture, or two.
"I'm not leaving," stated Duncan with finality.
"Well, I refuse to eat with you," retorted Louis-Marc vengefully.
"Eat with YOU? Whatever for?"
"Never," said Louis-Marc, not quite sure how to rebuff *whatever for.*
Another pause.
"I could play cards, though," said Louis-Marc, somewhat slyly.
"Of course. Our return match. Well, I agree. This would be an
excellent time to teach you another costly lesson."
"Fine. But poker, this time. My house, my game."
"Poker?" sneered Duncan. "I haven't played since high school."
"Same for me with baccarat."
"Poker it is, Sir. Where do we play?"
And in no time at all, the two fathers-in-law were sitting on
opposite sides of the antique card table in Louis-Marc's study, open-
ing brand new decks that Louis-Marc had presciently purchased just
that afternoon; and apportioning Eighteenth Century, gilded poker

disks that outdated Duncan's *Monte Carlo* chips by a good hundred years.

"We'll start with twenty thousand each, like last time. And you'll mark me down twenty thousand for the cheque Josette got from you. I am very sorry about that, by the way..." said Louis-Marc sincerely.

"Those things happen," shrugged Duncan. "But now you'd be in for forty thousand if you lose. What have you got to back it up?"

Louis-Marc took a deep breath. "My house."

"This?" laughed Duncan. "How much is it worth? Twenty five thousand? Thirty?"

"Are you crazy?" snapped Louis-Marc. "I wouldn't accept less than one hundred and eighty?"

"You're not serious. For an apartment in the East End?"

"A *walk-through*, Sir. And now we call it the Plateau," Louis-Marc proudly.

"So be it," said Duncan, remembering the whole block of handsome, Parc Lafontaine triplexes his father had bought for a penny in the old days. "Deal."

If we could picture a cinematic jump-cut, we would see the two antagonists, still at it, about seven minutes hence. We would find Louis-Marc with a generous helping of chips, and Duncan down to only a few.

Louis-Marc took another peek at his hole-card — they were playing five-stud. — and shot Duncan a crafty look. "I tap you," he said. "How much have you got there?"

"Just about five thousand."

"Five thousand it is, then." Louis-Marc threw in five impressively large chips. They landed right in the middle of the pot. "Are you in?"

Duncan closed his eyes and pushed all his chips sloppily into the pot. Louis-Marc opened up his hole-card: an Ace of Spades to join the Ace of Diamonds in his open cards. Duncan groaned as Louis-Marc gleefully gathered the pot, quickly formed the chips into piles, and added these to the rest of his piles.

"Okay, then. I've won back my old twenty thousand, and I'm up twenty for today. You don't have to pay now. Some other time will do." Louis-Marc made to stand up.

"Not so fast. We never said anything about quitting after twenty thousand. We continue. I'll take more chips. Give me fifty thousand."

"Fifty? Oh, big shot. And where's your collateral?" bellowed Louis-Marc as he pushed new piles of chips to his opponent.

Another jump-cut: This time Louis-Marc is sitting behind an enormous pile of chips, Duncan sporting a very modest pile.

Louis-Marc was showing two pairs on his four open cards. Two Queens and two very pretty deuces. Duncan was showing a sequence of four cards to a straight. An eight, a nine, a ten, a Jack. Louis-Marc took his usual, highly annoying, last peak at his hole-card. He smiled, brimming over with confidence. Surely a bluffing posture, speculated Duncan, who had a Queen in the hole, giving him the straight.

Louis-Marc peered at Duncan, and tossed some weighty chips into the pot, using the reverse-flip, backhanded move that landed, once again, precisely mid-pot. "Ten thousand bucks," he stage-whispered.

"I only have eight-five," said Duncan peeved.

Louis-Marc removed one large and one slightly smaller chip from the pot. "True, it's table-stakes. Sorry. Only eight thousand five hundred, to you."

Duncan hesitated. Louis-Marc looked at him benignly. "In, or out?"

"You know you can't bluff me," jeered Duncan.

"Who's bluffing? I have the full-house," winked Louis-Marc.

Duncan threw in all his chips. "The hell, you do!"

Louis-Marc slapped open his hole-card with a screech of joy. "The hell, I don't!" he yelled, as he scooped the pot with both hands. The card was a Queen, the last available Queen in the deck. Full-house beats a straight.

"Horse-shoes, Louis-Marc. You got horse-shoes deep inside your rectum."

"Yes, but they are actually made of platinum. Platinum horse-shoes," laughed Louis-Marc, perusing their score sheet. "Maybe diamond horse-shoes. According to my little piece of paper, after the twenty I used to owe you, now you owe me a hundred and twenty thousand dollars."

"Give me another hundred grand," demanded Duncan tersely.

At that moment, Josette's voice rang out from the dining alcove. "We're ready! Come on, you guys."

Louis-Marc stood up. "You heard the lady. Let's go eat."

"I'm not hungry, thanks. I'll wait here."

"Come on!"

"You go. I'm fine."

"You know, Duncan, I can't stand your guts, and you can't stand mine, but is that a reason to miss out on the best roast goose in the universe?"

Duncan stood up slowly and followed Louis-Marc to the table.

Epilogue

The Happy Ending!

MID-JUNE, 2000

The baby, a healthy, cuddly little girl named Maria-Josette, is now six months old. She lives with her parents in a beautiful, third-storey walk-through on *Parc Lafontaine,* presiding over a leafy view that will turn white in winter.

Her grandmothers, Maria and Josette, are in Mykonos on a week's getaway to celebrate the glut of good fortune that has been regaling them. Their kids settled down, their grandchild a treasure, their status as preferred co-baby-sitters inalienable, their husbands attentive and romantically recharged. All of it had been so good, it was overwhelming. They are on Mykonos to put it in perspective, examine it in the clear, crazy, Cycladic light, and digest it, find a way to make it last.

Her grandfathers, Louis-Marc and Duncan, are co-baby-sitting Maria Josette tonight. To pass the time, they are playing killer poker, which is not unusual for them. They have been getting together for head-to-head poker on a regular basis, ever since their scrappy encounter last Christmas Eve. Louis-Marc is now ahead by three hundred and seventy thousand dollars — three hundred and ninety counting the recouped twenty grand he had originally lost at bacarrat. Not one real penny has yet to change hands. It's all on the score-card, and Louis-Marc has stated that he wishes to be paid when he reaches a million. Unlike poker, baby-sitting is very unusual for them. This, their first attempt has been necessitated by their wives' Mykonos escapade. They are very nervous. Babies, they know nothing about. They are involved in a monster hand: some sixty thousand in the pot already, before the fifth card. The baby makes a small noise from her crib. They both drop their invaluable hole-cards in terror, and rush to her bedroom to see if she is alright. She is. She is just testing her power over them.

Her parents, Ari and Arletty, are out on the town. Sort of. They are at the park, rehearsing the pivotal scene of a play they've written together, entitled *Love In The Age Of Confusion*. The scene is a kind of verbal tennis game, inspired by the ball-and-racketless tennis routine at the end of Antonioni's *Blow Up*.

Maria-Josette's honorary uncle and aunt, Ben and the very pregnant Anita, are waiting for them at *La Crevetterie*, but Ari and Arletty decide to do one more run-through, right there under the stars:

[ARI and ARLETTY are dressed in thin white fabrics loosely cut. They are shoe-less on the grass. They dance-walk around each other, like two boxers looking for an opening. They are smiling.]

ARLETTY
Love-fifteen. Your serve.

ARI
I forfeit the game. You're too good.

ARLETTY
THAT is a different game. And you're way better than me.

ARI
Let's stop playing altogether.

ARLETTY
And just be happy, you mean?

ARI
For the moment.

ARLETTY
Okay.

ARI
Even though there is no reason?

ARLETTY

Yes... No! Wait.

ARI

Too late. Fifteen all. Your serve.

ARLETTY

I hate this game.

ARI

ZAP. ZAP. ZAP. Sorry. Against the rules!

ARLETTY

Rules? Silly! There are no rules.

ARI

Oh, I forgot.

ARLETTY

Fifteen-thirty. Your serve.

ARI

Fine. Alright. Imagine this: A fireplace blazing. A table loaded with your favourite dishes...

ARLETTY

Poutine! *Yes, I'm afraid it's back to* poutine.

ARI

A bottle of Pernod fresh from the freezer. So cold it could slice your heart. A soft rug to lie on. With me. Powerful music...

ARLETTY

Bach's *Chaconne for unaccompanied violin...*

ARI

...not Motown. Okay. I look at you. I touch your cheek. My hand catches fire. You smile, then you part your lips. I vapourise. I become breath. You suck me in. You have me inside you forever. I become you. You walk the earth, like a god, all powerful, alone, yet together.

ARLETTY
That was an ace. Good shot! Thirty all. Go ahead. Serve.

ARI
I pass my serve. You serve.

ARLETTY
No. There will never be a clear winner. This game will last forever.

ARI
One more volley. Please. Serve.

ARLETTY
Okay. here goes. We have three babies. The twins are born exactly thirteen months after little Maria-Josette. The first boys in my mother's family since 1648. We name them Louis-Marc and Duncan. We live in a big and fully equipped flat on Parc Lafontaine. We're not really living off our parents, but all of them are squeezing money into our palms at every opportunity. I'm keeping track of every penny and fully intend to pay them back, if I can only stop getting pregnant all the time. Anyway, money is no longer one of my hang-ups. I butter Duncan up, and he gives us millions, with which we open a movie studio. We hire Depardieu to do juicy little bits in our movies. How am I doing?

ARI
Wonderful. Your point. Thirty-forty. My serve. Your game point.

ARLETTY
Wrong. That was terrible. I lost that point. As loser of the point, I serve again. It's thirty-forty. Your game point.

ARI
I protest.

ARLETTY
So noted, but you are over-ruled. Ready? Here I go:

We get everything you always wanted. We make two movies. Starring me. They both become super hits. The Palme D'Or. *The* Oscar. *A sep-*

arate Oscar for me. Best Actress. I get intensely depressed. And I commit suicide. I'm dead. You get to love me forever, and there is nothing I can do to stop you. You win. Game. Set. Match.

                                        ARI
Why? WHY???

                                      ARLETTY
Because I couldn't continue. I don't have the patience to live out your fantasies for the rest of my life. I'm dead. And then I'm reborn. Instantly. I start again.

                                        ARI
And what do I do?

                                      ARLETTY
You fall in love with the new me. You learn from your mistakes, and you behave like a person, instead of a tired old cliché. You understand me. You don't crowd me. You don't try to own me. We become friends. You never wear penny loafers again.

                                        ARI
Really? Oh, that's great! That's wonderful.

                                      ARLETTY
Yes. It is.

                                        ARI
So, there is after all, some kind of hope.

                                      ARLETTY
Oh, yes, my darling. There is always some kind of hope.

[ARLETTY laughs. ARI laughs with her. They circle each other again. She catches him. She hugs him. He struggles and fights her off, briefly, before he surrenders to her, and hugs her passionately. They kiss.]

❋

CURTAIN

Montreal
September 19, 2001

About the Author

Byron Ayanoglu has written fourteen stage plays, all of which have been mounted in various cities (Toronto, New York, London, Edinburgh, Prague, Montreal). His most recent play, *Food,* was mounted to rave reviews in Montreal, in February 2001. He has worked as a food-journalist for almost twenty years, with long stints as the restaurant reviewer for *NOW* (Toronto), and for Montreal's *The Gazette.* On the side, he has written countless food/travel articles for those two publications, as well as other venues, such as *The Toronto Star, Menz Magazine, Gault-Millau,* and *Sposa.*

He has appeared on many food-related TV programs, most notably as the host of a five-part series for PBS. He is the author of two Montreal restaurant guides, the most recent of which, *Montreal's Best Restaurants* (Véhicule Press, Montreal, 1999), was on *The Gazette's* Best Seller list for forty weeks. He has four cookbooks, only one of which, *Byron's New Home Cooking* (Penguin/Viking, Toronto, 1992) is out of print. The other three include *The Young Thailand Cookbook* (Random House, Canada, 1994), which was re-published in 1996 as *Simply Thai Cooking* (Robert-Rose, Toronto); *The New Vegetarian Gourmet* (Robert-Rose, Toronto, 1995), and *Simply Mediterranean Cooking* (Robert-Rose, Toronto, 1996), the latter two of which were translated into French for the Quebec market. He is currently writing a non-fiction book, *Crete On the Half Shell,* about that legendary Greek island and its famous, long-life diet for HarperCollins (Toronto).

He resides in Montreal and is still, at age fifty-five, living life to the fullest.

AGMV Marquis

MEMBER OF SCABRINI MEDIA

Quebec, Canada
2001